TRICKS OF THE TRADE

I'll do anything—anything—if you keep quiet about this. If the board finds out, my days as a doctor are over!" Dr. Eric Potter cried.

"Would you really do anything?" Dr. Elaine Drexel said as she led him to a laboratory with hundreds of glass containers of varying sizes.

"What was your preoperative diagnosis? Here's one that should fit your case," she said pulling a jar from the shelf. "This should take care of your incorrect prognosis—all I have to do is switch the specimen."

"Elaine, I'll be grateful to you for the rest of my life!"

"You'll be more than that, Eric. You'll be my husband."

He lowered his eyes as she continued, "You'll diagnose a terminal disease, perform the necessary surgery while I'll make sure the 'correct' slides go to the lab. Your patients will recover with remarkable speed, and in a few years you will have an incredible reputation—with an enormous following. And I will be the rich and famous Mrs. Eric Potter . . .

BESTSELLERS FOR TODAY'S WOMAN

THE VOW (653, $2.50)
by Maria B. Fogelin
On the verge of marriage, a young woman is tragically blinded and mangled in a car accident. Struggling against tremendous odds to survive, she finds the courage to live, but will she ever find the courage to love?

FRIENDS (645, $2.25)
by Elieba Levine
Edith and Sarah had been friends for thirty years, sharing all their secrets and fantasies. No one ever thought that a bond as close as theirs could be broken . . . but now underneath the friendship and love is jealousy, anger, and hate.

CHARGE NURSE (663, $2.50)
by Patricia Rae
Kay Strom was Charge Nurse in the Intensive Care Unit and was trained to deal with the incredible pressures of life-and-death situations. But the one thing she couldn't handle was her passionate emotions . . . when she found herself falling in love with two different men!

RHINELANDER PAVILLION (572, $2.50)
by Barbara Harrison
Rhinelander Pavillion was a big city hospital pulsating with the constant struggles of life and death. Its dedicated staff of over-worked professionals were caught up in the unsteady charts of their own passions and desires—yet they all needed medicine to survive.

Silent Partners

ALBERT KOVETZ, M.D.

ZEBRA BOOKS

KENSINGTON PUBLISHING CORP.

One

New York City
August 1968

Dr. Eric Potter slouched in the armchair bored by the seven o'clock evening news. His head sagged exaggerating his double chin. As he got up to turn off the TV, the phone rang.

"Dr. Potter?" a deep female voice asked.

"Yes, this is Dr. Potter," he said assuming a formal tone out of his drowsiness.

"Dr. Drexel, here," she said and Potter immediately recognized the hard emphasis on the *r* she always put to her name.

"I just finished cutting that hysterectomy specimen you removed today. You better call your lawyer," she said and he almost caught a slight bit of laughter before he heard the click followed by a dead line.

At first, he had no reaction except for a vague feeling of weakness around his knees. His very pale skin flushed only slightly. Before he put the phone down, his ample cheeks were fully flushed. There was a sickening feeling of weakness that made him tremble.

There was no doubt in his mind that it was Dr. Elaine Drexel who called. That emphatic *r* in her name which she pronounced with a smirk. But it could have been her poor idea of a joke.

Dr. Potter was unmarried and lived alone in a sparsely furnished three-room apartment. The living room he was standing in had a couch and the easy chair. There was a desk where he sometimes worked and a few bookshelves which hung inexpertly at an angle.

He went over the desk frantically looking for the staff directory of University Medical Center among a pile of journals and newspapers. He thumbed through the listings but could not find Elaine Drexel's name. She was a junior staff pathologist recently appointed. He decided to try the Pathology Department through the hospital switchboard hoping she would still be there.

The hospital operator rang through to the Pathology laboratory. After ten rings, someone picked up the phone.

"Dr. D*r*exel," the voice answered and with a

sinking feeling Potter knew immediately it was the same person who had just called.

"What do you mean 'I should call my lawyer.' What's going on?" he said with barely controlled anguish.

"You really fucked up this time, Potter and I've got you dead to rights," she said with sinister glee. "You removed a pregnant uterus today with a viable fetus. It was viable until you put your hands on it."

There was silence for a moment while he let the import of what she said sink in. His hand covered his eyes and his legs vibrated uncontrollably.

"You're lying!" he said, "This is your idea of a bad joke. I don't believe it!"

"You'll believe it tomorrow when I show that specimen at organ recital. Then you'll be out on your ass."

"Wait! Stay there! I'm coming right down. I don't believe it," he said with waning conviction.

His apartment house on the East side was eight blocks away from the medical center. He ran all the way, huffing and puffing because of too much weight and a total lack of regular exercise.

"Let it be a bad joke," he prayed as he ran but he knew he had been too hasty in his decision to operate. It wasn't because he was overworked. Just the opposite was the case. After more than a year in practice, the volume of surgery he hoped for just hadn't materialized fast enough. He had a small income from working in the clinic but the money from his practice barely met expenses.

His practice expenses were high for he dreamed

of a high society type of practice. All the rich matrons coming to him, fawning on his great skill. But it was all taking too much time.

He was able to control his breathing but not the sweat pouring down his face as he entered the Pathology laboratory where Dr. Elaine Drexel was waiting.

She had thin flat hair cut short around her ears. As she looked into the microscope, Potter thought it was a man from the squareness of her broad flat shoulders. She only glanced up briefly from the microscope as he stood there beside the table wiping the sweat from his face.

Next to the microscope, there was a plastic specimen bucket resting on the table. When she looked up again she put her hand over the bucket, almost caressing it, and then handed it to Potter. He pulled his hands away. She laughed at his gesture of refusal.

"So you don't believe it," she said menacingly, "well come over here!"

She led him to the sink and opened the plastic bucket. The acrid formaldehyde singed his nose but didn't seem to bother her. The specimen was a gray mass about six inches long with slender tubular wings that were the fallopian tubes. It had been cut deeply along one surface which she now opened like a book.

"Take a good look," she said sticking the acrid specimen under his nose. He backed away as the formaldehyde brought tears to his eyes and he coughed violently. He blew his nose into a handkerchief then was able to look carefully at the specimen resting on the sink top.

Attached to the lining was a three-inch tadpolelike structure. Dr. Drexel put a large magnifying glass over the specimen, clearly demonstrating a humanoid head disproportionately large compared to the fishlike body.

"Oh, my God, I'm ruined," Potter turned away banging his hands on the desk next to the sink. There were more tears in his eyes, not all of them from the formaldehyde that permeated the room. Dr. Drexel could not repress her smile at his discomfort.

"Oh, my God," he sobbed again, "they'll chew me up and spit me out when they see this. It can't be!" he moaned, "There must be some mistake."

"You made it!" she said with angry disgust. "Did you get a urine specimen for a pregnancy test on this twenty-three-year-old girl? Couldn't you tell she was pregnant? Did you even care?"

"That's easy for you to say now sitting here in the lab," he stopped sobbing but there was still some hurt in his voice. "The lab tests were negative, I swear! But now . . ., now they'll crucify me. All those bleeding women . . ., all they care about is their bleeding wombs like it was the Holy Grail. You can't understand, can you? Your heart is just breaking over this poor woman and her baby. You don't feel the least bit sorry for me!"

"I don't give a shit about this or any other baby, you prick!" she said livid with rage. "I only want to see one of you get just what you deserve. You're not the only one around here who has taken out a normal uterus. But they always manage to get around it somehow. A small fibroid, irregular menstruation, always some excuse. But not this time!"

He stared, awed by her visceral outrage. Her pale white face had become livid with tiny dilated capillaries that were first red, then almost purple. She took off her thick-lensed glasses and her wideset small eyes burned with hate. She was very thin, almost completely flat-chested. She was as tall as he was. She trembled with anger as she pulled the sides of her short, thinning black hair and, turned away from him.

He made a move to the door, totally dejected and hopeless, then turned back toward her.

"But why," he begged, "why are you doing this to me?" It seemed irrational that there could be any way out of this but he sensed something irrational about Dr. Drexel.

"You arrogant fat slob," she said to him disdainfully as she turned. "Do you think it's just you? It's all of you that I hate. All of you trying to pull the wool over every woman. Don't you think I know how you all feel about me. I'm as good as any man in this department, better than most, but that won't help me get tenured or move up to an endowed professorship."

He felt heavy and awkward, although he never thought he was fat. He never was a charmer, never really comfortable in a social setting with women but Dr. Drexel's bitterness gave him some hope.

"Nothing is absolute," he said. "There are woman professors at the school. Don't always take the hard line." His hands extended pleafully begging her to see some hope in return for some hope for him.

"Those charming womanly dilettantes who have rich fathers and rich husbands," she said sarcastically. "Even the talented ones who can afford to take fellowships while I have to take any available job just for the money to live!"

"I'll help you, I swear!" he jumped in. "I'll do anything. I'll be your strongest supporter, I'll give you money. I'll do anything you want but please, there has to be another way," he sobbed letting his head droop and his shoulders shudder.

His performance was horribly pitiful, so self-indulgent that she almost dismissed it with disgust. She felt no pity for him but he did abate her anger for the lack of a formidable opponent. He was right about one thing. The staff would chew him up and spit him out and then go back to business as usual. She would gain nothing because he was not important; just a sacrificial goat to show how tough they could be.

"Would you really do anything?" she said, her voice hard so there would be no question of who was in control.

He moved toward her with his arms outstretched as if to embrace her. She picked up a long wooden pointer and stuck him in the gut holding him at bay.

"Don't touch me, you pig! Don't ever touch me!" she said. "You will do everything and anything I say."

"Yes," he said frightened, not knowing what she could do for him but willing to sacrifice anything for another chance. "But how? I mean what can we do now?"

"Come with me," she ordered. He followed her down the hallway to a locked room which she opened. At first glance it looked like a large storeroom with many rows of steel shelves. He soon recognized he was in the Pathological Museum. There were hundreds of glass containers of varying sizes. All were filled with formaldehyde and each contained some part of a human body removed and stored here for reference and teaching.

"What *was* your preoperative diagnosis?" she said bitingly. "I remember, carcinoma of the uterus. Here are a half dozen carcinomas. Let's see, hmm! Here's one that should fit your case," she said pulling a jar from the shelf. "And here's one with a fetus! You're not the first," she laughed at him.

Potter now understood how she would save him. He held up his short stubby fingers with great joy and with difficulty he restrained himself from hugging her, mindful of her fearful reaction earlier.

"Elaine, I'll be grateful to you for the rest of my life, I swear!" he said with the deepest sincerity.

"You'll be more than grateful, Eric," she said, "You'll be rich and famous."

He was puzzled. He ran his hand through his unruly hair with obvious nervousness. His flabby thick lips twisted with concern.

"Come, Eric, sit down," she said with a touch of softness that one would expect a teacher to use on an errant child. He sat in the chair while she sat at the edge of the desk with one foot on the floor.

"You will be the busiest gynecological surgeon at University Medical Center. You will also have the best results of any surgeon here," she said looking straight at him.

Like a child, he was eager to please, losing some of his discomfort when it seemed he had a supporter.

"Elaine, if you switch this specimen this one time, I know I can do it. I know I can make it just as you say."

"You egotistical fool!" she scowled as she stood up banging her fist on the desk. He jumped about one inch and pulled himself back in the chair as she bent forward toward him.

"It'll take you years and years to build up that kind of surgical practice if you can do it at all. How many hysterectomies have you done in the past year? Six? Seven? You could be doing that many in a month. Even more in a few years."

She walked away from him letting the idea sink into his mind. She could see he was mentally calculating, with some help from his fingers, the six-figure gross income from over a hundred hysterectomies a year.

"Where are all these patients coming from?" he asked.

"From where this one came!" she said holding up the bucket with the specimen. "All those poor women with their painful periods; those women who think they bleed too much or too often; those women who are so fearful of getting pregnant! You can save them all."

"And you will provide the proper specimens to present to the Pathology Department. It's impossible!" He waved his hand dismissing the idea and buried his head in his other hand as he feared she might renege on her current promise.

"Nothing's impossible!" she said coming back to the desk.

"Where will you get the specimens? There are only six on the shelf."

"Come over here," she ordered as she moved down the aisle to the back of the room. There were three foot lockers against the wall. She flipped on the lights over this part of the room. The rectangular containers were about two feet high and four feet long. They looked like refrigerators because of the handles in the center of each of them and the rubber insulation between the lid and the base. They were merely airtight and watertight boxes.

Formaldehyde vapors rose quickly as she opened the middle one. She lifted out a preserved forearm and dropped it back in to one side like someone rummaging in a tool or storage box. There were hands and feet carefully dissected, with the major arteries and nerves tagged for identification. There was a spinal column and spread among these larger bony parts were hearts, lungs and assorted vital and nonvital organs in various stages of dissection.

This anatomical foot locker contained many specimens used for demonstration and teaching. It contained duplicates and triplicates of diseased organs that many medical students, interns and residents used for reference and study. Dr. Potter had seen this before. It still wasn't enough to do what Dr. Drexel proposed.

"So what?" he said dismissing the collection and

14

walking back to the desk. Dr. Drexel slammed the top down and followed after him.

"That's only the reservoir!" she said. "In a hospital of this size we get fifty to sixty diseased uterine specimens a month. They all come down in these plastic buckets. And after they are examined and small sections taken for microscopy, they are all incinerated. Just leave it to me. I'll put in the cancerous specimens at the right time. I can easily switch the buckets and even more easily switch the small pieces and the slides. I won't even have to read them myself."

"Are they all going to be cancer? Is that what you're going to call them?" he said softly and unhurriedly as he thought about the possibilities.

"They ain't nothing until I call them," she said. "It's just a piece of meat until some pathologist names it."

"But why cancer? Why not a few fibroids or endometriosis?"

"Who would refuse surgery if you said they had cancer?" she said as if it was the most natural thing in the world. They were no longer reacting to each other emotionally. They were two professional colleagues discussing some technical manipulations with a neutral effect. They exchanged ideas in the lingua franca of medicine. They were speaking Medspeak which required no moral indignation nor verbal intonations.

"The diagnosis is dependent on the microsections," she said, "even if the gross specimens look normal. The other pathologists won't pay too much attention to the 'gross.' If they can't see the cancer with the naked eye, they'll take random sections. It'll be simple to substitute pieces from malignant specimens that were discarded. Microscopically, all cancers look more or less alike."

"What if the patients want a second opinion or they have the surgery at another hospital after I tell them they have cancer?"

"I can do the same thing with Pap smears. I can give you the right slides if some other doctor wants to see them. But more than likely the report will be enough and it would be more than unlikely for someone to repeat the Pap smear. And if they do, so what? Pap smears vary all the time. It's a matter of interpretation."

"But what if they operate on the basis of a false report and take out a normal uterus," he said with a little anxiety creeping into his tone.

"That happens. There are such things as false negatives and false positives. Besides, what surgeon is going to blow the whistle on himself after he takes out a normal uterus? He made the final decision, didn't he?" she laughed a bit. "But all that won't happen. We'll start slowly at first but soon your reputation will blossom. You're an adequate surgeon and should have no complications taking out normal uteri. It doesn't take too much skill to remove a normal uterus. Your patients will recover with remarkable rapidity from their cancer surgery. And in seven or eight years, you will have the best survival records for any series of uterine cancer."

"And what do you get out of this?" he asked lowering his eyes.

16

"I get you, darling," she said without a smile or the least bit of warmth. "We'll be married after a proper courtship and I'll get half of everything you earn. We will become a devoted couple, the famous surgeon Dr. Potter and his wife, Dr. Potter. But don't ever touch me!"

Two

Hadley, Massachusetts
August 1979

The ten-year-old boy stopped crying but the black streaks stained his cheeks where he had wiped away the tears with his dirty hands. He sat quietly on the examining table while his mother held the broken arm in the set position.

"Just like that, Mrs. Toma," Angie said as she wrapped the arm in soft cotton gauze. "It's not a bad fracture. In eight weeks it'll be as good as new again."

Billy Toma watched the young, pretty woman

wrap the wet plaster gauze around his arm. Her delicately slender fingers gently worked the plaster into a firm mold. Her two hands massaged the plaster round and round his forearm and in long graceful strokes up and down the arm, giving it a uniform smooth surface.

He kept glancing from this magic performance, which changed the soggy plaster to a perfect cast of his arm, to the intense blue eyes and slender eyelashes of the woman. Her eyes followed her quickly moving hands. Billy forgot his fear and his pain. She moved closer to him as she smoothed the cast near his elbow. He enjoyed her faint perfume.

"There you are, Billy," Angie said with a bright smile. "Just hold that arm on your lap like this until I get you a sling."

She took the arm from the mother, who was impressed as much as Billy was by Angie's skill and attractiveness. Angie gently rested the arm, then she tousled the boy's hair before she left to get the sling.

"She's pretty for a doctor," Billy said to his mother.

"She ain't a doctor," his mother said.

"She's not?" Billy's eyes opened in childish surprise. "How come she doesn't wear a uniform like the other nurses."

"She ain't a nurse either," the mother said holding her son around the neck and lightly stroking the cast with her fingers.

"Then what is she?" he asked.

"Don't ask so many questions! How's the arm feel?" she said.

"Okay."

"Then next time, don't ride your bike like a maniac!"

Angie came back into the room carrying a heavy brown cotton cloth that she fashioned into a sling around Billy's neck.

"Go into the next room. Terri will be right there to take some more X-rays. After Dr. Connors sees the films, you can go home. Mrs. Toma, bring him back next week so I can check the cast."

She turned back to Billy, raising her arm over her head.

"Simon sez, 'raise your arm'! Simon sez, 'wiggle your fingers'! Simon sez, 'hands down and go into the next room.' "

The boy complied with all the commands, demonstrating that the cast was not too tight nor were there any injuries to his muscles and nerves.

Dr. Connors stuck his head in the doorway. His full head of white hair curled up at his neck. The lines in his face and heavy bags under his eyes were a legacy of thirty years of many nights of interrupted sleep and long days. Still his eyes projected an elflike alertness.

"Angie, could you come in here, please?" he said softly. "How are you doing, Billy? Are you still playing Evil Knivel?"

Billy smiled, tucking his chin into his chest with shyness. Angie walked into the hallway with Dr. Connors. They were in the central foyer of an old Victorian house Connors had converted to a clinic complex. The large living room with its centrally placed fireplace was the waiting room. There were only three patients waiting there now.

The kitchen was completely rebuilt as a clinical laboratory with two full-time technicians working there. A new addition to the building built about ten years earlier contained examining rooms and the X-ray suite. Dr. and Mrs. Connors lived upstairs in a very comfortable, large apartment which was more than adequate for them since their two children had been married.

"Do you recall the Secino child?" Dr. Connors said quietly in hushed tones so no one could overhear them.

"Why, yes, I saw him twice in the past four weeks for an upper respiratory infection." All the happy wrinkles in her face, so prominent when she exuded joy, now disappeared. Her skin had a creamy smoothness with a touch of natural color in her cheeks. She brushed her thick black hair back around her ear in a nervous sort of concern for the Secino child.

"I've seen him for the same thing," Dr. Connors said, "as a matter of fact, I've seen him four times and came to the same conclusion. He's in examining room two. Take a listen to his chest. I think he has a murmur that I never heard before."

When Angie and Dr. Connors entered the examining room little John Secino was sitting quietly on a chair, very uncharacteristically for a three-year-old boy, swinging his feet under him. His mother had been talking to him softly but stopped when the door opened.

"Hi, Angie, he's back again," Mrs. Secino said, happy to see Angie and a little distraught because

John had to see the doctor again. She and Angie had gone to high school together. John was her second child and she was a year younger than Angie.

"Hi, Pat, how's big John?" Angie said as she reached into the pocket of her long white clinical coat to pull out her stethoscope. John Secino, Sr. had graduated from Laconia High School with Angie nine years earlier.

Angie held out her arms to little John. He came off the chair to her and she lifted him onto the padded examining table against the wall. She kissed him on his bare chest as she put him down, which made him giggle from the tickling sensation.

Angie put a gentle hand lightly on his chest as the little boy stared up at her confidently. The hand on the chest gave him assurance of her gentleness and gave her an opportunity to feel the rhythm of his heart as she searched for a "thrill." A "thrill" is the tactile equivalent of a murmur heard with a stethoscope. She then listened for several minutes with the stethoscope before giving him a playful kiss on the neck. The boy reached out and gave her a big hug around the neck in return.

Mrs. Secino was smiling expectantly. She was very worried about little John. The affection between Angie and her son lifted some of that worry momentarily. Angie looked at her while she hid her own feelings. She said nothing.

"Mrs. Secino, you can get John dressed now and I'll see you in my office," Dr. Connors said.

He and Angie walked back into the foyer to resume their conference.

"What do you think?" he asked.

"There's a definite murmur over the second left intercostal space. I don't know how I could have missed it," she said pushing her hair back.

"I don't think it was there before," he said showing her the chart indicating the number of times he had listened to the boy's heart.

"It sounds like it might be pulmonic stenosis," Angie offered.

"Possibly, but it's very rare. We won't worry about that now. I'm sending him down to Children's Hospital. It may have been there before," he said referring to the murmur, "or that valve may be getting tighter."

"If they're going to do a cardiac cath, maybe I should talk to Pat," Angie said with concern.

"They probably will but I wouldn't say anything now. They have to do some preliminary studies and they might decide against it, so let's wait. I'll talk to her."

"What happened with Mrs. Montague last night?" His eyelids sagged as he looked at the floor.

"Oh, poor Mrs. Montague," Angie said. "I told you this morning."

"What happened between you and Dr. Lindsey?" The sparkle came back to his eyes as he pursed his lips.

"You know Mrs. Montague," Angie said, "she never complains about anything. Seventy-eight years old and she's never been in a hospital! When she called me last night because her belly hurt, I went right over to her house. After I examined her, I called the ambulance to take her to Laconia

Hospital. Then I called Dr. Lindsey to tell him she was coming. Lindsey called me back about ten o'clock to say she didn't have anything but gastroenteritis. So I went up there to check her again. I told him she had appendicitis and he better crack her."

"Did he give you a lot of static?" Connors asked with a wry smile.

"Not the second time. He came about a half hour later and was grumbling a little but we opened her about midnight. You know her appendix was ruptured. Come to think about it, you knew this morning. How did you find out?"

"Lindsey called me about ten-thirty. I told him that if you said she had appendicitis he better operate."

"Oh shit!" Angie said with her hand over her mouth.

"What's the matter?"

"I thought I really convinced him, that's all," she said with a slight tremor to her voice.

"Well, forget it. He's only been here a year. When he gets to know you better, he'll listen more carefully. I think he'll listen to you from now on."

"As soon as he opened the belly you could tell from the smell it was ruptured. You should have seen the way his eyes bugged out," she said smiling.

"You stayed to scrub with him, huh?" Connors said with mild annoyance. "It's not like it was six or seven years ago, Angie. They have plenty of doctors over there now. You don't get anything out of it. Medicare won't pay you for assisting and the hospital won't pay you. It just isn't fair! I'm going to talk to the hospital about paying you whenever you scrub. It saves them money."

"I don't do it that much," Angie said.

"That's beside the point," he said with a wave of his hand. "Don't bother to go up there to see her this afternoon. I'll go. I want to have a talk with the hospital administrator. You take the afternoon off after you see these patients."

Dr. Connors was gone by the time Angie finished seeing the last three patients. She sat alone in her office staring at the two diplomas hanging on the wall. One was from University Medical Center simply stating that Angelica Palmeri was a graduate Physician's Assistant. The other was a license from the Commonwealth of Massachusetts permitting her to practice as a physician's assistant.

There was nothing left to do but she didn't feel like getting up. Because of Mrs. Montague's appendectomy, she didn't get to bed until after two A.M. and she had come to the office at eight just as usual.

Helen Davis, who was sort of the office manager and clerical major domo, walked in. She was surprised to find Angie still there.

"I thought you had left," she said.

"I'm too tired," Angie said with a forced sighing breath.

"Well, go home and go to sleep," Helen said, tidying up the desk.

"What did he mean 'take the afternoon off.' This is Wednesday. The office is closed anyway on Wednesday afternoon. I think he's getting senile," Angie said laconically.

Helen looked up at Angie and saw her very tired face and droopy eyes. She saw a touch of irritability she had seen so often in Dr. Connors when he missed a good night's sleep.

"I think you're a little senile. It's your Wednesday to be on but Dr. Connors said he would take all the calls until tomorrow."

"Did you tell Dr. Aldrich? He'll be relieved he doesn't have to cover me today," Angie said wearily.

"Dr. Connors didn't say anything about that. He just told me to be sure you went home early today."

"They don't get along because of me," Angie said, becoming more animated.

"It's more than just that," Helen assured her. "When Aldrich came here two years ago, Dr. Connors offered to take him in, let him share this office. But he just wanted to go it alone, he said, but I think he thought he was too good for us."

"That's not what I heard," Angie said stretching her arms over her head. "He didn't want to work with a Physician's Assistant, at least not the way Dr. Connors does. Maybe I should quit and make life easier for Dr. Connors."

"You'll do nothing of the sort!" the usually undemonstrative Mrs. Davis said. "I've been with him for more than twenty-five years. You saved his life when you came to work for him. He was killing himself and couldn't get anyone to come to Hadley. Now there's Aldrich here and there's another one opening up in Dyer, plus they've got about ten new doctors over in Laconia. I don't know where they all came from!

"If Aldrich doesn't like you seeing his patients, well . . ., Dr. Connors doesn't like the way Aldrich sees our patients, so it's even!"

Angie was about to hang up her white coat when the buzzer sounded indicating someone had come in through the front door. Then they heard the painful call: "Doctor! Doctor! Help me!"

Angie and Helen ran out to the foyer. Betty LeDonne was leaning against the door clutching her protuberant pregnant abdomen. Angie immediately noticed the blood streaming down the inside of her leg.

"Angie, help me!" Betty cried holding one arm out to her. "Oh, the pain," she groaned.

Angie ran over to her and put the outstretched arm over her shoulder. "Help me get her into the examining room," she said to Helen who came to her aid with a calm that matched Angie's.

As soon as Betty LeDonne was on the table, Angie asked Helen to call the ambulance, "And tell them if the ambulance is out to send the fire truck!"

The patient was sweating profusely but her skin was still warm. Angie peeled off the woman's cloth coat and placed a blood pressure cuff around the arm. The pulse was strong and regular.

"What happened, Betty? Take it easy, everything will be all right now," Angie said calmly.

The pain had subsided on its own as Betty became calmer. She was breathing more easily and could speak more slowly.

"I don't know, Angie, I don't know. After six

babies, I never had one like this. I was home doing the laundry when my water broke. It ain't time yet but I figured I better go to the hospital."

She stopped while Angie took her blood pressure. When Angie removed the stethoscope from her ear, she wiped the woman's forehead, which was beaded with sweat.

"It feels much better now," Betty said gratefully. "That pressure is gone," she said touching the lower part of her abdomen. "I finished putting away the laundry and then got in the car to go to Laconia."

"Where's Henry?" Angie asked referring to Betty's husband.

"He's working. Don't call him, Angie. He gets so upset just when I'm havin' a baby regular. This is gonna be a tough one." She said it with a little smile so Angie could see the space from her missing front teeth.

"I thought I could make it to the hospital. It's only fifteen miles and there was no pain. Just the water broke. When I started drivin' the pains started and I knew I couldn't make it so I came here. I think it's all right."

Just then Angie could feel the abdomen become rock-hard with a contraction and the pain contorted the woman's face.

"Breathe deeply, slower! That's it," Angie assured her. The belly softened and the pain relented. "I'm going to examine you . . ., just hold on," she said as she went over to get a pair of sterile gloves from the drawer.

"I don't understand it! Six babies and I never

had any trouble. I should be able to do this by myself," Betty said unconvincingly.

Helen Davis came back into the room. "The ambulance is on its way," she said.

Angie slipped off the woman's underpants and put her gloved hand into the vagina. She looked up quickly at Helen Davis who immediately recognized that there was something dangerous going on by Angie's expression. Angie didn't remove her hand. She stayed at the foot of the table.

"Betty, don't push," Angie said with some distress. "Breathe slowly and don't push when the pain comes," she said changing her tone to sound more reassuring, but she couldn't calm her own inner feelings.

"Okay, Angie, I'll try," the woman on her back responded in the same calm tone but there was a small tear in the corner of her eye. "What is it, Angie?"

"Helen, get me a tubex of Demerol," Angie said maintaining her hand in position inside the vagina.

"I can't. The narcotic cabinet is locked," Helen said helplessly.

"My purse is in my desk. The keys are in there," Helen scurried out of the room. There was another contraction. Betty LeDonne held on to her belly and Angie's arm stiffened. The pain lasted about thirty seconds while the patient breathed deeply trying to cooperate with Angie's instructions.

When the spasm was over, Angie said, "The cord is prolapsed. The cord is coming before the baby. Everything will be all right but I have to hold the baby back. He's pushing the cord in front

29

of him. I've got to stay like this until we get you to the operating room. You're gonna have a cesarean."

"Oh, my God!" Betty said clasping her hands together. Then she crossed herself. "That's it! No more babies after this!"

Helen came back with a syringe of Demeral and handed it to Angie. "I'm giving you this shot to slow down the pain and relax you so you won't push so hard. Helen, get an alcohol sponge and wipe her leg."

Helen turned around to open the drawer where there were packets of alcohol sponges wrapped in foil. Betty LeDonne lifted her head and smiled at Angie. "Could you tell it's a boy up there?" she said.

"No, I can't tell. I just said 'him' for no reason. But everything's okay. The baby's okay and you're going to be okay."

Angie stuck the needle in the spot where Helen washed the thigh with alcohol. Then they all waited for the ambulance.

Angie felt the ropelike umbilical cord passing through the fully dilated cervix. She also felt the baby's head pushing against her hand as she tried to keep it out of the canal and prevent if from compressing the cord and cutting off its own lifeline. It was easier now without the contractions but when the labor pain reached a crescendo, Angie feared she would put her fingers through the soft pliable skull of the baby. Her hand slipped a bit because of the blood that was oozing from the uterus. It wasn't much but it might get worse.

Angie had never done this before. Her heart was pounding but she maintained her outward calm as she tried to recall what she had read and what Dr. Connors had done on a similar case. It helped tremendously to let the patient feel more relaxed. Five minutes later, the ambulance attendants arrived. The Demerol had not taken effect yet.

Angie held up her free hand as the two men dressed in blue uniforms positioned the stretcher alongside the examining table.

"Take it easy now," she warned. "The umbilical cord is prolapsed and I have to hold the baby back like this so I'm part of the patient, get it?"

The two men looked at each other, not fully understanding why but they would take Angie's word for it. A large sheet was draped over the patient and Angie's arm.

They made it into the ambulance without a mishap and were on their way to Laconia Hospital. The Demerol took effect and the labor pains caused less of a reaction in Mrs. LeDonne. Still each time the baby threatened to push through and trap the cord. After six babies, the patient's cervix was pliable and floppy. The head could probably come through without touching the side walls but the cord would definitely be trapped, cutting off the blood supply to the baby before it could breathe.

In spite of Angie's warning to the driver to take it slow and easy, he took a curve too sharply and too fast. She lost her balance and the slipperiness of the blood and mucous in the vagina made her hand come out. Almost immediately, a forceful contraction of the uterus ensued.

When she regained her balance and lifted the covering sheet, the baby's head and face were outside the vagina. The baby's face was bluish-black because the cord was wrapped three times around its neck. Like a small boa constrictor or some vile lichenous weed, it was strangling the life from the child. The child had to breathe on its own for the placenta had already separated.

The cord wouldn't give as Angie tried to unravel it. She took a scissors from the emergency kit and cut the three strands of cord around the neck. It broke loose, popping off like tense rubber bands, splattering blood over Angie and Betty LeDonne.

Betty LeDonne's hands gripped the sides of the stretcher. Her knuckles and fingernails were ghostly white from holding on so tightly because of the pain. She did not cry out or make the smallest sound. She knew instinctively that Angie was struggling with some disaster or else she would have been at her side trying to comfort her. She knew she could only help by lying as still as possible.

Angie rapidly found the two ends of the cord still in continuity with a pumping heart; one to the baby and one to the mother. She clamped these, staunching the flow of blood from each of them.

The child was still not breathing. Mucous and blood clogged its nose and mouth. Angie wiped the mess from these openings with a gauze. She inserted the tip of a suction aspirator to clear the air passages. Holding the child by two ankles with one hand, she turned the baby upside down and pinched its rump. When it started to cry, the blue color gradually gave way to a brightening pink.

The baby's loud cries reached the front cab of the ambulance and the driver pulled over.

"Hey, what happened?" the blond youthful attendent said as he opened the back door.

"We had a baby!" Angie said exhausted.

Mrs. LeDonne had almost fainted from the pain and the Demerol. She was sweating profusely but just managed to open her eyes.

"Angie, what is it?" she asked weakly.

"It's a girl!" Angie said with what little enthusiasm she had left.

"Thank you, Angie." Betty said and then closed her eyes again.

Mother and child arrived safely at the hospital and were turned over to the hospital staff in good condition. Of course, the new baby girl was named Angelica.

Angie's dress was covered with blood which soaked through to her underwear and skin. One of the nurses got her a green O.R. dress to change into. She wanted to see Mrs. Montague but skipped it because she was too tired. Connors was supposed to see her anyway. The ambulance took her back to the office and then she headed home in her own car.

When she was fourteen years old, Angelica Palmeri fell in love with the most promising freshman quarterback in the history of Laconia High School. Two years passed before she got down to the serious business of planning her life with Tommy Mazzini.

Everyone told her not to rush into it and she

assured everyone that she wasn't. It wasn't going to happen tomorrow or a year from tomorrow but after she had finished nursing school and had a good-paying job. Then she would marry Tommy, save all her money and live off his salary until they had enough money for a house. It was her way of showing how serious she was and how she could plan for the future.

They all told her she was beautiful. Her thick black hair and blue eyes attracted many men, but at sixteen she could only feel embarrassed by the thought of men looking at her soft young body. They told her she should go out with the other boys who asked her so often. She said it wouldn't make any difference in the way she felt about Tommy. Her heart was set and her mind had been carefully made up. She had no intention of changing her plans.

Some things did change even before she graduated from high school. Tommy was second-string quarterback in their senior year. Angie felt very bad about it but Tommy took it gracefully. He was the best cheerleader on the bench. At the time, she only thought it was wonderful and considerate of him to act that way. Years later, she knew that he just didn't try hard enough to be number one. The truth was that he just didn't care.

Perhaps she didn't recognize the difference because she was wrapped up in the excitement of her new plans for a career. She wasn't going to be a nurse. She was going to be a Physician's Assistant. Her mother really couldn't see how that was different from being a nurse but jumped at the chance of driving a wedge between her daughter and Tommy Mazzini. If she could change her mind about nursing then she could also change her mind about Tommy.

Angie explained that it was like being a nurse only better because you learned to do what doctors do. She would become an extension of a doctor's eyes and ears and even his hands and mind. A "P.A." learned how to take a medical history and to do a physical examination. From there, it was an easy step to making diagnoses and prescribing treatments within the limits set by the doctor for whom she would be working.

"Hey, who's gonna pay to see you when for the same money they can see a real doctor, eh?" her mother asked, worried about the practicality of her choice. "If you wanna work like a doctor, then be a doctor. You're smart enough and somehow it'll work out."

Her mother's words kept her awake all night. "Then be a doctor" and "it'll work out" kept coming back to her with mocking obsessiveness. There was a pleading sincerity in her mother's tone that Angie didn't understand.

After all, the plans she made would make her something like her mother only more progressive. Angie wanted to be a mother, a wife and something more than both.

Perhaps her mother didn't completely understand what she meant to do. Maybe it was just her mother's way of separating her from Tommy for reasons Angie couldn't understand. That would be the result if she followed her advice to be a doctor. Four years of college, four years of medical school, one year of internship; nine years that weren't in her plan at all. Maybe that's what she meant by "it'll work out."

Angie wasn't sure. There was no way her family could help her financially. She was the oldest of five children. Her father had a good job as a foreman in a plastic factory in Laconia. Although she never felt poor, she knew there was no money left at the end of the week. Besides that, there was no guarantee that she could get into medical school even if she tried.

On the other hand, she knew she would be accepted into the Physician's Assistant Program at University Medical Center in New York. She also had an excellent chance of getting a full scholarship with maintenance. It would only take three years, which was exactly the same time it would take to be a nurse. It was the other thing her mother suggested that bothered her more. Could she get a job in Laconia when she finished?

Laconia is a small manufacturing town in north central Massachusetts. There were eight physicians and thirty-two saloons serving a population of fifteen thousand who went to the bar rooms four times more often than they went to see a doctor. Despite this or perhaps because of it, the doctors had more work than they could handle. All of them worked at the community hospital of sixty-five beds which adequately served the needs of Laconia as well as some of the surrounding smaller communities.

The next day Angie set out to canvass the opinons of these physicians abouts P.A.s Five of them didn't know what she was talking about and after she explained it, they didn't think it was a good idea. The other three knew about P.A.s but weren't sure it would work in Laconia. At any rate, they weren't interested in having one work for them.

If her mother hadn't raised the question, Angie would not have made the survey. Ironically, if her mother had not caused a spark within her when she suggested Angie could be a doctor, the survey would have convinced Angie to become a nurse.

But once said, ideas cannot be unsaid. Angie was determined to be more than a nurse. Dr. Connors was her last chance to keep her new plan intact. He practiced in Hadley which was only fifteen miles from Laconia. He was so busy that he had no time to visit any patients that might have to be hospitalized in Laconia. So he referred them to doctors at the hospital in Laconia or sent them to Boston.

It turned out that he had been thinking about getting a Physician's Assistant so he could follow his patients at the Laconia Hospital but he couldn't find anyone willing to come out to the "boonies." He was sure there would be a place for Angie in Hadley when she finished her training.

With this amount of encouragement, she was sure once again about the viability of her plan. She went to the P.A. training program at the University Medical Center in New York City and completed the program with high honors.

Despite numerous opportunities all over the country, including an offer to stay at the University, she went back to Hadley, Dr. Connors and married Tommy Mazzini.

Tommy worked regularly for the first few years they were married but after he was laid off during a mild recession, he didn't seem able to get a job. So they weren't able to save all her salary. Angie was never quite sure what the problem was as she was kept so busy working for Dr. Connors. She was well paid for her time and although she had enough money to support them both, they never bought the house. They still lived on the second floor of a garden apartment complex.

Angie wasn't surprised to find the apartment door unlocked but her weariness made her feel acutely disappointed that Tommy was home. It had become harder and harder for her to discuss his future. She had become increasingly important to the Hadley community in her job with Dr. Connors. He had become increasingly despressed by his inability to match her stature.

She threw her blood-stained dress into the bathroom hamper. Her mind was made up not to discuss Tommy's job or anything else because she felt so tired. Without calling his name, she walked into the bedroom.

Tommy was there. Sitting up next to him in the bed was Sheila Flanagan. Both of them tried to hide their nakedness by pulling the blanket up to their necks.

Angie slumped against the door staring at the

two guilty-looking people in her bed. She didn't feel any anger until she noticed a can of Budweiser sitting on her walnut night table and the overflow ring that stained the veneer.

"Sheila, why do you always have to be such a goddam slob?" Angie said with bitter sarcasm. She completely ignored Tommy. She didn't even glance at him as she walked around the bed to wipe the night table with the hem of her O.R. dress. She picked up the beer can and dumped the remaining contents over Sheila.

"Get the fuck out of my house!" Angie said forcefully but with equanimity.

Sheila squealed as the cold beer dripped down from her disheveled brown hair. She dropped t. blanket covering her droopy large breasts. Angie turned and started walking out the door.

"Fuck you, Dr. Angie," Sheila said hatefully.

Angie stopped and turned back to her. For a moment, Sheila seemed frightened that she might come back and really attack her but when Angie stopped, Sheila gained some courage.

"Dr. Angie, ha-ha! The only doctor I ever heard called only by her first name. You phony shit!" she laughed.

"Get out of here before I bust your head open," Angie screamed at her.

"Hah! Do that and you'll have to fix it," Sheila taunted her. "The great healer, the savior! Business must really be slow so you're out to make some on your own. Maybe Dr. Aldrich is taking away all the patients. At least he's a real doctor."

Tommy had barely reacted to Angie's appearance when she first came in. He didn't say anything until Sheila's words started to sting Angie.

"Cut it out, Sheila!" he said giving her a shove that almost knocked her off the bed. "Get dressed and get out of here!"

Sheila smiled a nasty smile but got up openly displaying her nakedness in front of Angie. Angie ran into the bathroom and locked the door.

She almost started to cry until she heard Tommy and Sheila arguing.

"When are you going to tell her?" she demanded.

"Get the hell out of here right now!" Tommy said with a ferocity Angie had never heard before.

Angie washed her face instead of crying. She thought about the past few years with Tommy and realized there wasn't much between them. When she heard the apartment door slam, she came out of the bathroom. Tommy was sitting in the living room in his jeans and T-shirt. Angie sat down across the room from him.

Tommy sat with his elbow resting on the arm of the couch. His muscular arm bulged softly. He couldn't look up and face Angie. Angie felt the anger leaving her as she saw that Tommy had not changed physically since high school. Neither had she very much. But what she recognized was the schoolboy who was out for a joy ride. The kid who felt everything was okay as long as everyone had a good time.

"Tommy," she said softly but he didn't look up. "Tommy!" she now ordered him and he looked up with a hurt expression. His black hair fell in a ringlet on his forehead. His brown handsome eyes had the hurt expression of a hound dog.

"Tommy, you knew that I would be home this afternoon," she said softly again.

He nodded like the guilty child he was.

"You want a divorce?" she asked.

"Angie, I didn't want—" he started to sound pleadingly apologetic and Angie couldn't stand it anymore.

"Tommy, go home to your mother!" she said. Then she went into the bedroom, slamming the door behind her.

When she heard the apartment door open and close as Tommy left, she felt a great sense of release. She wasn't angry at Sheila anymore. It was Tommy's style to get someone else involved in an unpleasant chore. He had acted out the scene in place of coming to Angie and facing the fact that their marriage was over. She couldn't put all the blame on him. She didn't want to admit it either so Sheila had done them both a favor.

The next day she went to work as usual. It was now obvious to her how little her marriage played in her daily life in Hadley. People at the office had stopped asking her about Tommy for some time. Perhaps they knew long before she did that the match wasn't meant to work.

Dr. Connors was already in his office working on some papers when she got there at eight o'clock. She sat down in front of his desk planning to tell him about the breakup with Tommy.

"Mrs. Montague will have a tough time for a while but I think she'll pull through if she doesn't get a pulmonary embolus or something," he said looking at her over the top of his spectacles. "And by the way, we're not going to refer any more patients to Dr. Lindsey!"

"Why not?" she asked, surprised. She didn't particularly like Lindsey but he was reasonably competent. By now her own problem was pushed aside temporarily.

"He made a big stink about your being on call and referring patients on your own. You were perfectly right only he would have missed the diagnosis without you. For some reason, this made him mad."

"Did he say anything to you?" Angie asked without real concern.

"He didn't say anything to me. He went to the hospital administrator," Connors said with obvious indignation. "I went in there to talk about them paying you for scrubbing with the surgeons and came out with egg on my face. I was told that the Executive Committee was going to vote to forbid anyone but a licensed physician to write orders or do the histories and physicals in the hospital. That is a deliberate slap in the face! Five years ago they were delighted to have you."

Angie felt a painful lump of anxiety in her throat. This news hurt more than yesterday's revelations. The breakup with Tommy seemed almost trivial compared with the implications of this. She couldn't speak and she didn't want Dr. Connors to see the hurt in her eyes. Too much had happened in the last twenty-four hours for her to hide her feelings. She got up and went to her own office.

She tried to piece together her life in Hadley. Some of it was good and some bad but she felt she was being squeezed by the tide of events. It could only get worse.

She pulled out the letter she had received from Martha Daniels about a week earlier. In a very friendly letter, Martha had asked if she wanted to come back to work at University Medical Center in New York City. She hadn't had the time to answer it. If she had, she would have said no definitely but now everything seemed so different. Now she had nothing to lose by leaving Hadley.

Dr. Connors still needed her. She worked hard doing all the things she was capable of doing and Dr. Connors appreciated her ability. She was also accepted by the patients. If they still thought of her as Dr. Connors's nurse, it didn't bother her in the least as she went about the business of diagnosing and treating their ills.

But what seemed to be happening suddenly was the culmination of things which had gradually developed since Angie started working. Dr. Aldrich, a new general practitioner, settled in Hadley, drawing off some patients. That was okay because Dr. Connors was getting old and wanted to slow down more.

There were now fifteen doctors in Laconia including a few specialists. It was the local effect of the national policy which had increased the number of medical schools from 87 to 116 and the annual output of M.D.s from 7000 to almost 14,000. With the military draft abolished and the government's pressure to produce more primary care physicians, the P.A.'s role in rural health care seemed doubtful.

She wanted to get away from Hadley and Martha's letter was the escape hatch. She was surprised that she was needed at the University. Once more national policy had its local effect but this time it worked in Angie's favor.

National policy now decreed there were too many physicians. There was no longer any need for Foreign Medical Graduates. The liberal immigration policies of the sixties were clamped down suddenly, making it almost impossible for "FMGs" to come into the country.

The immediate effect was most strongly felt in the large urban centers. Particularly hard hit were the surgical services and the surgical training programs with a pyramid. The pyramid system allowed for a large number of junior residents who did all the unexciting but essential "scut" work like recording medical histories and physicals, being the second or third assistant at surgery, which meant little more than holding a retractor referred to as an "idiot stick," and anything else the senior residents didn't want to do.

The pyramid system assured that when the chief coughed, the juniors jumped. The chief resident was a survivor of the pyramid which each year dropped off the less qualified and less attentive. The "FMGs," also known as "foreign bodies," helped fill the base of the pyramid.

With the supply of "foreign bodies" shut off, there weren't enough American graduates interested in surgery to keep the University surgical program oiled. There weren't enough potential surgeons who were willing to risk three or four years of very hard work at the bottom of the pyramid without a guarantee of getting the last two years at the top where the high surgical skills were learned and practiced. Besides having to know everything, a surgeon must finally know how to cut. A surgeon who can't cut is like a pitcher who can't throw.

With the government's pressure on the medical schools to produce more primary care physicians and fewer surgeons, the base of the pyramid was threatened. P.A.s were designed to fill a rural need in medically unsophisticated regions. Now they were needed to fill an urban void.

Three

New York City
September 1979

University Medical Center on the island of Manhattan was an island unto itself that interrupted the canyon walls of buildings stretching north and south, east and west. There was an unimpeachable air space on all sides of the thirty-five-story tower hospital extending from a base that covered three city blocks along First Avenue.

Halfway across First Avenue, after the light had changed halting the traffic, Angie felt she had crossed an invisible boundary. Perhaps it was only a breeze coming off the East River but she felt it was a physical barrier reminding her she was in the realm of University Medical Center.

Nine years earlier, New York to her was a vast unexplored archipelago. It remained that way for the three years she spent studying to be a Physician's Assistant at one of the greatest medical complexes in the world. It was a hospital, a medical school, a school for nurses, research laboratories, clinics, laundries, its own electric generating plant, huge kitchens and a place of employment for thousands of people.

She tried to remember if she had felt this invisible isolation of the Medical Center from the rush of the city around it when she was here nine years earlier. It was different then for she was only planning to be there for three years. She had her whole life planned so the Medical Center and New York were just a passing phase; a means to a different end. Now she was planning to make this the center of her life.

Martha Daniels, the supervising P.A., had told her to come to her office which was room 368F. It had sounded so familiar that she thought she knew exactly where it was. Now, in the main lobby with its high arched gothic ceiling, it seemed so strange and foreign to her. She felt conspicuous standing there carrying her suitcase. No one paid any attention to her as visitors and employees hurried through the corridors around her.

Actually, nothing had changed in the forty-year-old building with the distant ceiling lights in the main corridor giving off shadowy lights and the feeling that it was a cathedral rather than a hospital. The chapel on the main floor added to this effect.

Angie walked along the length of the chapel wall with its stained glass windows as she recalled the elevators off to the left of the main corridor served the "F" pavillion. The sign beside the elevator door said "Patients, staff and carts only." She wasn't staff yet so she decided to take the visitor's elevator on the other side.

The building wasn't a shrine and the daily wear and tear was quite evident in the peeling paint and worn woodwork. The solid hardwood borders on the walls were an extravagance of the thirties when the hospital was built.

Angie was about to knock on the door of room 368 when it swung open. A young-looking bearded man in a short white cotton coat breezed by her. She didn't have a chance to ask if she was in the right place as he was quickly gone around the corner. She peeked into the room lined with gray metal lockers. It could have been a male locker room so she hesitated to go in.

"Hello," she called out tentatively. There was a scraping of chair legs against a linoleum floor out of her view. A moment later, Martha Daniels came out to greet her.

Martha's thick rubber-soled shoes barely squeaked so Angie was slightly startled by her sudden presence. Martha had straight black hair cut shoulder length instead of the Afro she had when Angie last saw her. Her smooth brown cafe au lait skin was slightly rouged. There was a small brown mole on her left cheek near her upper lip that looked as if it was pasted on except for the fine hairs growing there. She held out her arms and smiled as soon as she saw Angie.

"Don't stand there like a doorstop holding the door open. Come on in!" she said wagging her hands at Angie.

Angie's suitcase snagged against the door as she made her way in against the spring-loaded door. She felt her spirits rising because of this unexpected warm greeting. When they had been together before, they hadn't been very close. Angie was a year ahead of Martha and was somewhat of a loner, concentrating on her studies while thinking of the day she would return to Hadley.

"Don't tell me you came here straight from the bus depot," Martha said, taking the suitcase from Angie. "Never mind, just leave it against the wall and let's go into my office."

Martha led her into a cubbyhole of a room which had just enough space for a small desk with a chair behind it and one in front of it. There were no windows in either of the two rooms Angie had entered.

"This used to be the janitor's storeroom and closet space until the union complained and they got one with their own bathroom," Martha said, suppressing an embarrassed laugh.

Angie smiled, responding to Martha's lighthearted informality.

"It's better than nothing," Angie said. "When I was here before, there was no place for us to go. The nurses wouldn't let us into their lounge and the doctors certainly didn't want us hanging around. We had to take our breaks in the visitors' lounge."

"In some ways things haven't changed too much," Martha sat back sighing just a little bit, "but they are getting better as they come to depend on us more and more."

"How many students are in the training program now?" Angie asked.

"There is no training program for P.A.s anymore," Martha said as she dropped a pencil she had been toying with on the desk, "not one student P.A. left. They are really schizophrenic about P.A.s. The Medical Board doesn't know if they want them around or not. When the Federal training money ran out, they dropped the program."

Angie couldn't hide her surprise and disappointment. She also felt a little wary about her own position. She came to New York as soon as she could decently arrange it. Dr. Connors didn't raise any strong objections when she told him she was leaving.

"Cheer up," Martha said, seeing the furrowed frown contorting Angie's face, "when they is down, we is up! The Medical Board almost had a fit when they couldn't match all the surgical interns they wanted. Besides the manpower shortfall, the interns and residents now have a union too. So they don't work as many hours as they used to. Everyone has a union except us, but we have Dr. Arthur Comerford!"

If Angie had forgotten Dr. Arthur Comerford from her student days, the name came back to her quickly when she entered the hospital. There were signs indicating the directions to the Comerford Pavillion, the Comerford Radiology Department and the Comerford Research Laboratories. All this and more was in recognition of the large amounts of money that the Comerford family had donated to the University Medical Center. Angie knew the name but she couldn't quite picture him, although she concentrated very hard.

"Cheer up, honey," Martha smiled, "it can all work to our advantage. Where are you and Tony going to live?"

"Tony?" Angie said with a squint in her left eye. "Oh, you mean Tommy! That's all over with," she said with an inappropriate smile because of the mistaken name.

"I am sorry," Martha said lowering her eyes. "Not if that's what you want, Angie. I mean I'm sorry for sticking my foot in it like that. I should have known something like that, well . . . , when you said you were coming down so quickly."

"It's okay, Martha. It was a clean break," she said slapping herself up and down as if she was slicing, "and the patient is mending. But I still had to get away."

"In that case, your coming is twice blessed," Martha said with a big smile pushing her cheeks upward giving her eyes an exaggerated almond shape. "I need a roommate so if you have no other plans, you can move in tonight."

In her rush to get away from Laconia, Angie had not even considered where or how she would live once she got to New York. She had saved enough money to live on for a couple of months and certainly enough to get by with until she settled into her job. But she was also lonely and afraid. Martha's welcome more than lifted her spirits. She felt she had come home.

"But why twice blessed?" Angie asked forgetting to put up even a little show of protest about imposing on Martha's hospitality.

"The second reason just went out the door when you came in," Martha said waving her hand in that direction. "That was Ted Painter and he just told me he was quitting. You're starting to work tomorrow! A gallbladder at eight and a hernia to follow."

Angie's jaw dropped open and her eyebrows shot up in disbelief. Her blue eyes sparkled with excitement because she now really believed that she had the job.

"But Martha," she still protested anyhow, "I don't know anything about a gallbladder operation. I worked for a G.P. who didn't do any major surgery. I . . . , I only scrubbed occasionally."

"Well, you know how to scrub. Just show up in the operating room on time and they'll put you where they want you," she said referring to the surgeons. "You don't have to know a thing. Sometimes the less you know, the better they like you."

"Okay, if you say so," Angie said taking a deep breath, "but remember, I need this job and I don't want to get kicked out of here the first day for screwing up."

"There's nothing you can do to screw up in the operating room. Leave that to the surgeons!" Martha assured her glibly. "And no one can fire you except Dr. Comerford. He wants to see you in his office at three o'clock. Meet me back here when you get through and I'll take you home."

Angie started to make her way over to the "A" building through the corridors of the third floor. Halfway there, she met an obstacle which wasn't there six years ago. The sign said "Authorized Personnel Only—Burn Unit." She backtracked to the "F" building and returned to the lobby.

The "A" building and Comerford's office was the Jansen Pavillion. It was characteristic of Arthur Comerford not to have his office in the Comerford Pavillion. Years ago he admitted publicly that he was embarrassed to have his name sculptured on the walls all over the Medical Center. He said it made him feel like a girl with a bad reputation who had her name written in the public toilets.

More deeply, he felt he was benefitting too directly from his family's charitable donations when he used the hospital facilities like any other staff member. It was an unnecessary form of self-effacement. Arthur Comerford was a well-trained surgeon. His forty years on the surgical faculty of the University and the hospital staff were marked by constant devotion to caring for patients and improving the quality of medicine and surgery. Yes, it was true: no one would ever dare to suggest the exclusion of a Comerford from the staff. He wasn't the best and the brightest but he combined his intelligence and wealth to make his judgment the surest.

On his sixty-fifth birthday, after competently

completing a colon resection for cancer of the bowel, he dramatically announced his retirement from the operating room. He was still more than adequate but he knew he wasn't indispensable. His real worry was that no one would have the guts to tell him when to quit so he took it upon himself to jump the gun.

A week before that, his wife handed him an envelope addressed to him. The ink had faded and inside there was a dirt-stained letter he had written to himself in 1944. Many years ago, he told his wife that this would be her birthday present to him. She was to give it to him a week before he turned sixty-five. This was the letter.

Normandy, France
August 4, 1944

Dear Arthur,

If you are reading this letter as you are supposed to, then you and Beatrice have had a long and good life together. It also means that you have survived this war and the shelling which is coming closer and closer to the hospital is of no consequence so I can ignore it.

I have learned why some officers are referred to as "Blood and Guts So and So." Four days ago there was a "big push." I can't remember if we were pushing them or they were counter-pushing us but for fifty-seven straight hours I was up to my elbows in blood and guts.

The first boy they brought in had half his face blown away with the eyeball dangling by the optic nerve. I know you will never forget this so I'm not stirring up painful memories. The wound was caked with filth and mud from where he had fallen. I cleaned it up thoroughly and stopped all the bleeding. I debrided all the dead tissue, including removing the eye. If he gets back to the States, a good plastic surgeon should be able to reconstruct his face but I am fearful of a cavernous sinus thrombosis with infection. Maybe if this new penicillin drug is half as good as they think it is, he'll survive. I know he wouldn't have a chance if it depended on sulfa.

After that they came faster and faster. I cut off a lot of limbs. If we had more time and better equipment maybe we could sew up some of those torn arteries and save some arms and legs.

After the first twenty-four hours, I can't remember anything too clearly. Just that there was a lot of sewing and cutting; cutting and sewing. I know some died on the table. Someone grabbed my arm as I was carefully closing a wound. They stopped me because the patient was dead and I didn't even realize it.

I finally got some sleep and recovered. When I made rounds on the postop patients, I couldn't remember many of them at all! I couldn't remember operating on some of them but I did! Some were patched up reasonably well but a few were in a sad state. There would be wound abscesses, wound openings and some will have to go back for more amputations where gangrene is setting in.

Don't be shocked. Remember the nurses told me that these were some of the worst cases and it's a miracle they're alive at all. Some miracle!

I feel like I've aged a lifetime from those fifty-seven hours. At the end, I couldn't remember a thing. Maybe I still did my best and it was the best those boys could get here and now. Maybe I will rejuvenate myself but I feel very old now.

Remember this, Arthur! When you get old you start doing things by rote and memory. What you think you are doing may only be a memory of what you once did. This time in your life may be like those last few hours in the battalion field hospital.

Don't keep on working in the dark!

Respectfully,

Arthur Comerford, M.D.

Capt. USA (MC)

He carried that letter with him through France and Germany. When he got back home he gave it to his wife, Beatrice. Over thirty years later, she returned it to him unopened, just as he had asked.

He had forgotten about the letter and was not one to take impertinent advice from young surgeons just starting to practice even when they signed off "respectfully." It was not in his mind to let go of the reins, to move from center stage and become a character actor in the surgical suite, but he did. He did it because of this advice from the only person who could make him do something he really didn't want to do.

Angie stopped in the washroom to freshen up a bit. Her shoulder-length black hair seemed unruly, so she tied it in a bun which came unraveled. She settled for a ponytail but decided she needed some eye shadow to keep her from looking like an aging teenager. Her yellow cotton dress still looked fresh except for the creases and wrinkles in the back from the long bus ride. Despite Martha's assurances that she had the job, she still wanted to make a good impression on Dr. Comerford.

She sat nervously in his anteroom while his secretary, who was busy typing, ignored her. Although Comerford had stopped operating, he was still very busy with teaching, administration, fund raising and keeping an eye on the Physician's Assistants.

Dr. Comerford did not get up when she came into his office. He merely indicated where she should sit as he opened her file containing her application and personnel data.

"Well, Mizz Palmeri, how much surgical experience have you had since you left the Medical Center," he said quite formally. His balding gray hair, white moustache and knitting of his equally white eyebrows combined to make the question seem like a challenge.

"Mizz Palmeri" also made her uncomfortable. She had become used to Mrs. Mazzini or just Angie.

"Not much in the operating room," she said letting out a nervous sigh, "but I've seen a fair amount of surgical cases. Dr. Connors had a very large general practice but referred all his surgery. We worked up quite a lot of cases, you know, gall bladders, colons. The patients always called us first, so we saw all the acute stuff and—"

She stopped as she realized she was going on and on more rapidly for no reason. Comerford had asked her a simple question. She turned red as she felt her answer was excessively long by the way he was looking at her.

"I take it that you did a great deal of independent work when you were with Dr. Connors," he said, sounding more sympathetic. "Don't take on too much responsibility here. Use your judgment, but work a little bit below your true abilities and experience. You'll be working a lot with interns and residents. Actually, they will be supervising some of your work. Think twice before you voice any criticisms and then come to me or Martha Daniels.

"As a student, you had a knack for asking some very good questions, much to the embarrassment of the staff at times. You looked too young to be a house officer so I assumed you were a medical student. You're in a very different position now. Don't be frustrated when you're ignored or your opinions are dismissed."

He stood up and held out his hand. Angie shook it.

"Thanks for stopping by and good luck!" he said.

She left with mixed feelings but the most astonishing thing to her was that Dr. Arthur Comerford actually remembered her. It always seemed to her that she was invisible when she was a student at University Medical Center.

Four

Belief in invisibility is a great defensive armor. Unlike disappearing, the believer still functions and interacts with the environment, but with a false sense of invulnerability. The more one feels vulnerable, the greater is the belief in invisibility.

"I just don't believe he really remembered me," Angie said.

She was sitting on the floor next to the square coffee table in Martha's living room. Martha sat on the white couch with her smooth shapely brown legs tucked under her and covered by a long robe.

"What's the matter with you girl?" Martha said

with her voice rising in surprise. "Of course he remembers you! Ted Painter suddenly announced he was going to quit a few weeks ago. Well, the first thing Comerford did was to ask me if I knew what you were doing. I almost blew it for you. I said Angie Palmeri has a one-track mind. She couldn't be pulled out of Laconia by an earthquake. Then you called and made a liar out of me."

"I made a liar out of myself in many ways," Angie said softly as she stared into her teacup. "I made promises to myself about things I knew nothing about. When it came time to keep them, it was like I never made them."

"Don't lay that on yourself," Martha said, "it was a dream. We all have dreams we wish for but it's not a promise. Don't feel guilty because your dreams didn't come true."

"I don't care what you call it. The main thing is I lied to myself," Angie said, lowering her eyes self-consciously once more. "It took me awhile to figure this out. I thought I was doing . . . , well, you know . . . , smart and independent. . . ." She looked up at Martha, who was listening attentively with her head at an angle. Martha waited for a more satisfactory explanation.

"I did all the things I set out to do," Angie said proudly tapping her chest with her finger as she sat up straight. "It should have worked," she said, slouching back on her heels dejectedly, "but I wasn't doing it for myself. That was the lie. I thought I was doing it for Tommy or my mother or Dr. Connors. In the end, it didn't seem to make much difference."

"What about you and Tommy?" Martha asked.

"Tommy is the sunshine kid. Nothing bothers him and he never gets angry," she said wistfully. "I don't think he ever really loved me. I don't know. Am I beginning to sound like I'm feeling sorry for myself?"

"Not yet but you're working up to it," Martha said.

"Well, I don't. I feel sorry for Tommy because — well, not really sorry. He's a happy person but I did force my dreams on him," she said raising her eyebrows. "Not that he didn't accept it but he didn't want to own it. He wanted it to be put in his lap. As long as I planned it and worked it out Tommy went along. It wasn't his fault. He never promised anything more."

Angie sipped her tea while Martha shook her head negatively.

"Even then I thought it could work," Angie continued. "I liked being the breadwinner, the decision-maker. It's so strange how two people . . . , how the same thing can look so different to two people. I said okay, let it be. I liked my work very much but it was no use kidding myself. Tommy's formula for happiness needed no friction and no goals. Maybe he's right but—" Angie stopped, not sure of what was right.

"But nothin'," Martha assured her. "You can tell someone about your dreams but you can't make them share it. You don't need any excuses and that's what you're searching for now. Nothing happened except that you grew up and your experience caught up with your dreams."

The progression of Angie's first day in New York outpaced her ability to plan. It was exhilarating to be carried along by events. It was the difference between shooting the rapids and paddling along a placid stream.

When she left Laconia that morning she admitted to Dr. Connors that she might be back within a week. She didn't believe they were ready to take her back at the University so readily. She didn't know where she would live or if she would like living in New York alone. She planned to look at the situation objectively before she made a commitment to University Medical Center.

Within a few short hours after arriving, she had the job, a friend, a roommate and a place to live. She was caught in a white water current and was enjoying the sensation.

The next morning she still had the same sensation as she and Martha walked into the operating suite at 7:15 A.M. The nurses were already there preparing the rooms for the ten cases scheduled to start at eight o'clock.

Large packages of sterile linen and surgical tools were wheeled into the different rooms from the sterile supply cabinets and storage areas. Orderlies were moving out the stretchers from the central hallway of the operating room to bring in the patients. The anesthesiologists and the nurse anesthetists were checking their equipment: valves, gas tanks, all sorts of tubing and hoses, small carts with drugs and syringes.

This seemingly chaotic activity resembled in spirit the start of a horse race or the assemblage of settlers before a nineteenth-century western land rush. But there was no race at all. Once each case began, it would proceed at its own pace. Later, each room would change occupants in a calmer, slower-paced manner as each case finished and the room prepared for the next one. In this staggered way, each room would gradually empty and fill until the end of the day only one or two remained active.

An unpeopled operating room retains the silent echoes of its past and future much like an empty football stadium or darkened theatre stage. The props are set needing only actors to bring the drama to life.

In the center stands the table not even two feet wide covered with sheets tightly tucked under its plastic covered mattress. An unlikely place to rest the body except in unnatural sleep induced by drugs. The table tilts in every direction. It goes up and down. It bends and flexes at the head and foot and in between. All this to exaggerate and contour one's anatomy for exposure to the surgeon's knife.

Gears, levers, ratchets and drive shafts hide beneath this pedestal standing beneath a giant saucer-shaped bank of multiple spotlights. Electronic machines programmed to monitor and control the vital functions of the body stand silently waiting in dumb repose.

But when Angie and Martha came in, the machines were just warming up. Their knobs were turned and tickled, waiting for a human body to start them pulsating.

Martha led Angie through a glass-partitioned door into the office of Roberta Beeson, R.N., O.R. supervisor. Mrs. Beeson could be seen through the glass with her head down working on some report. Her head was covered with a green cloth bonnet, as were all the other heads in the O.R. She looked up through bifocals that had a thick lower lens magnifying her eyes. Her thin lips did not part with a smile for the two younger women standing before her desk.

"Mrs. Beeson, this is Angie Palmeri, our new Surgical Assistant," Martha said presenting Angie proudly.

"Well, another one! They're getting prettier anyway," Mrs. Beeson said rather stiffly. "I suppose you want me to find a locker for your friend here. I don't have any left unless she wants to change with the men."

"Oh, c'mon!" Martha said obviously annoyed. "There are three empty lockers in my row and Mary Ellen left last week so there's one more."

"Martha, don't get hostile," Beeson said cracking a weak smile for Angie's benefit. "The directive from Dr. Comerford says there are six lockers for surgical assistants. She can have Ted Painter's locker."

Martha stared angrily at Mrs. Beeson while Angie stood by embarrassed by the whole scene. Martha unslung her bag from her shoulder and together with her coat she placed them neatly in an empty chair as if she were getting ready for a fight.

"Mary Ellen's locker is a nurse's locker and

reserved for her replacement," Mrs. Beeson said defensively. "I won't have any of my girls doubling up. The other three lockers are for the medical students. You can take it up with Dr. Janeway if you don't like it!" Beeson ended with an assured finality which didn't change Martha's attitude one bit.

"You can get another locker in there," Martha said tapping her finger on the desk. "Move one in from the men's room!"

"Where'll I put it, in the john!" Beeson said sarcastically. "When I first came here thirty years ago, there were no woman surgeons or female medical students. No . . . , there was one but she never came to the O.R. Now there are twenty female surgeons between the house staff and the attendings plus the medical students. That nurses' room was built for thirty and now there are over fifty! Over sixty counting the recovery room. What am I supposed to do?"

"This stinking hospital has a budget of over a hundred million dollars a year," Martha said, redirecting her anger, "you'd think they could find one more lousy locker!"

"It's not the locker, it's the room. I've been screaming for more room for years but it's always priorities. And the women's room is way down on the list," Beeson said with a mixed air of triumph and defeat. She won her point with Martha by invoking the treachery of the system.

Martha and Angie left without another word. It seemed rude to Angie the way they left but she didn't want to show any disloyalty to Martha.

No one else was in the locker room as they entered through the door marked "Nurses." Martha no longer appeared to be upset as she pulled two green cotton O.R. dresses from the pile marked medium and threw one to Angie.

"Don't worry about it. I'll speak to Comerford today and tomorrow you'll have your own locker," Martha said confidently.

Angie was suspicious of Martha's confidence. She started changing her clothes and stuffing the locker she shared with Martha.

"Is Comerford going to concern himself with something this trivial?" Angie wondered out loud. "I mean, why don't I just throw my clothes in one of these empty lockers and give you my valuables!"

"This ain't trivial!" Martha stopped undressing momentarily to emphasize the point. "It's a matter of territorial rights and respect. Anytime a nurse tries to nudge you, you better hold your ground. Nobody wants your job more than a nurse."

"I know that well enough," Angie said shaking her hair into place after pulling the green cotton dress over her head. She pulled down the top part that was caught on her bosom. "But I don't want to bother Comerford about it. The one thing I got from our short meeting yesterday was that I shouldn't make any waves."

Martha brushed her hair into place as she smiled at the mirror on the locker door.

"I know just what he meant," she said. "Don't argue with the medical staff. They know more than you do. But this is different. Besides, that's what he does around here now. He settles all these petty squabbles and some of the bigger ones.

"Everyone around here is fighting for the available resources. All the surgeons want to start at eight o'clock but there are only ten rooms and fifty surgeons. Some surgeon comes up and says he's got an acute appendix that's going to rupture. He wants to bump the schedule but it's only because he's got office hours or it's his afternoon off. Bam! Arthur decides! And in this case, Arthur will make sure you get your own locker."

"Oh, so it's Martha and Arthur," Angie teased.

Martha burst out laughing at this unlikely coupling. She quickly regained her control and became serious.

"Nobody calls him Arthur except his wife," she said. "In something like this he'll always stick up for us. The nurses are always trying to get us under their thumb. But we're not nurses' aides. We're physicians' assistants and never forget it! Besides, he really likes you. He told me if Beeson won't give you a locker I should let him know," Martha winked at Angie.

Angie reddened because she still hoped her invisibility would protect her.

"If things are so tight in the O.R., why doesn't he just build a bigger one with some of his money?" Angie quipped.

"He may just do that," Martha said. "There's some talk of moving the G-Y-N service to a separate facility but in the meantime, I'll see to it that Arthur gets you a locker."

They returned to the central hall of the operating suite. Martha picked up a Xerox sheet with the day's printed schedule. Under the column marked Assistants, Angie saw her name listed under Maguire who was a first year resident.

Much of the earlier hectic activity had subsided with only an occasional exit or entrance into one of the operating rooms by the circulating nurses. These nurses went in and out to get some drug or needed piece of equipment. Almost all the patients scheduled for eight o'clock were on the tables. Between the rooms on each side of the central corridor, men in green caps and masks were scrubbing their arms and hands over wide, deep sinks.

Martha and Angie slowly walked down the corridor studying the schedule. They were dressed in the uniform of the day and of everyday in the operating room: green hat, helmet type for long-haired persons which were one time called nurses' caps; green cotton scrub dress, limited to women but some women chose to wear green pants and shirts like the men; white rubber-soled shoes worn only in the O.R. or any old shoes covered with paper overshoes.

Dr. Edsall just finished the final rinse of his hands and arms, letting the excess water drip off his elbows into the sink. His arms were held up in parallel obeisance to prevent the water from draining from his elbows to his hands. As he started toward the room where his patient was asleep and where Dr. Maguire was already painting the abdomen with povidine, Martha called out his name. He stopped while still keeping his hands up.

"Dr. Edsall, this is Angie Palmeri, the new Surgical Assistant," she said and was about to add something else.

"Very good, come on and get scrubbed," he said quickly and then walked into the room.

"You heard it, Angie! Get scrubbed. I'll meet you in the cafeteria at noon," Martha said as she gently maneuvered Angie to the sink and left her.

Angie looked at the wall clock over the sink as she began washing her hands to be sure she took the full ten minutes as prescribed by ritual. When she got into the room the patient was already completely covered with sheets except for a small window exposing part of her abdomen. By the protruding curve of the sheets, it was easy to see that the patient was obese. At the head of the table, the sheets went up forming a screen which separated the surgeons from the anesthetist.

Dr. Edsall had already made the incision. He and Maguire were busy applying hemostats to the bleeding wound. The nurse at the table kept handing the hemostats to both men as they silently held out their hands after applying the clamps.

Angie stood there silently dripping water down her elbow with her hands held high. Her arms began to feel heavy but no one paid any attention to her as Edsall continued to deepen the incision. Angie thought of Comerford's warning not to be frustrated if she was ignored.

The circulating nurse put her hand on Angie's back and pushed her gently toward the table containing instruments and linen.

"Doris," the circulating nurse said to the scrubbed nurse at the table to get her attention. The scrub nurse turned half around as she continued to hold out hemostats for the surgeon to take. At the same time, as if she were being pulled in two directions, she picked up a sterile towel from the table and handed it to Angie. Angie reached for it.

"Watch it! You're dripping on the table," the circulator said anxiously as she pulled Angie backwards. Edsall and Maguire kept their heads down and continued working.

Angie dried her hands and arms carefully then dropped the towel into the outstretched arms of the circulator. She stood there as before while the three people around the table ignored her once more.

"I need someone up here to hold back this skin," Edsall complained as he looked up to see what was keeping Angie. "This woman's a whale! Look at all this blubber," he said holding the patient's thick layer of skin and fat between his thumb and forefinger.

"Give me those big Wheatlanders and get her dressed so we can get on with this," he said to the scrub nurse. She handed him a pair of instruments resembling ice tongs used to carry blocks of ice but only much smaller. The tips of these retractors were like sharp rakes pointing in opposite directions. The rakes were inserted into the fat on each side of the wound. With a rachet at one end, the Wheatlanders were opened, spreading the wound edges far apart.

While Edsall worked, the scrub nurse handed Angie a folded gown to put on. Angie opened it upside down and the collar fell below the table top.

"Drop it, just drop it on the floor," the circulator said sounding like a scold to Angie. Edsall looked up to see what was happening. So did Maguire and the scrub nurse. Angie wondered if the gown had been deliberately handed to her that way.

"Doris, do you have another gown there," the circulating nurse asked.

"No, that was my last one. There's one on the shelf behind you," she said innocently.

"Just put some Kellys down here," Edsall said, pointing to the patient's abdomen below the wound, "and help her get dressed."

The nurse placed a half dozen large clamps on the spot indicated and stepped off a foot stool she was standing on. She was no more than five feet one. Now that Angie could look down at her she seemed much less formidable. The nurse pushed the table aside and took the sterile gown held in a half opened package by the circulator. The gown was shaken loose and the bottom fell downwards as she correctly held the front of the gown for Angie to slip into. The circulator tied the back as Angie put her hands into the rubber gloves held open for her by the scrub nurse.

The gloves were too small and pinched her hands painfully. Angie said nothing about the poor fit. Doris stepped up on her stool resuming her position at the table while Angie again waited silently unsure of where she should be.

"Stand up over here, honey," Edsall commanded, pointing to his left shoulder. Angie was too tense to resent being called honey by a man she not only didn't know but one whose face she had never seen. Besides, she still had enough composure to find it amusing not to argue with a masked man holding a knife.

She walked around the instrument table toward the patient's head. The patient's right arm was resting on an extension which partially blocked her approach. She could only squeeze in sideways without breaking sterile technique.

Her hands barely reached to the operative field. Edsall was only a few inches taller than she was but he had very broad shoulders and thick arms straining against the cotton gown. His elbows seemed to take up all the room she needed. He saw Angie's contortions from the corner of his eye. She was leaning backwards to avoid his moving elbows. She could feel her buttocks pressing against the armboard.

"Can you get a little closer?" Edsall asked impatiently.

"I can't move," Angie said, "the arm is pressing against me."

"Harry, move that arm out of the way," Edsall said looking at the sheets draped upwards in the anesthesiologists domain.

A woman stuck her head around the side of the sheets as she pulled the earpiece of a stethoscope from her ear.

"What did you say?" she asked.

"Where the hell is Harry?" he asked, surprised to see the nurse anesthetist instead of Harry who had started the case.

"He took a coffee break. What's the matter?"

"Nothing! How's everything up there?"

"Fine."

"Would you please move the armboard out of the way?"

"Sure."

The nurse anesthetist adjusted the arm so Angie could move closer to the table. Edsall handed her the handles of two large curved Deaver retractors which arced down into the wound out of Angie's sight. He set her hands just where he wanted them. She still had a problem keeping out of his way. The Deavers slipped and he readjusted them. To keep the retractors just as he wanted them, Angie had to arch her back forward and keep her elbows up in a most uncomfortable, straining position.

The pain in her back started immediately. Soon the too tight rubber gloves were interfering with the circulation in her fingers as she pressed against the steel handle of the retractor to maintain the proper angle. Once more she was ignored as Edsall worked in the deep wound to free the gallbladder from its attachments.

About fifteen minutes later, which seemed like hours to Angie in her cramped position, the Deaver started to slip. She had not moved a muscle from that contorted position. Now, as she tried to adjust her hands to compensate for the slippage, she lost her balance. The Deaver flew up out of the wound and Angie fell back against the armboard. She let go of the retractor.

Edsall and Maguire were forced to look up from the deep ditch they had carved in the patient's belly. Edsall replaced the retractor, holding it until Angie moved back into position to take the handle.

"Son of a bitch!" he cried out when he examined the inside of the wound. "Get me a zero silk on a big needle. The fucking liver's lacerated! Get the suction in here!"

The curved nozzle of the suction tubing started pulling out blood that could be seen through the transparent hose attached to the bottle hanging on the wall. The scrub nurse handed the heavy silk suture attached to a large curved needle. Angie couldn't see what he was doing but after two passes with the needle and some tension on the sutures, the suction hose made a pulsating irritating sucking sound but no more blood passed through the hose.

"Why didn't you give me a Deaver with a sleeve?" he said to Doris.

"It's not on your card," Doris said slightly irritated.

"Well, get me one now," he said calmly.

"There aren't anymore," the circulator told him. "Do you want me to put it on your card for the next time?"

"Yes, I want all the heavy retractors covered. Get me a Harrington."

The circulating nurse hurried out of the room. Edsall wrapped a thick muslin pad around the steel blade of the Deaver retractor and carefully placed it against the liver. Angie couldn't see what was going on but he was having trouble exposing the deep inside of the wound. Her back and hands ached but she dared not move.

A few minutes later the circulator came back. She unwrapped a large gray metallic retractor that was almost twice the size of the Deaver. The curve of the blade started out round like the Deaver close to the hilt but then became a straight tongue sticking out from the end of the curve. It was twice as heavy as the Deaver but when Edsall placed it in the wound, Angie felt it resting more comfortably. He set her hand into position and she held it with much less tension in her back and less pressure on her pinched fingers inside the ill-fitting rubber gloves.

"That's much better," Edsall said with great relief. "This woman really is built like a whale. Maguire, see if you can tie off the cystic artery."

Until then Maguire had been doing little more than Angie, albeit much more intimately as conditions in the interior of the wound varied. The small cystic artery was the main blood supply of the gallbladder. Edsall was delegating an important responsibility to the first year resident, who was in a better position to tie it from his side of the table.

So simple in conception, it was within the experience of anyone who had ever tied a package or a shoelace. A simple loop around the end of a tubular structure held in the tip of a long metal clamp.

The two-zero silk was thick and heavy compared to six-or seven-zero silk used to suture the eye but it was gossamer compared to postal twine. It was about the same size as the cotton thread used by a seamstress to baste a hem. A hem that falls or a package that unravels can be a disappointment, but an artery that slips its ligature can be the death of you.

It's not too hard to imagine the ligation of a small artery at the bottom of a deep wound. The base of the liver presses in from the top and the bowels threaten to engulf the exposed area. Two hands can fit in completely obscuring the view and leaving no room to turn and move the hands.

It's not hard to imagine it but it takes a lot of practice to do it right. Only the artery must come within the loop. A piece of fat will eventually slip out leaving the artery loosely tied, able to retract, able to start pumping blood out through the cut end.

Maguire took the long silk ligature from the nurse. Holding one end between his thumb and middle finger, he bent the ligature over the tip of his index finger. The other end was held taut in his other hand like the string of an imaginary bow. Keeping the ligature tight, his right index finger slipped down along the clamp until he could feel the curved tip. Then he knew he was around the artery and brought the ligature back to the surface where he made a loop of the two ends. Holding the two ends taut, he tightened the loop keeping steady pressure on both strands until he was sure it was snug around the artery.

Edsall held the clamp gently. "Okay?" he asked.

"Okay," Maguire answered.

With literally blind faith, Edsall opened the clamp releasing the artery now held by one loop of silk. Maguire made a second loop switching the ends from one hand to another so the two loops would lie flat against each other and not unravel. And then a third knot was made.

Maguire retracted the wound again for Edsall to inspect. He brushed the artery with a gauze pad to test the efficiency of Maguire's handiwork and was satisfied.

He removed the large retractor Angie was holding. The aching numbness of her fingers did not subside immediately. There was nothing for her to do but watch as Edsall and Maguire closed the wound with a series of sutures. When the muscles were closed together, Edsall stepped away from the table and removed his gloves.

"You come over here," he said to Angie as he pointed to his place at the table. "Help Dr. Maguire close the skin."

He started to leave but turned back to Angie.

"What's your name again?" he asked pleasantly.

"Angie Palmeri."

"Well, Miss Palmeri, thanks for your help. Thank you everybody," he said and left.

The three people remaining at the table shifted their feet around coinciding with a great lowering of the tension in the room. Maguire started suturing the skin while Angie stood by idly.

"Do you want to sew?" Maguire asked her.

"Sure," she said.

Doris handed her a straight needle with silk attached and a forceps. She copied Maguire's stitching with which she was quite familiar.

When they removed all the sheets, it was the first time Angie wondered about the person lying there unconscious of all that had happened. Angie didn't know anything about her, except that she was very obese and no longer had a gallbladder. This wasn't at all the way she had hoped the job would be.

Gratefully, she removed the restricting rubber gloves. She vigorously opened and closed her fists to improve the circulation.

Five

The black woman in the blue cotton uniform of the hospital's food service department wouldn't let Angie into the employee's cafeteria. Angie had to change into street clothes when she left the O.R. In her green slacks and sweater with nothing to identify her as an employee, she was barred from entering.

Angie concentrated on the bulletin board outside the cafeteria. Someone was offering a refrigerator for sale; another had a stereo set on the block. There was an announcement for group tickets to a Red Sox-Yankee game. Maybe she would go to cheer for the Sox just to upset some people here who were all probably Yankee fans. Actually, she didn't really care, having never set foot in Fenway Park.

Her concentration made her feel invisible. She ignored the unpleasant woman at the door and was ignored in return. Several white-uniformed people walked in and out of the cafeteria ignoring them both. Finally Martha showed up. Angie simply followed her into the cafeteria without a word passing between Martha and the woman guarding the door against intruders.

Angie wondered if Martha had winked or given some signal to the woman but it was no longer important once she was on line waiting to choose her food. Martha was also in slacks but she wore a short white coat over her blouse. Besides the shoulder patch with the Medical Center seal on her right sleeve, an identification badge with her picture hung loosely from her lapel.

"How did things go?" Martha turned to ask Angie and then looked over the food counter. "I'll take the fried chicken, please," she said to another blue-uniformed employee behind the counter.

"Didn't you hear the screaming?" Angie said.

Martha looked at her with a squint and a frown, not sure of what Angie was talking about. "What are you going to eat?" she asked.

"I'll have the meat loaf and the green beans," she said quickly. "Didn't you hear Dr. Edsall bellow when I tore the liver?"

They kept moving along the line picking up a salad, coffee and tea. After they paid for lunch and were seated, Martha asked:

"How badly was it torn?"

"I couldn't tell. I wasn't anywhere near it," Angie said sipping her tea.

"Did he yell at you?" Martha asked. She had heard nothing about the case at all.

"I certainly hope not!" Angie said with some discomfort. "If he talked to me like that I'd hit him with the Deaver."

Angie sat back in her chair slouching over her food and let out a deep sigh.

"I didn't know who he was yelling at. I was so friggin' scared," she said. "I think he apologized before he left."

"I don't think Paul Edsall apologized," Martha said. "Before I forget, right after lunch you have to get your I.D. badge," she said tugging on her own.

"What's on the schedule after that?" Angie asked expectantly.

"Take your time filling out the personnel forms. Angie, I really appreciate the way you stepped in today. Anyway, take off after that and I'll meet you back at the apartment."

"Is that the whole job?" Angie asked disappointed at the prospect. "Is my whole career going to be looking at the back of some surgeon's head while I hold on to the idiot stick? Level with me, Martha, why did Ted Painter leave?"

Angie put a forkful of green beans in her mouth. She chewed hard and quickly filled her mouth again with the green vegetable. Stuffing her mouth with food was a reaction to stress acquired in early childhood. She did it to please her mother while waiting for an answer to some special request her mother was likely to refuse.

Martha sensed the anxiety because of her own experience rather than from Angie's eating habits. Martha's professional experience was limited to University Medical Center and the rest of her life was New York.

She envied Angie her small town origin; for the opportunity she had to work with one small town doctor who came to depend on her; for the single-minded determination Angie had displayed as a student.

Martha's dreams, so much more basic, seemed almost cynical when compared to Angie's. She wanted shelter, food and clothes. She wanted them with dignity. After that came the pursuit of happiness, which did not include any rigid long-range plans as Angie had made. Still she envied her purpose because her own seemed so selfish.

Martha's light skin didn't make her feel less black. It sometimes made her invisible but not insensitive. New York gave her invisibility and security and Angie's return convinced her more than ever that she was doing the right thing.

If Angie Palmeri couldn't make it as a semi-autonomous Physician's Assistant in a small rural town, where did that leave Martha? If Angie couldn't find enduring love and happiness with all her carefully laid plans, Martha was content to sit back and let things happen.

"Ted Painter would like to be a bare-foot doctor in rural China," Martha said. "He didn't like the regimentation and the limitations placed on him here. I don't know why he ever came here in the first place. He's going back to the Peace Corps."

"Maybe I rushed into this job too quickly," Angie said pushing her plate away leaving half the food. She had felt so hungry just a little while earlier. Now her stomach churned uncomfortably.

"I ran away from Laconia but I can't run away from myself," Angie said.

"What is that supposed to mean?" Martha asked warily.

"I am very sympathetic to Ted Painter's viewpoint. I want my life to have some meaning. I—"

"You want to be in the spotlight," Martha chided her. "You want people to depend on you. You don't want anything for yourself?" Martha said, looking at her from the corner of her eye.

"I didn't say that," Angie replied.

"You don't have to! It's the way you planned your whole life. You always said you did this or you did that for Tommy or your mother . . ." Martha was excited and stopped to take a breath. "You never admit what you want to do for yourself. What does Angie want to do?"

"I want to be involved with people," Angie said, matching Martha's assurance temporarily. "Not just the kind of relationship I had with Dr. Edsall this morning. It has to—" Angie put her hand to her forehead as if she had pain there. Her counterargument weakened. "I have to feel my being there makes a difference. Even if it doesn't really . . . , so long as someone else thinks it does."

"I don't think we're on the same wavelength," Martha said. "When I say do it for yourself, you come back with what someone else thinks you're doing. That's all different. This is University Medical Center, not Laconia Community Hospital. That's different too!"

"It's not that different," Angie said sitting back feeling more comfortable. "On a scale of zero to a hundred, with hundred being perfect, how would you rate the best hospitals in the country?"

"This is the best!" Martha said emphatically. "I'd give it a 94 or 95."

"How about the worst?"

"I wouldn't know. Have you been at the worst?" Martha said smiling.

"Maybe you won't believe this," Angie said, taking a long look at Martha, "but the difference between the worst and the best isn't more than ten points on a scale of zero to a hundred service for service. And service for service," Angie held up her thumb for emphasis, "Laconia is as good or better than University Medical Center."

"I don't believe it," Martha said. "Where would you have your gallbladder removed, here on in Laconia?"

"Neither!" Angie answered quickly. "But taking all things into consideration, I would pick Laconia. Dr. Weston has done more gallbladders there than anyone at University Hospital. He's a Board Certified surgeon who trained at Massachusetts General. And there's something else you haven't considered. It costs three or four times as much here as it does in Laconia. With the money I save I could spend my convalescence in Bermuda."

"Oh, come on now, there's a lot more to it than

that," Martha said with her voice rising defensively. "There's so much more here. Of course it costs more. What about the house staff?"

"We're talking about a gallbladder, not a renal transplant," Angie reminded her. "Who needs the house staff to learn how to tie an artery in my body? And I want the surgeon who opened me to see me every day and to be there first if I do have any trouble. On gallbladders, I'd give U.M.C. a ninety and Laconia a ninety-six. Don't get me wrong. If I needed open-heart surgery or a transplant, there's no question that I'd come here. They don't do that sort of thing up there."

"Well, you're here now but are you going to stay?" Martha said, then finished her coffee.

"What's on the schedule for tomorrow?" Angie asked feeling victorious.

"How about a hysterectomy? I was trying to let you get your bearings but if you're so hot to get involved, you can work up Dr. Potter's patient this afternoon and scrub with him tomorrow."

Angie spent the next three hours in personnel getting her identification badge and filling out the multitude of papers needed to make her a full-fledged citizen of University Medical Center. Martha wasn't just being nice when she told Angie to take her time. She meant the process would take time and Angie wished she hadn't complained.

All the things she was anxious to get into would come along in the natural course. There would be many patients to work up, patients to see and follow from week to week in the clinic. There would be ward rounds with the house staff and private patient rounds with the Attending Surgeons. Her time would be severely rationed as she attended various educational conferences with the medical staff.

There were endless conferences scheduled. Almost everyone showed up for Grand Rounds to hear the most difficult and most interesting cases presented. Mortality and morbidity rounds presented the mistakes: esoteric and common. Plus there was a large selection of specialty rounds to attend if one were interested in the latest technical and clinical advances and research.

The personnel process took longer than she expected. Everyone she met assured her that what they had to say was absolutely essential. The Director of Personnel took a half hour to tell her what a big happy family the people at University Medical Center were. He talked at length about how every department meshed but finally admitted he wasn't sure where the Surgical Assistants fit in the organizational chart. He was bothered because he didn't know the chain of command. He broke down completely when he admitted he never had received an evaluation report on any Surgical Assistant and didn't know who was supposed to send it to him.

Other personnel workers explained the Health Insurance Plan, the vacation and sick benefits, life insurance, the Credit Union and the Pension Plan. There was a new person for each category to explain the great benefits of working for University Medical Center.

As the afternoon ticked away, Angie paid less

and less attention as she thought about meeting her first patient. Going to work for Dr. Connors had been much less complicated. He was the Director of Personnel, Health and Welfare, Vacations, Pension Plan and the Employee Health Clinic.

This last item was a bit of friction that existed between Angie and her former employer. Dr. Connors never had a routine annual physical examination himself. Before Angie came, the last time he had his blood pressure checked was ten years earlier when he took out some life insurance. He said he didn't believe in it because "how are we going to find something wrong when you're well when we have so much trouble finding the cause when you're sick!"

At University Medical Center an annual physical examination was required for all employees so Angie didn't have to ask. She was told to call the Employee Health Clinic to schedule one for herself.

Six

Angie felt more secure and confident wrapped in the white cotton jacket with the emblem of University Medical Center. It identified her as a member of the community. She could use the staff elevator and move about unchallenged.

Without hesitating, she walked past the counter of the nurses' station to the rack of metal folders containing the patients' charts. She was noticed but not acknowledged by the nurses writing notes and preparing medications. She ran her finger down the rack until she came to Helen McCrae's chart.

"Hello, I'm Angie Palmeri," she said to the nurse

writing at the desk. Angie clutched the metal chart to her body with two hands waiting for a response.

The dark-haired nurse who was about the same age as Angie turned her head slowly. She read the I.D. badge hanging from Angie's lapel but said nothing.

"I'm here to see Mrs. McCrae," Angie said cheerfully but it was greeted with a potent indifference which communicated hostility.

"I'm a new Surgical Assistant," Angie tried again, this time extending her hand. "I just started working today."

The gesture accompanied with Angie's bright warm smile broke the ice as she refused to be ignored. The nurse stood up embarrassed by her initial coldness. She returned the greeting.

"I'm Sue Barrett," she said. "I thought you were one of the medical students. Well, er, nice to meet you." She shook Angie's hand quickly. "You look very familiar. Who did you want to see?"

Angie decided not to tell her she was a student here once. It wouldn't have mattered and she could feel the frost creeping back between them.

"Mrs. McCrae, what room is she in?" Angie asked businesslike.

"Oh, she's a nervous wreck," the nurse said as she went back to her writing. "She's in 734. It's right on the chart you're holding."

Angie looked at the front of the chart. There was a small tag at the upper right hand corner indicating the room number.

"Could you set up for a pelvic examination?" Angie interrupted her writing once more. The nurse looked up quickly this time.

"All the stuff you need is in the treatment room," she said and returned to her writing. Angie started down the corridor.

"Wait a minute," the nurse called after her. Angie walked back to the counter where the nurse was now standing.

"Dr. Potter doesn't want the house staff to do pelvics on his patients when he's not present," she warned Angie.

Angie felt slighted but the nurse was obviously worried and sincere. House staff usually referred to interns and residents who were physicians in postgraduate training. It was not clear if the prohibition applied to Angie. Still, there was something artificial about Angie's examination of this patient.

Helen McCrae had already been fully evaluated by Dr. Potter so Angie's job was somewhat a duplication of effort. There was a law that required every patient to have a physical examination when they came into the hospital. Maybe it wasn't a law but the practice was well entrenched, so every patient was examined the day they came into the hospital and the findings recorded.

It was possible for the patient to develop an acute condition such as a sore throat or even pneumonia. Angie's responsibility was to check on these things. The real reason for the hospital admission was the responsibility of Dr. Potter.

Helen McCrae was a thirty-two-year-old housewife and mother of two children ages seven and ten. Her temperature, pulse, respirations and blood pressure were normal. Angie found out this much from the nurses' notes in the chart. She also learned from reading the front sheet of the chart that the admitting diagnosis was adenocarcinoma of the uterus: cancer of the womb.

With this much information available, Angie felt her role was insignificant. The actual history could be a variant of three or four typical ones. Angie assumed that the diagnosis was established by a Pap smear and a D and C done earlier. It was so unlike the role she played while working for Dr. Connors.

Often she was the first person to whom the patient presented the complaints and symptoms. By careful questioning, a comprehensive story was developed bringing in things the patient considered trivial and excluding the unimportant. It was a process of discovery, sometimes complicated, sometimes obvious. The history of the case she was required to get from Helen McCrae seemed superfluous to Angie. It had already been figured out and the diagnosis established.

Helen McCrae was five feet four, about as tall as Angie, but she had delicate features, which made her appear more petite. She had big blue eyes sitting above clear high cheekbones. Her hair was a sandy, natural blond hanging to her shoulders. When Angie came into her room, Helen McCrae was sitting on the side of her bed staring at her long delicate fingers as she nervously rubbed the thumb of one hand over the other.

734 was a private room with a partial view of the East River. Just a band of the waterway could be

seen through the space between two rows of buildings at a rather sharp angle. The standard hospital furniture filled the small room: a contorting mechanical bed driven electrically by pushing the buttons on the side, a metal dresser and night table painted in a soft brown, outlets for oxygen and suction in the wall and a long cable resting on the bed to call the nurse.

"Are you Mrs. McCrae?" Angie asked.

"Yes, I am," she said smiling and seemingly pleased to see Angie.

"I'm Angie Palmeri and I'm here to do your history and physical."

"Yes, I know," she said.

Angie wondered how she knew but didn't want to ask. She was glad to find such ready acceptance. Mrs. McCrae knew because the hospital brochure said someone on the staff would see her for just that reason.

"Isn't it awful?" Mrs. McCrae said with resignation. "You just never know. I feel perfectly fine."

"I know," Angie said, "but that's probably a very good sign. What made you go to Dr. Potter?"

"He was recommended by someone in Jim's office. That's my husband. He should be here soon. We just moved here from Chicago a few months ago and we didn't really know who to go to. Jim's been so busy with his new job. It was really a big break for us. I don't think he's had time to think how serious this is."

"Did you have abnormal bleeding," Angie asked.

"Some," she said preoccupied.

"Why doesn't he think it's serious?" Angie asked,

sensing her preoccupation.

"All he says is don't worry, everything will turn out fine," Mrs. McCrae said, sighing wistfully. "They never tell you, do they?"

"Nowadays they do," Angie assured her. "What did they tell you?"

"Dr. Potter told me I had cancer." Her voice was steady but an unmistakable twitch marred her face when she said it. "I didn't believe it. I thought it was those birth control pills. After Michael was born—I have two, Michael's the youngest—I started taking the pills and was on them for five years. I just worried and worried because I heard so many things about them. After I stopped, my menstrual cycles just came whenever they felt like it. My doctor in Chicago told me that might happen but that it would straighten itself out. It did. About three months ago it seemed to be regular again. Then last month, the month before last I mean, I missed my period. I was afraid it would start all over again. That's when I went to see Dr. Potter."

"Did you have a lot of bleeding? More often and a heavier flow?" Angie asked.

"No, I stopped completely. I thought I was pregnant," she said with a bittersweet smile. "With the transfer from Chicago I thought that would be the worse thing that could happen to me. We just didn't plan on having anymore children. Even my breast felt full like I was pregnant but Dr. Potter explained that that could happen from not menstruating."

"What kind of birth control were you using?"

"A diaphragm," she sighed again. "But even I know you have to use it, not leave it in the drawer. I thought I could get away with it sometimes. That's why I was almost sure I was pregnant. I hoped it was the other problem due to the pill. Dr. Potter told me my Pap smear was abnormal so I came in for a D and C a few weeks ago. That's when he told me. I wouldn't believe him. He was very nice about it. He gave me the slides and the reports to take for a second opinion. The other doctor said there was no question about it. So here I am. Boy, I wish I were pregnant!"

"How do you feel about the surgery?" Angie said sitting next to her bed. Helen McCrae had turned away from her to hide her distress. Angie thought she would feel better if she shared it.

"It's not the surgery that scares me," she said softly, turning back to Angie. "If they can't get it all out. Will you be in the operating room?"

"Yes," Angie said.

"Will you see me after the surgery?" she asked anxiously.

"Yes," Angie said.

"Will you . . . . tell what they find?" she asked childlike. "I can't seem to ask Dr. Potter the right questions when he's here. He seems so busy. Do you mind if I ask you?"

"Of course not. That's why I'm here," Angie assured her.

She completed the rest of the history-taking and physical examination leaving out the pelvic examination. As she was dictating the information Angie would have bet anything that Helen McCrae was pregnant. She would have bet anything but was not willing to bet on Mrs. McCrae's life. She couldn't deny the results of the Pap smear and the D and C so why stir up doubts in an already fearful patient.

As she finished dictating into the recording machine, Angie made a mental note not to put off her own physical examination and Pap smear.

Seven

Angie was in the operating room ready to scrub at a quarter to eight. As Martha had promised, she had her own locker due to Comerford's intervention. She went into room 8 where Helen McCrae was scheduled to have her hysterectomy. To her surprise there were a group of people in caps, masks and gowns already standing around a draped figure on the operating table.

For a moment she feared her time had somehow gotten screwed up. She had the terrible feeling she was late and had missed the chance to assist on Helen McCrae's operation. She had assured, almost promised she would be there.

In Laconia, she always tried to observe her patients during surgery. It made it easier for her to explain things afterward and to care for the patients when they returned. Often she actually assisted at surgery. One of Mrs. McCrae's deep concerns was that no one would truthfully tell her how bad it really was. She wanted the truth but was afraid to ask Dr. Potter, who seemed cold and distant. She wanted the truth but not the cold, hard facts.

Angie told her she would be there at surgery and she would see her many times while she was in the hospital. But this wasn't Laconia. Perhaps Dr. Potter was not in favor of Surgical Assistants getting so close to his patients just as he didn't like them to do pelvic examinations.

Finally, Angie decided there was no way for Potter to keep her from visiting Mrs. McCrae and answering any questions she asked. It was part of her job but to do it well, Angie had to get the facts first-hand. Then they would be her own facts which she could mold and present without distorting the truth.

Angie looked through the window into operating room 8. From the number of red-stained laparotomy pads and the amount of red fluid in the suction jar, she realized this operation had been going on for some time. It couldn't possibly be Mrs. McCrae under those sheets at a quarter to eight. She checked the O.R. schedule again. McCrae was posted for room 8 at eight o'clock.

She walked down the corridor, checking into the

other rooms as patients were being brought in on stretchers. Open-heart surgery in room 1 had already begun but the other rooms were still in the preliminary state of organized chaos.

Stretchers moving in and out, patients being transferred from stretcher to table with sheets dangling and uncovering prematurely to expose naked arms, legs, bottoms or tops; intravenous bottles hanging from poles with strips of tape stuck to the poles waiting to be applied when needed; oscilloscopes in the process of being attached to patients and recording interference in the process. All the rooms were filled and Helen McCrae wasn't in any of them.

Angie walked down the central corridor of the O.R. Suite toward the entrance and Mrs. Beeson's office. The door was closed but through the glass panel she could see a short thin man with dark thin and receding hair dressed in O.R. greens. The closed door made the room soundproof but the flagellation of his arms and body, the wide opening and closing of his mouth, the flaring of his nostrils and the crenellation of his brow produced a seriocomic pantomime of an angry and frustrated person.

Mrs. Beeson's reaction to this was also a stellar performance of restraint and injured innocence. Her eyes widened; she clutched her chest and swung her arms widely in dismay. Angie sat down on the bench just outside the door to wait.

Dr. Arthur Comerford came around the corner from the surgeons' dressing room. He wore the green pajamalike uniform of the operating room.

He had one that was much too long for him but at the same time it was very tight around his paunchy waist. O.R. pants come in small, medium and large. With some reasonableness, it was expected that anyone with a good-sized waist would have long legs to go along with it.

He had made some attempt to roll up the trouser cuff but it was futile. The pant legs covered his shoes and the lower edge in the back curled under his heel. Despite this ill-fitting costume, Dr. Comerford's carriage, his furry white moustache and alert blue eyes allowed him to maintain an air of authority and confidence. Angie thought of Adolf Menjou down on his luck in some old movie. Even as a hobo Menjou still looked elegant. Even in wrinkled, ill-proportioned pajamas, Comerford still looked important.

"Good morning, Miss Palmeri," he said. Angie stood up to greet him.

"Have you gotten everything squared away," he said and then noticed the silent dialogue going on through the glass window.

"Excuse me," he said before she could answer. He walked into Beeson's office leaving the door open. His action immediately disengaged the two actors as they turned to appeal to him.

"Arthur, they have done it to me again," the man pleaded.

"I have been trying to explain to Dr. Potter," Mrs. Beeson also appealed. "They started that dissecting aneurysm at five this morning and they're still at it."

"But why was my case bumped?" Dr. Potter

asked calmly without the anger and annoyance he displayed when he was alone with Mrs. Beeson. Only the tightness of his muscles at the angle of his jaw suggested frustration.

"They'll be finished soon," Comerford said, holding his hands up indicating patience was in order. "I decided they should use that room. If not you'll get started in the next available room. It shouldn't be more than an hour." The tone was matter of fact and enough to cool down Potter. Comerford added one more stroke.

"I want to speak to you about writing a paper on the excellent survival rates you've had with cancer of the uterus. They should definitely be published. It'll help us raise some money for that project I was talking about."

"Certainly," Dr. Potter said. He seemed hardly concerned about when the case would get started. "Let's go to my office and I'll show you the raw data. Mrs. Beeson can call me whenever they're ready."

Mrs. Beeson smiled an acknowledgement as they walked out. Then she slumped back in the chair and slammed her fist on the desk. She had put up with Potter's harangue trying to explain Comerford's decision to no avail. Then Comerford stepped in and raised his hand like Moses and the argument was settled.

Angie just sat there as Comerford and Potter walked past her. One of the circulating nurses crossed paths with them going into Beeson's office.

"They need a second assistant in room 4," she said to the supervisor.

Mrs. Beeson looked at the O.R. schedule, then said, "Where's McHenry?"

"He's scrubbed on the aneurysm in room 8 and they need someone in room 4 now," she said as if it were a common problem.

"Miss Palmeri, would you go and scrub in room 4. It's a neurosurgical case, an internal carotid aneurysm." It was a pleasantly put order.

Angie was a bit annoyed because she wanted to wait for Potter. She had promised Helen McCrae she would be there. Also she wasn't sure if Mrs. Beeson could assign her like this. On the other hand she had never scrubbed on a craniotomy and it sounded very interesting.

"What about Dr. Potter's case? Will I be through in time?" she asked.

"I doubt it but we'll find someone. Potter can do it without a second assistant anyway," Mrs. Beeson assured her.

Angie walked down to room 4 with a mixture of disappointment and anticipation. Her attitude changed to acute curiosity when she saw the anesthetized patient with the shaved head suspended beyond the edge of the table by a three-pronged device.

The head was completely shaved and only the smooth facial skin and fine bone structure suggested it was a young woman. But Angie wasn't sure. The patient's first name was listed as Adrian on the schedule but it could have been Adrienne.

The neurosurgeon was carefully painting the closely shaved scalp with brown antiseptic solution. Some of it dripped down into the ear of the suspended head. He carefully dried it with a gauze sponge. He was completely dressed in mask and gown; cap and gloves. It had taken him over an hour to position the patient exactly right so he could expose the correct area inside the unexpandable, rigid bony skull. Now he was making sure the skin was as clean as possible. Unlike the abdominal cavity and even the lungs and heart, the inside of the skull and brain have almost no tolerance for foreign invasions and infections.

Angie fixed her mask over her face and started to scrub. Alone at the sink, she scrubbed automatically, almost hypnotically up and down, back and forth between her fingers. Martha was scrubbed on the other aneurysm case. Angie wanted to talk o someone. She needed someone to tell her how she fit into this world. One thing was clear and it pleased her. They were anxious to have her back at University Medical Center because they trusted her ability. They knew her and could put her to work right away. They knew her but she felt like a stranger.

She made up her mind to get the right size gloves and to insist that the scrub nurse gown her properly. There would be no replay of yesterday's embarrassment.

When Angie walked into the operating room, the patient was completely draped with sheets. Only a small area of her smoothly shaved scalp tinted with iodine was exposed. The breathing tubes extended downward and then curved to the side where the anesthetists stood.

Angie was gloved and gowned without incident

this time. She took her place with the two surgeons, forming a ring around the exposed scalp.

"What's your name?" Dr. Peter Norwood said casually without looking at Angie. His eyes were on the scalp as he made a gracefully curving u-shaped incision into the scalp. Bright red blood flowed from the seams of the incision. Without apparent effort, he applied clamps to the edges of the wound one at a time. He seemed to be moving in slow motion as the clamps appeared in an evenly spaced row like a series of still photos.

"I'm Angie Palmeri," she said standing with her hands together waiting for instructions.

"Dr. Palmeri, this is Dr. Gross," Norwood said as he flapped the loose scalp backward exposing the underlying bone. All the bleeding was controlled.

"I'm a Surgical Assistant, not a doctor," Angie explained.

"Oh, one of those," he said without looking up. "Good, we haven't had one with us for awhile." He sounded pleased.

It seemed to Angie he was working very slowly and casually. It seemed it would take forever to get through this case at this rate. She was not aware that his hands never stopped moving; that each clamp was placed perfectly; that he never made a false move; that he never had to go back over an area once passed.

With an electric drill he made four equidistant holes in the bone.

"This is terrific," he said, handing the drill to the scrub nurse. "It cuts right through the bone but stops when it hits anything soft. I don't know why it works but it's terrific."

Dr. Gross helped him slip a flat thin ribbon of metal under the bone between two holes. A small hook engaged a narrow woven steel wire which was pulled over the flat ribbon that was there to protect the softer brain.

This steel wire was the Gigli saw. It looked like a very fine-chain necklace with eyes at each end through which the hooked handles were attached. Dr. Gross pulled the Gigli saw back and forth as it cut through the bone.

They repeated this between the next pair of holes. This time Dr. Norwood gave the handles to Angie.

"Keep your arms out so the wire isn't angled," he said as she began pulling it back and forth. It looked easy but keeping the wire almost flat against the bone required concentration and strained her biceps which ached terribly until she cut through the bone. Dr. Gross did the others and the bone flap was completed.

Underneath the bone, a tough connective tissue lining separated the brain from the skull. The dura mater was streaked with many small veins and arteries. Dr. Norwood coagulated these with the cautery before cutting across them and the dura mater.

Angie became more aware of his steady rhythm as he worked. There was no hurry to the even pace but it was constant and unrelenting even as he commented or handed off instruments to the scrub nurse. There were no unnecessary movements, no false starts or hesitations. And always his hands kept moving.

As if by magic, the brain suddenly appeared protruding through the large window Norwood had created. Angie had not been paying very close attention. She didn't have much to do and was thinking about Mrs. McCrae. She was not thinking about a brain but suddenly she was looking at the off-white, almost beige convolutions of the brain. The sight startled her. Here was a living human brain and it surprised and excited her.

"Okay, Palmeri, hold these very gently," Norwood said, handing her the handles of two retractors that curved under the bottom of the brain. In his slow, steady way, somehow unseen by Angie, he had insinuated these two curved flat ribbons of metal under the brain.

"Lift up gently," he said holding on to her hands, guiding them with just the right amount of pressure.

The brain wasn't as heavy as the liver. It had a firmer, dryer consistency which Angie could feel by the way the retractors held on to the undersurface.

She held on to the front part of the brain, the uniquely human part. Not the part that was similar to monkeys, chimpanzees or gorillas but the frontal lobes that were unlike anything in the world. Perhaps it contained the soul. If not the soul then certainly the ability to create new ideas and even new worlds. This piece of rubbery meat created music and paintings, memories and hopes. If the retractor lacerated this piece of meat, one could almost expect musical notes, numbers, scenes of happiness and sorrow to come tumbling out

106

never to be seen again.

"Son of a bitch, will you look at that!" Norwood said quietly as usual but filled with awe.

Dr. Gross looked in and pulled his head back. Angie had a chance to see for herself. The aneurysm of the internal carotid artery at the base of the brain was flat and broad. From its belly and its sides eight distinct arteries could be counted extending into the mass of the brain. It looked like some terrible insect, perhaps a spider or a crab, locked into the brain. Blood was oozing from its belly.

"There's no place to clip it," Norwood said. No one could detect any urgency in his voice. "I can't take it out. There are too many feeding arteries coming from it. Maybe I can clip it."

He placed a silver clip at the base of the insect where the blood was leaking. The prongs tore through the thin walls of the aneurysm increasing the bleeding. Dr. Gross suctioned the blood.

"Her pressure is dropping," said the anesthesiologist anxiously from behind the sheets. "What's going on?"

"She's bleeding, that's what's going on!" Norwood said with the first sound of annoyance he had all morning.

"I'll have to try the vinyl acrylate. Open one of those vials," he said to the scrub nurse. Then just as calmly he turned back to Dr. Gross. "I picked up two vials in Japan last year. You can't get the medical grade polymer here. You pour it right over the aneurysm and it cements in the whole thing."

The rare polymer was sealed in a blue glass vial

that had to be cut with a fine chisel at the neck of the vial. The liquid was very sensitive to light and air. It rapidly hardened on exposure.

The scrub nurse scratched the neck of the glass vial with a small file. Then she picked up the vial and using her index finger as a fulcrum, she applied pressure with her thumb. She was holding the vial too tightly and the glass vial shattered mixing fragments of glass with the liquid. It wouldn't pour as it rapidly hardened to a lethal mess of sharp glass fragments. Norwood took a deep breath.

"Her pressure is really down, 70 over 40," the anesthesiologist sounded a little frantic. "I'm giving her some blood!"

"Give it," Norwood said. "Honey, give me the other vial, please," he said, remaining calm as ever.

He carefully scratched the neck of the vial with the tiny file and then popped off the neck like a cork in a champagne bottle. He turned the fluid over letting it pour freely around the insect aneurysm. It seeped around the body and some of the arms clinging closely to the surface. Then it stopped flowing as it hardened. There was no more blood escaping from the aneurysm.

Norwood let out a long wistful sigh as if he had been holding his breath all morning. He had the kind of face that always seemed at ease but Angie could clearly see the difference now. The jaw muscles on the side were looser and the eyelids sagged. His shoulders were rounded instead of coat-hanger stiff. He gently removed the retractors and laid the brain back into the cranial cavity.

"You and Palmeri can close it up," he said stepping back from the table.

The closure of the craniotomy wound was much easier than the abdomen. The bone flap was set in place and the skin flap brought over it. Angie couldn't believe almost three hours had passed.

Martha was still scrubbed on the other aneurysm and Mrs. McCrae was already in the recovery room. Out in the corridor, near Mrs. Beeson's office, there was a surgeon still in his gown, gloves, hat and mask arguing with one of the pathologists.

The surgeon had just removed a piece of breast tissue; a breast biopsy for suspected cancer. He brought the specimen out to the pathologist, leaving the resident to close the small wound. The pathologist was Japanese, about thirty-five years old and with straight black hair speckled with gray. He wore metal-rimmed glasses and was holding the fatty tissue in his bare hands.

"Have you got enough tissue?" the surgeon said anxiously.

"I don't know yet," the pathologist said indifferently as he was mashing the specimen between his thumb and forefinger testing the consistency of the tissue. The surgeon was getting angry and agitated. He shook his head from side to side trying to display his annoyance.

"Is it or isn't it, dammit," he said. "Is it a cancer or isn't it?"

"I don't know yet," he said as his bow tie jiggled up and down as he swallowed hard.

"You're full of shit," the masked man said. "I know damn well there was a little nodule in there.

109

I know it's something."

The pathologist took a deep breath looking at the surgeon through the corner of his eye as he sliced the tissue with a free scalpel blade.

"It ain't nothin' till I call it!" With this rebuke, the pathologist left the O.R. with the specimen.

Eight

Angie walked into the recovery room to see Mrs. McCrae. The bed-stretchers were lined up along two walls opposite each other. Activity around each of the beds varied. When a new patient was wheeled into the room, two or three nurses converged on the stretcher. One immediately placed a blood pressure cuff on the new patient and checked the vital signs: pulse, blood pressure and respirations. Another nurse arranged the various tubes if any were in place: from the stomach, bladder or chest depending on the operation. Some patients still required heart monitoring via the oscilloscope.

Occasionally, a patient was brought into the recovery room and the anesthesia was not completely reversed. These patients still had the endotracheal tube in place and could not breathe on their own. They needed the most attention because a machine was required to keep them breathing. A kink in a hose or an unnoticed separation from the machine could lead to serious brain damage and death.

There were no seriously ill patients recovering at this time. The case of the internal carotid aneurysm Angie had just finished was still being reversed from anesthesia in the O.R. Helen McCrae's bed-stretcher was the last in the row of these four wheeled, lightweight beds that could be moved around easily. They were a little wider and the mattress was a little thicker than the conventional stretchers, so the patients were a little more comfortable.

Helen McCrae had her surgery done under spinal anesthesia so she was awake. She recognized Angie immediately even though she was drowsy from the sedation she had received.

"Hello, Angie," she smiled in a deep husky, almost inebriate voice.

Angie put her hand in hers and felt a warm response to the gesture.

"How do you feel?" Angie asked softly and smiled reassuringly.

"I don't feel a thing," Helen McCrae yawned. "Will the sensation in my legs ever come back? I can't move my legs," she said, totally unconcerned,

112

smiling like a drunk.

"In a few hours it'll all feel normal again," Angie promised.

"How did the surgery go?" Helen asked. "Did they get everything?" The sedation prevented her from feeling frightened but somewhere in her mind was the fear that the cancer Dr. Potter went after could not be fully eradicated.

"Helen, I couldn't be there," Angie said apologetically, "but I'll find out and talk to you later."

Helen accepted her promise as she would have accepted anything under the influence of the sedatives. Angie patted her hand and left her to the recovery room nurses.

The operating room suite had put on its midday calm. Unlike the morning rush, the central corridor was quiet. Only one or two nurses moving about to get some instrument or drug. Inside, the rooms were still filled with surgeons, nurses and assistants. Some nurses nodded a passing smile but she was mostly ignored.

Angie was feeling invisible again. This time it did not come from within but was in the attitude of those around her. It was as if putting on the operating gown and gloves gave her form that was recognized. The mask hid her face but without it she did not seem to exist. Helen McCrae knew her and that helped a little. Angie was sorry she couldn't keep her first promise to be at the surgery but she still had a chance to make up for it.

The coffee pot was still on in the corner of the instrument preparation room. The used instruments were piled on the counter top next to the sink. A mass of stainless steel retractors, carefully tempered metal forged in graceful curves, smooth and sharp angles, were all unceremoniously mingled with long and short fine clamps, stubby and right angle clamps. All this metal was dumped into basins waiting to be cleaned. The traces of blood clinging to the disorganized heap of metal added to the impression that it was the remnants of a head-on collision with no survivors.

Angie ignored the pile of hardware as she filled her styrofoam cup with coffee. Her attention was taken by the neatly stacked specimen jars and buckets on the counter on the other side of the room.

"Helen McCrae" was clearly labelled on the side of a six-inch high plastic container. She put down the coffee and unstacked the two smaller containers resting on Helen McCrae's specimen.

No one else was in the room to help her. She started opening the drawers and the cabinets until she found a pair of rubber gloves. The clean-up crew was out to lunch.

Angie dipped her gloved hand into the bucket of formaldehyde. The uterus had already changed to a dull brownish gray color because of its contact with formaldehyde. It was a firm smooth muscular mass that she turned over in her hands as she examined the specimen.

"What do you think you are doing?" Dr. Elaine Potter said in her usually deep voice full of reproach and tinged with anger.

Angie was more startled by the sound of the

voice because she did not see the tall thin woman come into the room.

"Put that damn thing back in the bucket!" Elaine Potter demanded. She held out the plastic specimen bucket and Angie complied by easing the uterus back into the formaldehyde. Potter's thin lips were tense, almost trembling with annoyance and anger.

"These specimens should have been brought down to me an hour ago," she said. "They are not to be handled in that manner. From the looks of this room," she said pointing to the pile of instruments in the sink, "it seems that you have more than enough work to keep you busy instead of playing with the specimens."

"But, I . . ., er . . ." Angie said in confusion.

"Never mind! Just help me take these to the lab," Dr. Potter said handing several specimen containers to Angie.

Angie had nothing pressing to do anyway. She did feel a little guilty about poking her fingers where she wasn't sure they belonged. She tagged along after Dr. Elaine Potter. Her anger had subsided but she was no more friendly than before. They delivered the specimens to Elaine's office and deposited them on the counter top.

Evidently this was not the general lab for processing specimens. Dr. Potter's name was on the door and the room was a combination lab and office. It was quite large enough. There was a desk set near the window and next to that was a table with a microscope. In the middle of the room was a high work table sitting like an island that could be approached from all sides. The work table was filled with laboratory glassware set up for some biochemical research. A deep double sink was on the opposite wall.

"Thank you very much!" Elaine said patronizingly and expected Angie to leave immediately. She remained hovering around the specimens while Angie made no move to leave.

Elaine Potter studied Angie more closely. She noted the bright blue eyes and long eyelashes without any makeup. There was an innocent curiosity in those eyes which did not allow them to turn away from Elaine's intimidating stare. It usually made the nurses and technicians vanish under its glare. She had not noticed this difference in Angie when she surprised her in the O.R.

"Is there something else you are waiting for?" Elaine said, raising her eyebrows to match her intimidating tone. It didn't have the hoped for effect on Angie. Instead of looking away, she looked at Potter with wide opened eyes and an ingratiating smile which forced Potter to turn away.

"Would Dr. Potter mind if I looked at McCrae's specimen?" Angie asked.

"I am Dr. Potter!" she said. "And what interest would that be to you?"

Elaine Potter looked at this inquisitive young woman again. She tried to maintain the same intimidating hauteur but her brow wrinkled with concern about the motive for the request.

Angie didn't see this change of expression as she was reading the name tag pinned to Dr. Potter's lapel.

"I'm a new Surgical Assistant. My name's Angie Palmeri," she said and then hesitated, not knowing if she should extend her hand. Elaine stood still with her hand on her hip expressing annoyed arrogance that made it clear that the gesture would not be welcome.

Dr. Elaine Drexel Potter was not too impressed by the title. She wasn't even impressed by surgeons. A Surgical Assistant wasn't even in her hierarchy of medical status but this intelligent, eager young woman made her think about it. She didn't feel the least bit threatened but an acquired instinct told her not to arouse any suspicions. Everything must always appear natural and routine.

Potter relaxed, leaning on the edge of the waist-high laboratory bench and placing herself between Angie and the specimens.

"I'm the other Dr. Potter around here," she said extending a coarse red hand with skin that was cracked and dry from years of contact with formaldehyde. Angie shook the hand placed in hers. It felt like a coarsened piece of balsam wood, cold and without life.

"Tell me about your interest in—what's the name?" the other Dr. Potter said turning to read the label on the bucket.

"McCrae. Helen McCrae," Angie reminded her eagerly.

"Whatever," Dr. Potter said folding her arms. "A Surgical Assistant has never come down to the Path lab to look at a specimen. Are you a relative of McCrae?" she asked pleasantly.

"No, nothing like that," Angie smiled. "We

117

talked when I was working her up and I promised I would be there for the surgery, which I was supposed to, but the schedule got screwed up and I had to scrub on another case." She stopped to catch her breath in the midst of this convoluted explanation. Dr. Potter listened attentively.

"I told her I would tell her exactly what was found," Angie concluded calmly.

"I'm sure Dr. Potter can do that," Elaine Potter said. "Is that why you were looking at the specimen upstairs?"

"Yes, but I didn't have much time," Angie flushed with embarrassment.

"How much time do you need?" Potter said sarcastically. "Do you know anything about Pathology?"

"Well, not really," Angie stammered a bit, "I have seen some really ugly specimens but Helen's looked good. I mean it was smooth and the cancer seemed to be contained."

"One can't be certain until the specimen is cut," Elaine said clinically. "Let me show you." She picked up Helen McCrae's specimen bucket and brought it over to the sink. Then she changed her mind.

"If you like, come back tomorrow when the uterus is more firmly fixed by the formaldehyde," Elaine said. "It's better to demonstrate when the tissue is completely fixed."

"I will if I can but perhaps it's better to just tell her the truth," Angie said despondently. "By that time I'm sure Dr. Potter will have spoken to her and I couldn't add very much. Thank you anyway."

Angie went out the door leaving Dr. Elaine Potter to wrestle with her motives for being there. It didn't seem likely that a Surgical Assistant knew anything about Pathology or could make any sense out of an isolated organ. Pathology was a laboratory science that couldn't be picked up just by experience alone. It was learned by study and comparison of many different variants of normal and diseased tissue. There was no time in the condensed curriculum of the Surgical Assistant to acquire even the rudiments of Pathology.

She dismissed Angie Palmeri as having nothing more than idle curiosity perhaps motivated by the chance to engage in some speculative gossip with the patient.

Dr. Potter examined the uterus over the sink. She tried to imagine what some inexperienced person such as Angie might think about this specimen. It was definitely larger than a normal uterus. That was a good sign for Potter. A cancerous uterus would be enlarged but other than that it looked perfectly normal. Not even a fibroid. She knew Angie could have learned nothing of value from her brief examination of the specimen.

Elaine cut the hollow organ open as she was almost about to do when Angie was there. A scissors with a six-inch blade was insinuated into the opening of the neck of the uterus. With two rapid strokes the thick-walled muscular organ was divided along one side exposing the contents. The sight mortified her. Her knees felt weak and a terrible flushing sensation filled her body. A few moments earlier she had almost shown this to

119

Angie Palmeri.

Experienced or inexperienced, genius or dullard, physician, layman or indian chief, the ten-week-old full-formed fetus could not be denied or explained away. The head was as big as the body but it didn't take a magnifying glass to tell it was a human fetus.

Just as she hid the organ below the murky formaldehyde, Dr. Eric Potter walked into the room. Elaine's eyes bristled with anger. She wanted to scream at his loathsome stupidity but restrained herself by gritting her teeth. There were other people in the adjacent offices. The power of her anger would have brought them running into her lab. She wanted to throw the acrid organ in his face but keeping the evidence in darkness was a stronger impulse.

Dr. Eric Potter was exceptionally jovial and ignored his wife's sour face and flushed skin. He could tell she was angry but it could have been any number of trivial complaints which he had gotten used to. His day had started out poorly when his case was delayed but it worked out well. It was an excuse for Dr. Comerford to sit down with him to discuss the paper he and Elaine would write on the surgical treatment of cancer of the uterus. The surgery had gone well and he was there to tell Elaine about his meeting with Comerford.

"Wait'll you hear what the old man had to say this morning," he said smiling and did a little jig. Living with Elaine, he had adopted her Spartan regimen. One noticeable effect was that he slimmed down considerably since they were married. His expensive blue suit tapered at the waist from his naturally broad shoulders. His jaw was angulated and smooth except for the dimple in his chin. It made him more attractive but not to Elaine who resented his good looks. It was a necessary asset as far as she was concerned. She could tolerate it as long as he remained the same old Eric she had married.

Only her interest in what Dr. Comerford had to say tempered her anger. She stepped away from the sink after carefully covering the specimen bucket. Even her glaring stare did not abate his good humor.

"The old man was really impressed with our data," he said smiling despite Elaine's disapproving face. "He kept on saying how wonderful the results were and that it showed how important surgical technique can be."

"It's my paper!" she said resentfully, "and at least when you're with me don't ever forget it! What else did he say?"

"That's the really exciting part!" Eric said waving his hands excitedly. "We talked about The Institute For Gynecology. Those were his words: The Institute For Gynecology. All the talk of the last two years is about to come to fruition. There's some problem about getting a Certificate of Need from the state but the money is all lined up and when Comerford money is involved nothing will stop it."

"Stop grinning like an idiot," she said very annoyed with his childish reaction. "He didn't offer it to you, did he?"

"He hasn't offered it to anybody," Eric said more seriously, "but this is also the first time he has talked about it so frankly to anyone on the staff. Up to now it has all been rumors and guesswork. But now it's definite. As far as I know, he's told no one else about it. It can only mean that he has me in mind for the directorship," Eric said, beaming once more.

"Stick that silly grin up your ass," she said striding forcefully in broad steps across the room toward him. He backed away a few steps but she was on him. His jaw became slack with fright because of her aggression. She grabbed his lapel as they stood toe to toe.

"Don't get so damned cocky," she said and let go of him. She walked back to her desk and sat down.

"Do you have any idea what it means to be the Director of an Institute, any Institute?" she asked focusing sharply through squinting eyes. He knew the question would be answered. He could see her anger giving way to the excitement of thoughts she was preparing to let him share. He had learned over the years to listen carefully and respectfully.

"The Director of an Institute is a prince among princes, a duke more powerful than the king," she began. "It is an independent fiefdom within the University. It is financed independently and Comerford's money is only the seed which will attract more from government and industry. University presidents will fawn on you with envy at your freedom."

The enormity of this vision of power and prestige frightened Eric Potter.

"You're absolutely right again," he said sadly. "I couldn't handle anything like that. There will be such fierce competition for this post both inside and out of the medical school."

"Stop jabbering like a fool," she said exasperated. She still had to present him with the specimen from McCrae's surgery but she didn't want to wilt his confidence completely.

"Once the Institute is established with you as its Director, there is nothing you can't do. Researchers and clinicians will flock to your side for just a tiny slice of the Institute's largess. You just have to nod your head or cough and pick the best ones. But always with the understanding that you are a silent partner in their work. You are responsible as the Director and should share equally in the credit."

"I think you're right, Elaine. Of course you are right!" he said with growing confidence. "There is no reason at all why I can't be the Director," he smiled at the prospect. "Arthur was truly impressed with the paper. He said this type of leadership can make the University even greater. He was talking about us, Elaine."

She didn't think it was necessary to remind him again that it was she who was making things happen; that it was she who had brought him to prominence and that it was she who would keep him from failing. But just to be sure he knew that, she pulled out Helen McCrae's pregnant uterus.

"Come over here, Eric," she said softly without a hint of reproach, "and take a look at this."

Eric complied. The uterus was closed as she held it in her hand. When he was close enough, she everted the cut edges and stuck the specimen in his face. He recoiled from the stinging formaldehyde fumes. It didn't take long for him to recover and see the fetus attached to the lining.

"Whose is that?" he said surprised, but his voice cracked. When things went wrong he had a habit of wishing them away in spite of his training and experience.

"This came from your patient, Helen McCrae," she said harshly. The evidence didn't demolish him as it might once have. He was chagrined, trapped, unable to come up with a good excuse but he felt secure.

"Don't be in such a huff," he said trying to sound conciliatory. "She is convinced she has cancer. I'm sure you can handle it like any other specimen."

"That's not the point!" Elaine grimaced. "We have to be more careful. There has to be no question about what we do from now on. They will be looking at you, watching how you work as your reputation grows," she said sarcastically. "We don't have to take risks like this! Be a bit more selective. I can still convince anyone there's a microscopic cancer but there is no way to hide this," she said holding the fetus up.

Eric Potter reddened as beads of sweat formed on his upper lip. He was not totally immune to the spectre of the dead fetus held up before him.

"Okay, okay," he said wiping his lip. "I'll cut down. I've been working too hard lately anyway. No one suspects anything about this case so please put it away. Incinerate it quickly with the other discarded specimens."

"I'm not so sure no one suspects," she said covering the specimen. She was more relaxed now that she had established her importance once more in the partnership. "Do you know Palmeri, a Surgical Assistant?"

"Never heard of him," he said.

"It's a she. Angie Palmeri. She was just down here looking for the specimen you removed today. Does she have any reason to suspect anything? Anything at all?" she asked calmly but she was massaging her hands nervously.

"I don't even know her," he said unconcerned, "but if you think she's a problem nosy body I'll keep her away from my patients."

"Don't do that," Elaine warned. "She's one of Comerford's Cuties. Let's not ruffle Arthur above all else. I think we're very close to what we want. Just be a bit more careful when Palmeri's around."

Nine

Angie's first week at University Medical Center had been a combination of whirlwind excitement and disappointing self-pity. She felt like a fifth wheel, used when necessary and then replaced on the shelf. There was no continuity or commitment to the way she worked. Yet as far as she could see, Martha Daniels was doing the same thing and it didn't seem to bother her.

Of course it wasn't fair for Angie to compare herself to Martha. Martha was a native New Yorker and at home in the Medical Center. It just seemed that everyone else had a place to be and a thing to do at a certain time. Angie did not know where she belonged in this new world. She had no incentive to initiate her own work. She only responded to the situation at hand but then Dr. Comerford had warned her that he was not looking for innovations from Surgical Assistants.

At the end of a hectic week, Martha's long smooth legs stretched out from beneath her short robe as she relaxed on the couch. The yellowish light from the table shining through the lampshade gave her skin a cocoa shade. The rest of the room was cast in shadows as the last hint of twilight faded.

"This is a crazy place, Martha, absolutely crazy!" Angie said as she slapped her thighs under her full-length bathrobe. Her hair, still wet from the shower, was covered with a towel.

Angie's complaint produced an indulgent smile from Martha. Martha knew she had wound her up and spun her loose like a top without time to give her directions.

"Where were you yesterday? Jesus!" Angie said sitting down in the arm chair and not waiting for Martha to answer. "I was supposed to scrub on a hysterectomy but assisted on an intracranial aneurysm instead. From then on the whole day was screwed up. It's a good thing you left that note telling me you wouldn't be home or I'd really have gone bananas."

"I'm really sorry about that but a friend of mine made me an offer I couldn't refuse," Martha stretched out sensuously recalling the evening.

"But how did you know you wouldn't come

home at all," Angie asked naively.

"That was the offer I couldn't refuse," Martha laughed and pulled herself up swinging her legs to the floor. Angie laughed also when she realized why Martha didn't come home last night.

"What happened to you yesterday?" Martha asked as she leaned over to get a cigarette from the coffee table.

"After I got through with surgery, I went to the clinic. I didn't know where you were. I walked into the clinic and this Dr. Wallace says I should see the patient in the third cubicle.

"I saw the patient and treated him. And then another and another just as if I were in Hadley. An hour later, Dr. Wallace comes back and wants to know where the first patient is. That's what so crazy around here. He thought I was a medical student and I was supposed to see one patient and present the case to him. It was a family practice clinic and there were some other medical students there.

"None of the patients had anything serious but he was really pissed because . . ., anyhow it's crazy how anyone with a white coat can step in and work in the clinic. By the time I found the Surgery clinic, everyone was gone."

"What time did you get through with the craniotomy?" Martha asked, taking a drag on her cigarette.

"That didn't delay me," Angie said. "I got into a long conversation with Dr. Elaine Potter," she said purposely omitting how they met.

"You had a conversation with *elytronic Elaine*?"

Martha said raising her eyebrows with impressed surprise.

"Electronic Elaine? I would hardly call her that. She's more like a cold fish!" Angie said.

Martha smiled broadly showing almost all her teeth. She leaned forward a little closer to Angie.

"Now get this!" she said. *"El-y-tronic,"* she sounded out the syllables distinctly." Dr. Ambrose gave her that name. Elytron is Greek for the fore-wing of certain insects which acts as a protective covering for the rear wings. Try to picture it. One set of broad wings folded over a more delicate set of inner wings. It's also an archaic reference to a vagina but only a Greek scholar like Ambrose would come up with something like that."

"I don't get it," Angie looked genuinely puzzled.

"It's like calling someone a putz," Martha said hoping the analogy would clarify the picture.

"A putz? Isn't that Jewish? I didn't know you spoke Jewish."

"In New York, everyone knows what a putz is!" Martha said but she could see from Angie's expression that not everyone in New York did.

"A putz," Martha explained, "is the Yiddish word for penis but it has nothing to do with that organ. It refers to someone's personality, character or intelligence in a very negative way."

"Oh, I get it now," Angie said shaking her head up and down, "Elaine is a female putz. I remember hearing that word before. Your accent is funny."

"Just forget it," Martha said with a wave of her hand. "What did you and Elaine talk about?"

"Just about pathology and how hard it was to know everything you had to know about pathology. Dr. Connors always looked at his patient's specimen whenever he could. He said even pathologists make mistakes and don't always admit it. He meant they don't describe things accurately all the time. If you ask them the right questions, you can get them to change their minds."

"I don't know anything about pathology and as far as I can see no one around here questions them. As they say, the specimen 'ain't nothin' till they call it'."

"I heard that in the O.R. yesterday. That Japanese Pathologist said it to some surgeon and it ended the argument. How come?"

"It comes from an old baseball story," Martha explained. "The pitch comes over the plate into the catcher's mitt and the umpire is a little late in making the call. When he does, he calls it a ball. Well, the catcher controls his temper. The next pitch is high and outside. Again the umpire is slow but this time he calls it a strike. On the third pitch, the batter swings and misses but the umpire doesn't say anything. The catcher is really mad now and he turns around and says sarcastically, 'Well, what is it? A ball or a strike?' The umpire says, 'It ain't nothin' till I call it!' "

"Where were you yesterday afternoon?" Angie asked. "When I left the O.R. you were still scrubbed."

"We didn't get through till four o'clock," Martha said shaking her head sadly. "That was a bitch! She was only forty years old."

"She didn't make it from the way you said that," Angie said.

"No, we never got her off the table. She had a dissecting aneurysm. The kidneys were involved. It even went up into her carotids. That's what really screwed her up. It went all the way up her neck on both sides almost to the skull and he just couldn't make the anastomosis. Everything just kept falling apart. The tissue was so friable it couldn't hold any sutures."

"That's really young for an aneurysm," Angie said.

"Dr. Trenton said it would probably turn out to be cystic medial necrosis after they finished the autopsy. It's a disease of the aorta where the middle of the wall is very weak, the lining tears and the blood tears through making a false passage. Fortunately, it's a very rare disease."

"Fortunately? For who?" Angie asked.

"Fortunately for the rest of us," Martha said, with a forced smile. Let's just forget about it. No more hospital talk. Jeannie's having a party tonight and she said to be sure you were there."

"I can't do that," Angie said stiffening her legs straight out in front of her and closing her eyes simulating great pain. "I'd rather have my gallbladder removed!"

"Come on, Angie! You're not going to be a long suffering pain in the ass, are you?" Martha said, amused by Angie's reaction.

Angie opened her eyes and relaxed her body. She was mortified by Martha's insinuation and tried to reverse the bad impression by joking about it.

"Whatever do you mean?" Angie said in a poorly managed falsetto, trying to comically imitate Victorian virtue. Instead of placing her hand over her heart, she pressed her breast from below vulgarly exaggerating its ample fullness. "I still happen to be a married woman!"

"Tell everyone that and they'll all be after you. There's nothing like an attached piece of ass floating around. It's a safeguard against permanent entanglements," Martha said casually.

"Really, Martha, I can't do it!" Angie blushed. "I'd be so awkward. It would feel so strange. I wouldn't know what to say if a man talked to me. Besides, I have nothing to wear."

"You don't have to say anything. Just blink those big blue eyes and let them do all the talking," Martha said to encourage her.

"Martha, how can you talk like that? You're not the type who pulls that kind of crap," Angie said seriously.

"Whatever do you mean?" Martha said fluttering her eyelashes and holding her left breast mockingly just as Angie had done.

"I mean you're too smart, pretty, intelligent and independent to stoop so low!"

"In case you forgot, child, there are some things you can't do independently," Martha said aggressively, keeping her eyes wide open. "And maybe you don't know it but there's a lot to be said about having someone love you just for your body. It takes a lot of pressure off the psyche."

"But—"

"But nothin'!" Martha slapped her hand down

on the couch so hard that Angie jumped. "You go put the hair dryer to your head and slip into a pair of jeans. We are goin' to party tonight!" she said snapping her fingers over her head.

"But I—"

"But nothing," Martha said more soberly. "You can't keep planning out every minute of your life. Just let it play out for awhile. See how it feels, let yourself be surprised. You tried it your way, now try mine."

Angie didn't have a comeback for that. She silently slinked her way to the bathroom. She turned the hot air on her head as she roughly and angrily combed the wet knots out of her long hair. She was the one with the chip on her shoulder and Martha was not afraid to knock it off. She felt like a child. As she pulled the comb through her hair she kept thinking, "I dare you to make me have a good time."

But as the hair dried, the knots loosened and the strands fell into place. She had been on the verge of tears, punishing her hair with the comb, as angry at herself as she was toward Martha for making her feel so childish. Then the comb moved more easily and gracefully through her hair. She began to relax and soften. There was a wrinkle at the corner of her eye that usually was there only when she smiled but she wasn't smiling now.

She took a closer look in the mirror. It was more like a crease than a wrinkle. She smiled at herself, not a happy smile but a facial manipulation to test her skin. Creases radiated from around both eyes like a star burst and all but one disappeared when the skin stretched back into place.

Twenty-seven was not the right age to start worrying about wrinkles. Her mother, who was almost fifty, had them under her eyes. She couldn't picture her without them. She once admired them because she thought it gave her mother's face character; some sign that she had lived an interesting life; somehow an overt expression of secret experiences which can only come with time.

Was this the secret, she wondered? Did each wrinkle appear with doubt and worry, fear and sorrow, a psychic tension diffused under a piece of loose skin?

She let her robe fall to the floor and stood as straight as possible. Her belly was flat and firm but she felt her hips were too broad and round as she pinched the skin at her side. She wished her legs were longer like Martha's but all in all she felt rightly satisfied with herself.

She moved around in the small confines of the bathroom feeling her mood loosen with the fluidity of her movements. Martha was right after all. There was some pleasure in not knowing, not planning each action. She could already feel the pleasurable anticipation of letting go.

They were both dressed in blue jeans and cotton blouses. Angie just finished putting on her lipstick while Martha stood at the light switch in the bedroom ready to leave.

"All set!" Angie smiled as she placed her lipstick in her purse. Martha turned off the light.

"Wait!" Angie called out in the dark and a second later the light came on again. She walked over to the dresser drawer and pulled out a small compact containing her diaphragm. She slipped it in her purse alongside her lipstick.

"It might not be that kind of night," Martha said referring to the diaphragm. "You don't have to change so radically so quickly. I mean, don't lose your head," she said worriedly.

"Me? Lose my head?" Angie smiled as she walked past Martha and flipped the light switch.

Martha followed her out to the hallway door. Angie turned around before she was about to open it.

"It's all part of my plan or else I would have left the stupid thing in Hadley," Angie winked at her.

Jeannie Tillman's apartment was only four blocks away. They passed a corner of the Medical Center along the way. It was more than a coincidence that so many of the professional staff lived so close to the Medical Center. The Upper East Side of Manhattan was expensive and ordinarily beyond the means of the salaried personnel. But the Medical Center through donations and discriminate purchases owned most of the land and buildings for several blocks around it.

This outer moat of real estate protected the Medical Center from encroachment of commercial New York. It was untaxable, secure and provided an added incentive to those who worked there. The rents were adjusted, the personnel were happy and no one could miss work because of bad weather and transportation.

When Martha and Angie arrived, the apartment was already filled with wall to wall people. No invitations had been sent. Only the word that there was a party at Jeannie's tonight. Also at Barbara's and Susie's who shared the apartment with Jeannie.

The sea of heads bobbed and produced a loud murmur of talk buried by the music coming from the living room. It was hard to tell where the living room began and the dining room ended except for the staggered walls and the open space made by the crowd for the couples who were dancing.

Above the din came a shout for "Dr. Glass" moments after the phone in the kitchen rang. A heavily bearded blond young man dressed in the white uniform of the Medical Center house staff made his way into the kitchen through the crowd. A long counter with a pass-through window separated the kitchen from the dining room. A collection of various kinds of alcohol in half gallon bottles were lined up along the counter.

The kitchen was packed with people coming or going to get a glass or some ice. The crowd avoided a small area near the phone which was left accessible to the many white-coated men who were on call. They were expecting a call from the hospital telling them someone couldn't breathe; someone was shot or stabbed; something was wrong with the patient who had a colon or a gallbladder removed. The call would come from another doctor. Someone lower down in the hierarchy, lower in the pyramid.

Rarely did someone higher up call on a junior. It was more than a breach of etiquette. It was a break in the chain of command which meant that someone had screwed up. It meant that the junior man wasn't on the ball. Something happened that wasn't picked up by the doctor in the hospital.

Martha and Angie were about to make their way to the area mapped out as the dance floor when the hairy Dr. Glass brushed his way across their path. He was halted in front of them by a taller clean shaven doctor in a white coat smoking a pipe.

"What's up?" the serious and weary-looking pipe smoker said to Dr. Glass.

"Mazur admitted a gunshot wound of the abdomen," Dr. Glass said excitedly. The other man, who was the Chief Surgical Resident and had spent the past seven years coming up the ladder, remained placid. He had seen many gunshot wounds and spent many sleepless nights over these and other emergencies. It was now his turn to let the others do the preliminary work as he had done. Dr. Glass was his junior resident; anxious, less experienced and more hungry to gain experience.

"The patient is twenty-two years old and stable," Glass reported. "He was typed and crossmatched for six units of blood. He also has hematuria. Should I get a pyelogram?"

"Get a pyelogram but don't move him over to X-ray unless you're sure he's stable," he said sticking his cold pipe away in his pocket. "I'll come over with you now. It's been too quiet tonight. Something else is sure to turn up before we get this guy to the O.R."

The two white-coated men engrossed in their own thoughts separated Angie from Martha as they walked out between the two women.

"Who was that?" Angie asked tilting her head toward the departing surgeons.

"That was The Lone Ranger and Tonto!" Martha smiled and Angie laughed.

"I heard that!" a tall man in an open-collared shirt and an expensive-looking blue blazer said, standing just over Martha's right shoulder. He was tall enough so he was able to extend his neck until he was cheek to cheek with Martha. "You have to show more respect," he added with good humor.

Martha didn't turn around but leaned backward pressing against him. It wasn't hard to do in the crowded room. She gently stroked and tapped his face trying to identify him with her fingers. Although Martha had been surprised by the intrusion of his deep pleasant voice, she knew who was standing behind her and she took her time with the tactile identification.

"There's only one person whose head could be this swollen," Martha said with one hand on the top of his head and the other under his chin. "It has to be Dr. Trenton!"

She turned around just as he began to blush a little. Otherwise he seemed to take the put-down gracefully. Martha moved away from him toward Angie.

"Angie Palmeri," she said sounding formal, "this is Dr. Peter Trenton but you can call him Pete or Trent when he has his small size hat on."

Dr. Peter Trenton's self-assurance was diminished as Martha introduced him to Angie. Such a reaction was rare for this thirty-eight-year-old surgeon who was considered one of the best young surgeons on the staff of University Medical Center. Martha realized it wasn't her teasing comments distracting him. His attention was focused on Angie. Someone grabbed Martha by the elbow and asked her to dance. Without a word but with a curious backward glance she slipped through the crowd to the living room dance floor.

"I heard you just started working here," Peter said, straining above the loud music. Angie could barely hear him. She cupped her hand over her ear and leaned toward him. He bent over and spoke loudly into her ear.

"I said I've heard a lot about you."

She couldn't recognize the scent of his cologne but it was senuously stimulating or else it was just the tingle in her ear as his lips brushed against her lobe. Perhaps it was the flattery of being recognized by a stranger. She still believed in her own invisibility. How could anyone as handsome and probably important as Dr. Peter Trenton know about her?

Despite the pleasant sensation she stiffened and recoiled from him. Her true courage didn't match the bravura she expressed to Martha as they were leaving the apartment.

"How could you hear anything about me?" she asked as the loud music stopped.

"From Martha and Dr. Comerford," he smiled. "You haven't been formally introduced to the surgical staff but people are already talking about you." Angie's eyes widened with embarrassment which made him add quickly, "You've made a very good impression so far."

"I haven't had a chance to do anything," she said, feeling he was less than sincere with his flattery. It didn't really matter if this was his way of coming on to her personally but she was bothered by what he might think of her professionally. Her face showed her concern.

"I really mean it," he said. "You stepped right into the O.R. the last two days like you've been here a long time. Dr. Edsall said a lot of nice things about you after that gallbladder you scrubbed on."

Angie covered her eyes and groaned internally as she thought about the lacerated liver. Thinking it was her own fault for letting the retractor slip, Trenton's compliment sounded sarcastic. It wasn't meant to be.

Trenton pulled her hand away from her eyes and held it in his.

"I very much agree with Dr. Comerford," he said in a deep baritone looking right into her eyes. "You and Martha and the other Surgical Assistants have not been given the recognition you deserve. I think you have been used when it was convenient and the time is coming when we will be more and more dependent on people with your kind of training."

Angie softened. Her knees felt weak and a warmth radiated from her thighs up her abdomen to her cheeks. It wasn't what he was saying but the way he looked at her. She looked back in the same way.

"Even Dr. Potter changed his mind today because of you," he said.

Angie blinked when she heard him say Dr. Potter. It broke the spell she had been under while looking at his eyes without really hearing what he was saying. Now she listened more carefully.

"Because of me?" she asked.

"Well, partly," he conceded. "Dr. Potter had been a strong holdout on the role of the Surgical Assistants. He didn't mind them in the O.R. but he has been very rough on them elsewhere. Of course, not openly since that would put him in direct conflict with Comerford. Now that it seems pretty certain Comerford will be able to put together his Institute, Potter may fall into line with whatever Comerford wants."

"That has nothing to do with me," Angie countered. "It sounds like he's just trying to soften up Comerford."

"I suppose so," he said, "everyone changes. At first even Comerford was very much against anyone but physicians doing clinical work directly with patients. He didn't want the Surgical Assistants here at all but with people like Martha and now you, he thinks it's a good idea. Most of all, he thinks you should be treated properly."

"That seems rather patronizing," Angie said, feeling hurt. "Martha's office could be compared to slave's quarters but we're not in chains if you noticed. We can leave any time. I think we can look out for ourselves."

"That's not much of a choice, is it?" He paused waiting for her reaction. He was trying to sound sympathetic but his raised eyebrows made her wary. She looked around hoping to find Martha for support.

"What I mean is, you have to work within a limited framework according to conditions set down by other people and—"

"Don't you have limits set for you?" she interrupted.

"That's different," he said quickly then stopped to think about it. "How about a drink?" he said looking at his empty glass. "Let's go into the kitchen," he said escorting her by the elbow.

The kitchen was empty and the air a little fresher. Angie leaned against the white refrigerator while he poured scotch into his glass. She imagined his broad, powerful back underneath his neatly tapered coat. His thick black hair extended over his collar as he leaned forward to pour. She wanted to reach out and touch his back or pull the hair as if both were too enchanting to be real.

It made her feel foolish to react this way and deepened her resentment of his patronizing attitude. From the back, he looked like her husband Tommy but then under the circumstances any tall dark man would have to remind her of him. Only it was different. It was the same kind of elation Tommy stimulated in her many years ago. But she was older now. She felt she could sort out these emotions and was better equipped by experience to control her feelings.

"Aren't you going to have one?" he said as he was about to sip his drink. He acted surprised to see her just standing there.

"I'll have Amoretto on the rocks," she said without moving toward the counter. He had expected Angie to make her own drink but wasn't the least put off by the request.

"Amoretto, amoretto," he sang as he tapped the bottles on the counter. "No amoretto. Scotch, gin, vodka or bourbon!"

"Scotch, just like yours," she said.

He fixed the drink. The kitchen was narrow and he was able to hand it to her without taking a step.

"We were talking about limits," he said resting his glass on the counter as he leaned forward and crossed his arms over his chest. Angie held the ice-filled glass to her lips but didn't sip. The slightly aromatic scotch made her anticipate the disagreeable burning sensation of the liquor. She regretted her choice, wishing she had asked for Coke.

"I'm limited by my own skill and judgment," he said, "and by performance. There are boundaries perhaps set by mutual consent but I can cross them when circumstances require."

"I can say the same thing about my job," she said swinging the glass away from her lips and pointing to him for emphasis. "Just different boundaries and different circumstances."

"It's not quite the same thing," he said unmoved by her resistance to his point of view. "You are much more vulnerable to criticism if you even approach those boundaries. For instance, just the other day Martha was scrubbed with me, I did this woman with a dissecting abdominal aneurysm. Do you know what that is?"

"Yes, it's caused by a tear in the lining of the aorta. The blood gets inside the lining and makes the tear worse."

"Very good," he said toasting her with his scotch. "Then you also know it is very rare in a forty-year-old woman. She was brought into the Emergency Room with a boardlike abdomen, hard and stiff and exquisitely painful. It could have been a dozen different things and the aneurysm was unlikely. Except there was an explanation in her case. She had a congenital weakness of her aortic wall called Cystic Medial Necrosis. Unfortunately, there is no way of knowing this until some catastrophe occurs."

"So you missed the diagnosis of a rare condition," Angie said anticipatingly. "In her condition an exploratory operation was necessary to make the diagnosis. Obviously I could never go that far."

"I haven't finished," he said annoyed at her presumption that he made a wrong diagnosis. "In this age of speciliazation, perhaps I should have called a vascular surgeon. But before we opened her, it could have been any number of things, such as a ruptured appendix, bowel obstruction, a ruptured tubal pregnancy. The point is since I crossed the boundary I had to do the best I could."

"Martha told me the woman died," Angie said without intending any criticism.

"That's beside the point of what we are talking about here," he said softly but was obviously stung by her words. "I was not criticized for anything I did as you might be. As long as I can document what I did, that I did it in a competent and professional manner it's okay. But if I left something out, if I failed to explore her abdomen then I'd be in trouble. In my case, the sins of omission and commission can be equally devastating. You can't be judged too harshly for not doing something on your own without direction. On the other hand, if you do anything which doesn't turn out too well, well you better have a doctor to back you up."

"You make it sound like we're nothing more than puppets," she said annoyed and hurt once more. "Do all surgeons feel this way?"

"Don't get me wrong," he said apologetically, "it's your welfare we're concerned with. We don't want you left holding the bag or blamed for something beyond your control."

"Who's we or is that the royal pronoun you're using?"

"I was giving you Dr. Comerford's viewpoint, which I agree with wholeheartedly. He means not to let you be a scapegoat or carry more responsibility than you should."

"I don't intend to but that doesn't mean I'll stop thinking or fail to have my own opinions," she said defensively.

"I'm sure you will," he said, "and it will continue to impress people like Dr. Potter. For some reason after you went down to look at that specimen the other day, it seemed to change his mind about you. I mean about Surgical Assistants in general. It showed some interest and he appreciated it."

"Did he or was he just accommodating Dr. Comerford? I haven't met him yet, only his wife."

"Ordinarily it would be hard to say," Trenton smiled, "but he did mention you when he changed his mind. I think he was genuinely impressed.

Comerford already thinks highly of him. He's gotten excellent results with his cancer surgery. Potter's a hard guy to figure out. I never thought he would do so well but I can't deny his results are the best around."

"And it's always the results that count?" Angie asked. Before Trenton could answer, Martha came in.

"What's going on? A private party?" she said looking from Angie to Trenton. "I want Angie to meet some other people."

"I'll call you," Trenton said to Angie. "Maybe we can finish this discussion."

Later that night on their way home Martha said, "Well, you got it on pretty good with Peter."

"Who's Peter?" Angie played dumb.

"Dr. Peter Trenton, that handsome rich surgeon you were talking to for so long. Don't act so cool!"

"Who cares? He's just another pompous jerk!"

"But he's a gorgeous pompous jerk," Martha laughed loudly.

Ten

Somehow the world organized itself for Angie. Actually the pattern already existed. She merely had to get into step with the rest of the world.

There was a pattern to the madness at University Medical Center. The constant flow of bright white coats through the corridors was matched with equally bright young faces of new nurses, technicians, residents, interns and medical students. They were all strangers in a cascading adventure which had been going on for years before they arrived; more likely for years before they were even born.

Events of the past caught up with the present as old ideas were rediscovered and competed with future trends. Older simplicity gave way to modern sleekness through wires, cables, computers, oscilloscopes and liquid crystal giving digital readouts. It was progress of a sort.

Every year there was someone and something new. The new faces were expected every year and were commonplace to those who remained. So Angie's new face was accepted along with the other newcomers to the hospital. The house staff, residents and interns, were transients. They were there for training, four, five or six years while some came and went in a year. People like Trenton, the Potters and Martha Daniels were just beginning to feel permanent. Dr. Arthur Comerford was to the manor born. And then there was Dr. Harold McDermott.

Harold McDermott was the oldest looking thirty-eight-year-old Professor of Surgery. Perhaps he looked that way when he was twenty and would remain unchanged when he was sixty. Perhaps it was his thick straight hair that lay effortlessly in place parted on the left side but always looking like it was put there accidentally. Its color depended on the light and sometimes the angle of the observer. At times it looked like dark gray flannel. If he tilted his head, it looked black. He wore wire-framed glasses with large convex lenses hiding his eyes and adding to the mystery of his age.

Three years earlier, he was the youngest man ever to be appointed Chief of Surgery at University Medical Center. His age alone was not so extraordinary. The man he replaced, Dr. Francis Wright, was appointed when he was thirty-eight and had been Chief for twenty-seven years.

By appointing young men as Chief, the hospital assured itself of continuity at the top barring premature death or disability. The hospital's by-laws required Dr. Wright to step down as Chief when he turned sixty-five but unlike Comerford he continued to practice surgery. If Comerford regretted his own decision and envied Wright, he never mentioned it. His decision was sealed in the letter to himself.

McDermott's succession to the Chair of Surgery was unceremonious but the change in the Department of Surgery was dramatic. Wright's ability and contributions to medicine and surgery were recognized internationally. Like McDermott, he had been a wunderkind who published over a hundred papers in the scientific literature before he was appointed Chief.

Dr. Francis Wright was an intimidator. He used his vast personal experience in surgery as well as his knowledge from constant study to dominate everyone around him. His conferences and rounds were a monologue which he interrupted only to ask questions. His favorite ruse was to call on an established surgeon who had not attended rounds regularly enough and ask him a question. When he faltered, as he might if he had not attended rounds with the residents where Dr. Wright discussed the problem, Dr. Wright then called upon one of the junior residents to give the correct answer. One upsmanship alone was not enough to sustain his leadership. He could solve difficult problems, was genuinely talented and was available to those who needed his help.

Harold McDermott was much more analytical than Wright. What Wright could learn about the stomach from doing a thousand gastrectomies McDermott could learn from ten or twenty. He wasn't that much smarter than Wright. It was just a difference in style, a different time when nonoperative treatments were improved so McDermott would never get to do a thousand gastrectomies.

Perhaps it was also the spirit of the changing times that made them different. An unchallenged authoritarian decision from the Chief was unacceptable. Whatever the result, public ridicule by the Chief was no longer justified.

This did not mean that McDermott could not dominate the conferences. He had his own storehouse of knowledge with which he could control the proceedings. He had facts, theories and statistics at his fingertips.

At Grand Rounds, Dr. Robert Trenton competently presented his case of the forty-year-old woman who had died of a dissecting aneurysm. He presented it clearly in a strong voice, pointing out the diagnostic problems along the way. It was an excellent exposition of logical alternatives in the face of an abdominal catastrophe.

Trenton presented this case from the podium of an amphitheater which stretched two stories above him. The gallery was semicircular with seats and desks for two hundred people. Surgical Grand Rounds attracted about one hundred and fifty: Professors, visiting attending surgeons, residents, interns, medical students, nurses and participants from the departments of Pathology and Radiology.

The assembly for Grand Rounds had a touch of Grand Opera as everyone had some costume to distinguish his role. Each actor joined his peers in an unmarked section of the auditorium. There was no formula for this. Nothing was ever written down or even mentioned. No one would ever ask a first year medical student to leave if he inadvertently sat in the first row next to McDermott, who sat close to the speakers lectern. It was not a snobbish seating arrangement but a practical and logical one.

Grand Rounds was participatory theater in which the audience was expected to comment and criticize the case presentations, to ask questions and learn so the same mistakes could be avoided or to learn how to do the right thing in the first place.

The chairman had the most to say or at least what he had to say affected the most people. McDermott could rise from his front row seat to face the audience with the least disruption or shifting attention of the audience. So on up the line, the professors, assistant professors, instructors and visiting attendings were arrayed in succeeding rows behind McDermott depending on how importantly their views would affect the policies at University Medical Center.

The full-time faculty walked in wearing their long white coats identifying their group. They filled the right side of the auditorium starting in the second row leaving the very first row for McDermott. Behind the long white coats sat the visiting attendings, private practitioners in business suits. On the left side, away from the lectern, there was an uninterrupted sea of white uniforms worn by interns, residents, medical students, nurses, technicians and surgical assistants.

Comerford usually sat next to McDermott but Dr. Wright always placed himself in the very last row. It was his conscious effort to avoid stealing the limelight from McDermott. After twenty-seven years in the front row, it helped him to suppress the impulse to stand up in front of the audience. It was not completely effective. When his familiar voice was heard from the rear, the entire audience swiveled in their seats. The reaction of the audience revealed that it was who you were rather than where you sat that was important.

Dr. Trenton's management of this patient's extremely difficult problem provoked a lot of questions and discussion. There was no criticism of the way he handled it until Dr. Francis Wright stood up to speak. He was twelve rows up. No one was behind him or higher than he. The entire audience strained their necks upward and to the rear in unison.

Dr. Francis Wright would have to be classified as a general surgeon but he pioneered in the rapid development of Vascular Surgery after World War II. In the past fifteen years his actual practice had been devoted almost entirely to it, including open heart surgery.

He began talking about the development of Vascular Surgery in America and particularly at University Medical Center. He discussed the problems encountered, the successes and the failures, the technical advances of materials for grafts and sutures. This was all a build up to the improved training of surgeons specializing in Vascular Surgery. It was evident that he thought Trenton had no business operating on this patient.

"I believe Dr. Trenton should classify himself as a Hand Surgeon," Wright boomed from the top of the auditorium. He remained standing, waiting for Trenton to take the bait. Like a multiheaded organism, the audience rotated toward the lectern. Trenton was prepared to defend himself but McDermott stood up.

"Dr. Wright, what exactly is a Hand Surgeon?" McDermott asked pleasantly. The heads swiveled to the rear.

"I mean Dr. Trenton wants to operate on whatever he can get his hands on!" Wright said clearly derogating Trenton's efforts.

There was a diffuse titter of laughter. McDermott waited until all heads were facing him again.

"I suppose according to you," McDermott said deferentially, "a Vascular Surgeon would operate wherever blood flows."

A louder ripple of laughter followed as the heads turned back to Wright.

"A trained Vascular Surgeon would have had much more experience dealing with this sort of case. Our results with over eight hundred aneurysms have consistently improved over the past twenty years. There is no reason for the younger surgeons to repeat the mistakes of the past when with advanced training they can learn to avoid them."

He felt satisfied with his speech as he sat down. The eyes of the audience turned to McDermott.

"I wholeheartedly endorse your last statement," McDermott said, "and indeed your results for atherosclerotic aneurysms are a yardstick to measure our performance. However," here he paused for effect to be sure everyone was listening, "we have yet to salvage a patient with a dissecting aneurysm of the type Dr. Trenton has presented. There were also some other diagnostic possibilities which were very well discussed. If we had to call in a Vascular Surgeon every time a blood vessel was involved, there's no limit to the amount of work they would do. It's possible they would insist on doing hemorrhoids also! Thank you very much, Dr. Trenton, and let's go to the next case," he said before the laughter had died down.

Surgical Grand Rounds was held every Saturday from nine until noon. On this bright sunny day in the first week of October, Peter Trenton had a date to take Angie sightseeing in Manhattan. It was three weeks since they had first met at the party.

They had one dinner date before this. It was soon after the party and they saw each other at the hospital. The dinner was pleasantly relaxed and the evening ended early. At the hospital Peter was merely polite and friendly but at the same time very reserved and distant. Martha had warned Angie to expect this attitude from him.

Angie insisted she didn't expect anything. She was through planning every detail. She said she was content to let things happen as they may. She was not anticipating anything. But she did find herself looking for Peter Trenton in the operating room. She memorized his schedule and tried to be available to scrub with him.

The dinner invitation was so casually offered late on a Wednesday afternoon that she thought he meant to meet her in the hospital cafeteria. But no, he said he would pick her up about six-thirty at her apartment. They went to a bistro on First Avenue that served some good Italian food. He offered her wine but said he wouldn't drink because he had a very full schedule the next morning, so she also abstained. She was home in bed alone by ten o'clock.

She told him she didn't know anything about New York. Despite spending three years in New York, she had not taken the time to explore beyond the limits of the Medical Center and the bus station.

He promised to take her sightseeing but didn't say when until three days before he was to present his case at Grand Rounds. So there they were walking hand in hand down East Fifty-second Street toward the Citicorp Center for lunch.

"You were very good today," Angie said enthusiastically as she hurried to keep up with his long strides. "Did Dr. Wright make you feel very uncomfortable?"

"Not at all," he said smiling. "Old Frank has mellowed quite a bit. It was strictly personal between the two us. I trained here when he was Chief. He wanted me to take a fellowship in open-heart surgery after I finished six years at University Medical Center. I had enough. I wanted to get out and make some money. He's never forgiven me for it."

They entered "The Mark," a five-story atrium in the middle of a sixty-story skyscraper that housed shops and restaurants. He led her around the central square of the atrium to an eating place that specialized in salads. It was self-service as they passed through the line picking up their food.

"Why didn't you take that fellowship?" Angie asked as they sat down to eat. "It wasn't only the money."

"Isn't that enough?" he said. "I was married, you know. Maybe he was right. The marriage didn't last. I was divorced after two years of practice."

"What happened?" Angie asked looking at him while she held a piece of lettuce suspended on her fork.

"I was too busy working at making money," he laughed and then sighed. "There were no more excuses I guess. As a resident I always had the pressure put on me. Afterward, I had no one but myself to blame."

"Are you sorry now you didn't take the fellowship?"

"Not at all. When I finished my residency I was drafted into the army. The Viet Nam War was still on. I knew I'd be drafted so if I did take it, it

156

would have to wait another two years. I had time to think it over. By then I had had twenty-five years of formal education. It was enough."

"Now that you're a busy New York surgeon making lots of money," she said lightly as she munched on the salad, "is it enough?"

"It's not enough," he said quietly, almost with humility as he lowered his eyes. "The money is never enough. Money is something the rest of the world uses to value itself." He looked up and spoke more aggressively. "Doctors are just part of that world. How much is the comfort of a Rolls Royce worth compared to the relief of pain due to a gallstone? Even that isn't important. It's not just the money. There are so many easier ways to make money and lots more of it if you're willing to put in this much time. And what do I have? There's no equity. It's not as if I owned a factory that I could sell. Have you ever held anyone's life in your hands?"

"Yes, I have!" Angie said, recalling her harrowing experience in the ambulance with Betty LeDonne. "And sometimes more than one at a time."

"You may have saved someone's life but you've never taken a life and dangled it with your skill and knowledge. I'm not talking about something like that dissecting aneurysm I presented this morning. That was life-saving or at least an attempt at it. It was a catastrophic event for which I had no responsibility. It didn't take much courage to make a decision because no decision would seal her fate. Even so it was still agonizing and Wright

157

made me feel more than uncomfortable. He was trying to hurt me, to make me feel guilty for not studying hard enough, for not having more training. If I thought it could make a difference, I'd quit right now but no one could have done any more than I did. That vessel was torn deep into the carotids! No one could repair that!"

"I didn't mean you didn't earn—" she started apologetically.

"I'm not finished," he interrupted and it was her turn to look at the salad. "Heroics is not what surgery is all about," he went on. "Any schmuck can be a hero. Sometimes there's not much difference. Surgery first of all requires that you know the natural history of the disease. You have to know what can happen if surgery is not done. Maybe not right away but even four or five years later when surgery may not be possible or the results not as good.

"Then you have to be right. The evidence is there in the bucket and you can't undo the surgery. But most of all, you've taken this whole human body and opened it on purpose. You have wounded it to get at the cancer or whatever disease lies beneath the surface. You have dangled that body over a precipice in a calculated risk to make it well again.

"And it's all done publicly right out in the open with people watching. No one compels so much attention as the surgeon for he alone decides to bring the patient to the operating room. Only the surgeon makes the final positive decision and only the surgeon takes the ultimate responsibility."

Angie pushed her salad bowl away feeling oppressed by her unintended criticism of Peter's motivation. She had never heard anyone speak this way about what she had come to feel was routine and casual. She was thankful she had never dangled a life as he put it.

"I owe you an apology," she said, "but not every surgeon feels this way about it."

"I wasn't offended by what you said about the money. I wanted you to understand why it was deserved and how it is earned. It's not a reward for good results. It's for being willing to try to make things better. The good results are the reason for trying again and again."

"If you won't be offended," she hesitated and then went on when he allowed that he wouldn't be, "what about those surgeons who do it over and over again? Dr. Potter, for instance. He does a ton of hysterectomies. I've scrubbed with him and worked up a lot of his patients. He does at least five a week, usually more. What's so attractive about him? He does so much more surgery than anyone else at University Medical Center."

"Why did you pick him as an example?" Peter asked with a wry smile.

"He does so many!" Angie exclaimed with her hands in the air. "I was curious so I looked in the log book. He does between twenty and thirty hysterectomies a month. How many patients would he have to see in his office to get that much surgery? What do you think is the ratio of office patients to surgery even for a specialist like Potter—ten to one? That's two to three hundred new patients a month."

"Interesting," Peter frowned while contemplating the figures. "I never looked at it that way but Eric Potter is exceptional. I don't know why. No one expected him to last. His first year in practice was a disaster. He had very few patients. And then gradually he started getting busier and busier. His statistics stood out like a sore thumb. We audited him over and over. I was on the tissue committee then. All his specimens were legitimate.

"You don't need that high a ratio if you specialize and get a lot of referrals. The screening is done by the referring physicians so your theory, if it is a theory—I'm not sure of your point—doesn't hold up. We also considered the possibility that he was fee-splitting to get so many referrals but there was no hint of that.

"Eric Potter has done a tremendous amount of work and I admit, maybe I was just envious. I was very suspicious he was doing a lot of unnecessary surgery. Not any more! It's all down in black and white and nobody can argue with his statistics."

"I'm not arguing with his statistics," she said, "I'm merely curious about his patients. Sometimes the physical examination doesn't jibe with the Path report and the specimens look different when I see them at organ recital compared to surgery when the're fresh."

"That, Angie," he said smiling condescendingly, "is a clinical impression. Your clinical judgment just isn't that good. It's not just you. It's true even for a very experienced doctor. A clinical impression is not a fact. It's a memory, an opinion that has to give way to the fact of a surgical specimen in the lab."

"All the same—"

"Could we drop the subject," he said pleasantly and stood up to be sure it was dropped. "No more shop talk. I'm off till Monday and . . . , finish your coffee and let's go."

She let the coffee stand. Although annoyed with his manner she was sympathetic with his wish. She also had had enough of shop talk. The schism healed quickly when he offered her his arm as they walked down the street.

They strolled the streets leisurely, occasionally looking in shop windows, joking about fashions and prices, people and things. The city itself, even with its stepped-down energy of a warm October Saturday afternoon, had a vital spirit strongly influencing their mood. So much better to share it between two people wanting to be drawn closer together.

Angie wondered who this man was who took her hand as they crossed the street. She kept looking at him while he stared at the sights. She knew well enough that she was being led around by Dr. Peter Trenton but now he seemed so different. As he walked along he stared at everything: the people, the stores, the cars. From the street to the tops of the skyscrapers his eyes wandered with curious bewilderment as if he had never seen it before. He seemed so different from the man who had just instructed her on the ethics of surgery. So sure in his tone, almost patronizing her, his whole attitude changed. He was the gawker, the novice enchanted by the commonplace of New York.

"Look at that," he said pointing to an office building several blocks away. "When did they put that one up?" he asked after scanning three hundred and sixty degrees to get his bearings as if he knew every building as a landmark.

"I don't know. Didn't they tell you it was going up?" Angie kidded him.

He picked up her lighthearted sarcasm and responded in kind.

"You're right. They don't tell me anything anymore. I've been too busy to keep track of things like that. I thought they finished building this city last year."

"How long have you lived here?" she asked.

"Where?"

"Here! In the city. How long have you lived in New York?"

"All my life except for two years in the army."

"You grew up here?" She tried to picture him as a child staring up at the tall buildings. "But how could anyone grow up here? Did you play in traffic for the fun of it?"

"Actually, I was born in Brooklyn. There were plenty of places to play without the traffic."

"I can't imagine growing up with all this noise and—" she sighed deeply, "all this . . . , it's so different from New England. In a small town and around it, there are so many places to grow up without car fumes. There are trees and hills. The changing seasons give you a sense of orderliness and continuity. You know instinctively people are part of nature. You don't know what I'm talking about, do you?" she asked disappointed by the faraway look in his eyes.

Perhaps she had offended him by the comparison when all she had wanted to do was to share some of her life as he was trying to show her his.

"I know what you mean," he said.

"You can't really," she shook her head. "Not anymore. Not as a child rolling down a snow-covered hill in winter or picking wild flowers in spring. Maybe I missed something you had in the streets of New York. It's hard for you to understand what it was like to be a child in the country. It's so different from the city streets."

"Maybe it was or maybe it wasn't," he said sadly, "but it's not there any more."

"What isn't there?"

"My street. Anyway not like I think it was. I wish I could make you see it as it was. . . ."

His street sloped steeply then flattened out in an alluvial plain when it reached the intersection. It was twice as wide at the bottom than at the top. At the very bottom, it was crossed by another street covered with cobblestones and trolley tracks. The trolley cars rattled noisily past his street occasionally shooting out sparks as its iron wheels scraped against some irregularity in the grooved iron rails embedded in the pavement surrounded by cobblestones.

In winter the hill was covered by snow that remained clean in those days when all the cars had gone to war. The air was clean and the few remaining cars posed no threat to the collection of belly-whoppers who zoomed down the icy, snowy street to the edge of the alluvial plain that began fifty feet before the trolley tracks. Still it was frightening to a child's imagination. One day his sled would carry him to those tracks where he would be shredded under the heavy iron wheels of the trolly. It was only a passing thought which lent greater excitement to the downhill run.

This world was made for him, he didn't doubt as he wandered up and down the hill and across the plain. There was a landscape under the concrete and macadam of the Brooklyn street. There was a landscape crowded out by the dirty, gray brick tenements.

The Atlantic Ocean flooded the lowlands forming estuaries. It created shallow bays not more than three miles from the street where he lived. These lowlands and bays formed ocean marshes and sandy beaches. The ocean plain was broad. In some places it extended for ten miles before the land began to rise.

The land began to rise on his street. It rose to the north, northeast and northwest. It continued to rise in rolling hills for miles and miles until it sloped down again to meet the East River on the other side of Brooklyn.

To the south and directly east and west, the land was flat. There was land under the concrete, macadam and cobblestones. There was land scarred by parallel iron rails that divided the plain from the rising headland. He found the land before he explored the concrete plain and the macadam hills.

Before the gray brick tenements had been built, before the land had been cleared, his block was a tiny dale, a saucer gouged out of the side of the land rising from the plain; gouged out by the glacier that receded from the plain over ten thousand years ago.

Geologists documented the terminal moraine and the exotic igneous boulders in Prospect Park only five miles due west. There was a giant boulder in the backyard of the tenement. In the backyard surrounded by other tenements. The boulder was enormous. Over six feet high and almost twice as wide. No one knew how it got there. No one asked and no one really cared. The glacier had eroded this tiny corner of the headlands and left the boulder when it receded. The glacier had gouged out a steep hill so the builders could not fill all the available land.

The block was saucer-shaped, more like a boomerang perhaps. The backyards of the tenements ringing this vale were divided into five different levels separated by mending walls. Not quite Vermont mending walls but rather varied. Some rock and mortar, one brick and one all concrete. This last one was as high as the tenement and kept the hill from sliding down.

This concrete wall was fifteen feet wide and rose straight up like a smooth cliff to challenge the most intrepid climbers. It was built to keep the earth back and prevent the foundation of the tenement on the top of the hill from eroding. But to five-year-old Peter Trenton and his friends, this smooth-faced colossus guarded the entrance to a vault containing untold millions. It could probably be moved by the right combination of open sesame

165

and hocus-pocus.

To the left of the wall, the hillside sloping down gently was covered with ragweed and a few stray sunflowers. The ragweed grew tall, green and straight and no one sneezed. The ragweed grew high, high as an elephant's eye, under the bright summer sky. This lush greenery with shadows and shadings cast off bright colors that reflected on the gray brick walls of the surrounding tenements. The succulent green leaves and bristley stems reached over his head. Peter Trenton and his friends were lost from sight, hidden by this green foliage pretending it was a jungle.

The orange monarch butterfly and green grasshoppers romped the hillside with the children. The tiger caterpillar crawled and munched from leaf to leaf. The top of this hill was a plateau occupied by a garage. But it was wartime and the cars were few.

After the war the number of cars increased. Oil began to seep down the hill and the ragweed died. And the caterpillars died. And the grasshoppers died. The hill remained brown all summer. Instead of caterpillers and butterflies, there were fleas and gnats, mosquitoes and cockroaches and the children didn't play there anymore.

It happened long before ecology became a household word and it was happening all over the world. The bright orange monarch butterfly also disappeared from London and was replaced by the black variety which blended with the grimy soot of the London landscape. Evolution was going on forever. It had a present and a future as well as a

166

past. The evidence is not only buried in the layers of the Grand Canyon or the Utah desert. It was there on that hillside in Brooklyn hidden by a ring of tenements that no one came to see.

He could have told her about Timbuktu or the North Slope of Alaska. Angie wanted to hear him speak in this way. She wanted him to talk to her about himself as he might not to anyone else. He searched her eyes for an approving response. It was so different than when he talked about surgery or the hospital.

They talked all day about each other. He listened as she told him about Tommy and he told her about his divorce. It all passed easily between them and was gone forever. She didn't recall when the street darkened or how they had arrived at the restaurant for dinner. They were expected as the maitre d' confirmed the reservation. He had it all planned.

Maybe she didn't need the *Sicilian Kiss*, one part amoretto with two parts of Southern Comfort on the rocks before dinner. Perhaps Martha's advice was enough: "Just let it play out for awhile. See how it feels, let yourself be surprised."

Maybe it was the red wine or maybe she was just tired from walking around all day but she didn't want to go dancing. She wanted Peter Trenton. Whatever he planned, it seemed to her he would never make it to bed with her tonight. So she suggested it first.

In the dark shadows of Peter's bedroom, Angie felt a warm, hard and very pleasant pressure under her lower lip. As her eyes opened slowly in the darkness, she was aware of the rhythmic flow of warm air gently caressing her upper lip and nose. She remained motionless while enjoying the syncopated sensation of Peter's breathing mingled with her own. Her sigh broke the tranquil beat.

She leaned back against the pillow. Without awakening, his lips followed her in sensual slumber. Her face now lighted from a distant source beyond the room retained that peaceful tension put there at the moment of release.

The silence was punctuated by the sounds of the city outside the window. City traffic in the early hours of a Sunday morning captured by still photography: the wounded shrill of a tire turning too sharply, the impatient horn and the tentative beep, the basso acceleration of a motor followed by a downshifting whine.

Monday morning didn't matter anymore. It was eons away. If he acted like a stuffed shirt, she would bite his ear. She tried it now letting her tongue gently caress the inner folds. He stirred and straightened as he pulled her over to him.

Eleven

She was right about one thing. Angie suspected Peter would revert to form at the hospital. His smile was polite and slightly embarrassed when they met in front of Mrs. Beeson's office.

There were other people around checking the bulletin board for the day's schedule. Angie was depressed by the cool greeting from Peter. Her stomach fluttered as her worst suspicions were confirmed. "He's a rat!" she thought. She didn't say a word to him and left him standing alone at the bulletin board.

As she was about to turn the corner a few feet

away, he called her name. She looked back and saw him purse his lips in a warm long-distance kiss. She walked away angrily. She hated his sly impudence. It couldn't go on like this she decided.

A few minutes later she found him alone at the scrub sink in the alcove off the central corridor where people were hurrying to get the surgical cases started. She walked up to him slowly and without a word she kissed him torridly in his ear, gently biting enough to hurt without causing any damage.

His hands and hairy arms were soaked and fully shampooed with brown iodine soap. He dropped the scrub brush in the sink and whipped off his surgical mask. His soaking wet arms engulfed her making her green cotton O.R. dress drippingly transparent and uncomfortable. He kissed her hard, which brought the traffic in the central corridor to a halt. An elderly patient on his way for a hernia repair sat up on his stretcher and raised his fist in salute.

"Attaboy, Doc! Give her one for me."

Angie was crimson from head to toe. She pulled away but he held her firmly.

"You see what I mean," he said pointing to the accumulating audience. "There's a time and a place for everything!"

He wasn't angry and he didn't mean to embarrass her but she had to walk all the way back to the dressing room past Mrs. Beeson to change her dress. When she returned on her way to scrub for her assigned case Peter was still at the sink. He held out his wet arms in an offered embrace. Angie turned away without a word.

Dr. Eric Potter was just arranging the draped sheets on the patient when Angie took her place at his side of the table.

"Scalpel," Potter said holding out his hand. He pulled the blade across the abdomen from side to side just above the shaved pubic hairline.

"She'll still be able to wear a bikini," he announced to no one in particular.

Angie had been stewing over Peter Trenton and thought he was speaking to her.

"I'm sorry, what did you say?" she asked Potter.

He was surprised by the question since he had said the same thing so many times no one ever bothered to respond. He was glad to have someone who was interested.

"This scar will be beautiful," he said as he continued to deepen the wound while the resident clamped the bleeders along the way. "That is one of the prime requisites for a successful surgeon. No matter what you do inside, the patients inevitably judge you by the scar."

"It's not unreasonable," Angie said pulling on the retractors Potter handed her. "It's one way to forget the experience if the scar is thin and not unattractive."

"I agree," he said as he continued to work. He split the muscles in their natural longitudinal plain and adjusted the retractors to keep the wound open. He reached in with a long sharp-toothed clamp to pull the uterus upward into the wound tethering the enlarged muscular organ by its lateral attachments.

"Those are really big fibroids," Angie said as she got her first good look at what they were there for. "May I ask you a question?"

"Sure. Long Kellys," he said to the scrub nurse as he held out his hand. He looked over his shoulder at Angie for a moment. He turned back to the wound as soon as the clamp was in his hand. Angie hesitated while he clamped the blood supply to the uterus.

"Go ahead, I'm listening," he said.

"Are you doing something different today? I mean last week on Marjorie Klein, remember, she had cervical cancer. When you mobilized the uterus it didn't pop out the way this one did."

"This is a big fibroid," he explained while he continued to clamp and tie inside the abdomen. "That uterus was much smaller. Actually, it was almost normal in size. The disease was limited to the cervix."

"I know it looked that way at the table but at the pathology conference it was much bigger. It looked completely different."

Potter's head snapped back quickly as he turned to Angie. He stopped operating and the flow of instruments and ligatures also stopped.

"Are you sure?" he asked calmly. "Did you get a chance to examine the specimen before it went down?"

"Er, no — it just was my impression . . . , it looked much smaller from here."

"It was," he said as he turned back to the wound and started working again. "What do you think,

Joe?" he said to the resident assisting from the other side of the table.

"About what?" Dr. Joe Gordon said while concentrating on the knot he was tying.

"You scrubbed with us on Klein. What did you think about the specimen?"

"Which one was Klein? I scrubbed on so many cases last week. I can't keep them all in my head. Was she the one whose husband had a vasectomy two months ago?"

"No, that was Jorgenson's case and her husband was mad because he didn't need it if she had the hysterectomy. Did you go to the pathology conference last week?"

"Which one?"

"The organ recital," Angie prompted.

"No, that's mostly for the medical students," Gordon said.

"The specimens do look different *in situ* than they do in the bucket," Potter said. "It's much better to leave it to the pathologists anyway."

He finished cutting away the last attachments of the uterus and lifted the free specimen out of the abdomen with two hands. It was a large bulky uterus with lumpy fibroids protruding on three sides. He handed it to Angie.

"Take a good look at this and then compare it with what you see tomorrow at the path conference," he said smiling under his mask.

Angie wasn't surprised by the size of this specimen. She had examined the patient and felt the enlarged irregular uterus when she did the pelvic examination. Her question was not about

173

this patient and Potter's answer did not satisfy her.

"It takes a lot of experience to judge these things accurately. Don't worry about it too much," Potter said as he stepped away from the table to let the resident close the abdomen with Angie's help.

Angie wanted to tell him she had lots of practical experience but she thought better of it. She just thought about it while she and Dr. Gordon sewed the peritoneum to begin the wound closure.

A few hours later Angie sat with Martha having lunch in the hospital cafeteria. Martha laughed out loud as Angie told her how she was soaked by Peter Trenton.

"I don't think it's funny," Angie said with a hurt expression on her face, "especially when I had to walk past Mrs. Beeson. Even she had a smirk on her face."

"I'm sorry, honey, but you asked for it," Martha said wiping her lips with a napkin and hiding her smile.

"I didn't ask him to embarrass me! I just couldn't stand that prissy—that phony kiss he tried to sneak by everyone. He acted like such a *shidrool!*" she said pinching her thumb against her fingers.

"A what?"

"A sh—" she waved the thought away with her hand. "If he had just said good morning instead it would have been so much nicer."

"Here he comes," Martha said as she spotted Peter heading their way carrying his lunch tray. He wore a long white coat over his O.R. greens. His hair was plastered down from wearing the pre-scribed cap all morning.

"For chrissakes, don't bite his ear again. He might take you under the table," Martha laughed.

Angie looked quickly behind her. When he arrived at their table she kept her head down pretending he wasn't there. The table was small, set against the wall and suitable for only two people.

"May I join you," Peter asked resting his tray on the table.

"I have to run," Martha said quickly as she got up taking her tray with her. "See you later, Angie."

Angie didn't object as Peter sat down. He carefully unfolded his napkin on his lap then threw some salt randomly on his food.

"Did you have a busy morning, Dr. Trenton," she asked pleasantly as she folded her hands over her plate.

"Average, how about you?"

"A little slow after a slam-bam start."

"Same here. I thought I'd have to cancel my whole schedule," he smiled as he looked up at her. The tension was broken as they both laughed about the scene in the operating room.

"I promise never to do that again," he said, "if you promise never to bite my ear in the hospital."

"I can't bite your ear anymore?" Angie asked with coquettish disappointment.

"Not in the hospital."

"Of course," she agreed.

"How about Wednesday night?"

"I can't. I promised Martha I'd go shopping with her but I'm free tonight."

"I can't. There's a County Medical Society meeting. And tomorrow night I have to go to this party for Comerford. It's a fund raiser for his new Institute. But I could leave early and—"

"I can't. I'm on call, which means I'll be in the hospital.

"Thursday, I've got to go to the surgical meeting. I'm giving a paper," he said disappointed as the week slipped by.

"Well, then Friday. Friday would be great," she said.

"Not Friday," he said shaking his head sadly. "I might as well tell you the truth. The second Friday of the month is for the most important meeting. But I'll meet you at Brogard's for a couple of drinks and then go to the meeting."

"What's so special about the meeting?" she said curiously.

"It's the monthly poker game. Très important!"

"Oh," she said letting her shoulders sag, "I wouldn't dream of keeping you from something as sacred as that."

"I'll meet you at six," he said pleased, "and we can go out for dinner Saturday night."

"Sure, why not!" she said shrugging her shoulders. After a moment she asked, "Does Potter really have a chance to be Director of the Institute?"

"It's almost a sure thing," Peter nodded. "There'll be a formal search committee and advertisements but Dr. Comerford has tapped him to speak at this party tomorrow night. I'd say he had his foot in the door."

"Do you think he's really good enough to run something as big and important as the Institute? I don't think he's that smart. Someone should keep an eye on him."

"I wouldn't say he's smart but he knows exactly what he's doing," Peter said as if he was offended. "He gets good results and he works hard. I don't know how he has offended you but it sounds very personal."

"It's not personal," Angie calmly insisted. "You seem to be taking it personally. I can't be too far off base if there was some suspicion about him a few years ago. You said so yourself that he was carefully reviewed by the tissue committee."

"Fine! But that is all water under the bridge," Peter said getting agitated and shifting in his seat. "If he does a lot of surgery it's because he's very good and his statistics prove it."

"What about his wife? Could she be helping him with his statistics?" Angie asked casually.

"That's ridiculous!" he frowned obviously angry. "I really don't know what you're getting at."

Angie leaned forward resting her elbows on the table. She spoke softly so no one could overhear and hoped it would calm Peter.

"Last week I scrubbed with him," she said, "and there definitely was a difference between what he took out and what they showed at the path conference. Couldn't his wife be helping him with his statistics?"

"Elaine? No way!" He seemed shocked by her implications. "I don't know what you did in Hadley but you're only a Surgical Assistant here. Potter has done over two thousand, close to three thousand hysterectomies and everyone of them had a documented satisfactory reason. When we reviewed his work we also looked at the pathology. We got out the slides and looked at them again. It had nothing to do with Elaine. She wasn't even there! And except for a few reports, she never even saw his work to begin with."

"Everybody thinks I'm a dummy around here," she said angrily, hurt by the way he lectured her. "Well, I have eyes and I look at what's going on, not after it happened, not reviewing slides and statistics but what is actually happening!"

"Angie," he said softly and seductively, "will you please forget about Potter. We were doing very well until you brought him up. I thought we were going to kiss and make up."

"Kiss my ass!" she jumped up and walked away leaving her dirty tray on the table.

"Hey, what about Friday night?" he called after her.

She came back and picked up her tray. She leaned over and kissed him on the lips.

"I'll meet you at six," she said and walked away with her tray.

Twelve

"*Que le ocurre?*" Angie asked smilingly but in poor Spanish to the brown-skinned woman sitting hunched over on the flat surfaces of the examining table.

The woman, her black hair a tangle of knots, looked up without moving her head. She flapped her shoulders keeping her hands crossed over her lap. Angie couldn't tell if she meant she didn't know what was wrong with her or if she just didn't understand the question.

They were alone in a narrow cubicle of the surgery clinic. It was one of eight in this section of the hospital's outpatient department. Each examining room was separated by a permanent wood and glass partition opening to a corridor connecting all of them so the doctors could move from room to room.

There were no doors or walls at one end that opened to this connecting corridor. At the other end of the stall, there was a door leading to the patients' waiting room. There was privacy enough except for the voices heard in the other stalls asking questions about pain and feelings, nausea and vomiting, bowel movements and bleedings.

There was privacy enough because eavesdropping requires a conscious effort. No one eagerly waits for the answer to "When was your last bowel movement?" heard over the thin partitions of the clinic. A psychological veil worked as well as any soundproofing.

Angie studied the patient's clinic record for some clues. Her Spanish was limited to a few phrases and she had little hope of getting the full story from the patient. The patient, Rita Algrin, was twenty-nine years old. Angie thought she could have been in her forties. The eyes were moist and dull with swelling of the lids especially on the bottom. The lips were thick but the skin around the rest of the face was drawn tight exaggerating the eyes and lips. In any language, she was unattractive.

"*Donde le duele?*" Angie asked.

"*Me duele aqui*," she said sitting back a little, pointing to her lower abdomen and spreading her legs. Her lips parted widely as she spoke revealing the absence of her two top front teeth. She tried to smile appealingly but it made her uglier.

"*Por favor*," she said, "*llame a un medico*."

Angie didn't catch the meaning with the words slurred one on the other.

"Any *sangrando?*" Angie asked.

The woman shook her head from side to side with her eyes closed. She bent over further indicating she was in pain but Angie already knew that. Angie went out to find Maria Rodriguez, the Spanish interpreter for the clinic.

Ten minutes later she came back with a petite young girl. Her straight skirt was too tight around her knees making it much more difficult for her to walk in her three-inch heels. Her feet moved rapidly in very short steps giving the feeling that she might topple over forward at any minute.

Even with the high heels she was still shorter than Angie. Maria's bleached blonde hair was neatly combed in perfect lines curving down the sides of her cheeks. Her face was heavily made up with light tones of pancake makeup and bright red lipstick.

Rita Algrin's jacknife position hadn't changed. When she looked up, it was obvious she knew Maria. She began a rapid exchange in Spanish with Maria while Angie stood by.

"She says she wants to see a doctor," Maria said in clear but heavily accented English. "I *esplained* you would examine her first and she said okay."

Angie knew she had been rejected and that it took some convincing to have her accepted by the patient. And then only by the promise that she

181

would soon see *un medico*.

"Ask her," Angie said unaffected by the slight, "if her menstrual periods are regular?"

A prolonged exchange ensued between Maria Rodriguez and Rita Algrin. For a while it seemed like an argument as the patient waved her hand over her head then pointed to her legs. Maria, applying some medical knowledge she had acquired from asking these questions for the medical staff, seemed frustrated then embarrassed. Finally, she used her hands like a conductor to halt Rita's flow of words. She asked her something very slowly and distinctly. The patient flicked her head to the side and shrugged.

"She says she's not sure when she had her last menstrual period," Maria said turning to Angie.

"What do you mean she's not sure?" Angie asked perplexed. "Did you explain it?"

"I *esplained* it," Maria said pleading frustration, "but I don't think she's too smart. She's a little coo-coo."

"Tell her I'm going to examine her internally. She'll have to lie down and put her legs up in the stirrups," Angie said as she removed a disposable plastic speculum from the drawer and moved the gooseneck lamp over to the front of the table.

Maria explained what Angie wanted Rita to do. There was another flurry of very rapid Spanish. With some soothing encouragement from Maria, the patient moved down on the table and put her legs up.

With the speculum in place, the light shone on a small drop of dried blood at the opening of the uterine cervix. Angie removed the speculum and placed her gloved fingers in the vagina. One hand on the abdomen pressed the womb against her fingers in the vagina. The patient remained quiet.

"Dolor?" Angie asked as she probed the pelvic contents.

"Si, aqui," the patient said taking Angie's hand and moving it to the right side of her belly.

Dr. Joe Gordon appeared behind Angie coming from the open connecting corridor. All three women looked up at his large frame topped with thick curly red hair. He was a third year resident, making him the senior physician at the clinic this afternoon. He wore a blue shirt and solid blue tie under his short white coat. His white pants were freshly starched. They only reached to his ankles about three inches from the top of his white shoes.

"What do we have here?" he asked as he folded his thick arms and leaned against the partitioning wall. His small nose and thick puffy cheeks exaggerated the curl to his upper lip when he spoke.

"I think she may have a tubal pregnancy," Angie said.

He stood up straight almost immediately and picked up the clinical record. After a quick glance he pulled on a rubber glove. Angie moved out of his way as he stepped between the patient's legs extended in the stirrups. He shoved one hand into the vagina and with the other pressed forcefully on the abdomen.

"Ai-eee," the patient screamed pulling away from him and scissoring her legs together.

"She's got P.I.D.," he said shaking his head and

extracting himself from the patient's legs. "When was her last menstrual period?"

"She's not sure," Angie replied without commenting on his technique.

"*Usted sangrando regular?*" he asked the patient.

"Si," she shook her head from side to side as she nervously pulled the blue striped hospital robe around herself.

"It's P.I.D.," he said pulling off his glove. "Get a GC smear and give her some penicillin."

"I don't think so," Angie said worriedly. "I think you were a little to rough. She didn't react that way when I examined her."

Dr. Gordon turned very red angered by the accusation and challenge to his diagnosis.

"Look at the damned record," he said picking up the chart. "1972, positive GC, '74 and again in '75. Three positive smears. She gets gonorrhea the way other people get colds. Don't tell me how to exam a patient! Just give her a big dose in the behind. Don't trust her to take any pills."

"But her history of gonorrhea makes her a set up for a tubal pregnancy," Angie protested. "I think she should be admitted and watched."

"If you think she has a tubal pregnancy she should have surgery today. This afternoon! Do you want to take her to the O.R. and open her?"

The question was directed toward Angie's impotence. He knew very well she couldn't operate on this patient under any circumstances. He wrote his recommendations on the clinical record, handed it to Angie and walked out of the cubicle.

After a minute of silence, Rita Algrin started

speaking animatedly in Spanish to Maria.

"She says," Maria interpreted, "she doesn't like him and wants you to be her doctor."

"I'm not a doctor," Angie said sadly. "Would you take her out to the nurse and explain to her about the shots."

Angie handed the chart with Gordon's written orders and started to leave.

"Also tell her that if she has any pain in her belly, she should go immediately to the Emergency Room."

Angie's instructions did little to salve her guilty feelings for not trying to be more persuasive with Gordon even if it did lead to a big argument. But it was too late now. The patient was gone. The advice seemed feeble since she had come to the clinic because of pain.

If it was a tubal pregnancy, any significant increment in the pain could be associated with abdominal catastrophe. The tubal pregnancy would rupture, rapidly spewing blood into the abdominal cavity. How much pain would it take to get Rita Algrin back to the Emergency Room?

Rita Algrin occupied Angie's thoughts as she worked through the afternoon seeing patients. Most of it was routine, which made it possible for Angie to work without consulting Dr. Gordon. She did want to call him in on a case of pelvic inflammatory disease just to show him what P.I.D. looked like. She decided to avoid a pointless argument. Besides, she didn't want to subject these women to his probing examination needlessly.

Angie wondered if she had presented Algrin in

the wrong way. Gordon wasn't that dense. Maybe he was more intent on proving Angie was wrong. That would be a poor excuse coming far below ignorance. But if it were the reason, what was it Comerford had told her — "work a little bit below your true abilities." No, sir! It wasn't that simple. Angie decided she would need more ability. A different kind of ability beyond her clinical training. If she was going to succeed by her own standards, she would have to become a manipulator. She would have to direct the attention of those with the power to do some good.

It made her uneasy having to think this way. She and Dr. Conners never competed. If she found something he missed, he didn't feel threatened, resentful or worried when she pointed it out. Of course, he didn't miss much. Maybe it was his experience that made him confident. Maybe it was inexperience that made Gordon so competitive.

The afternoon went by quickly as patients were ushered in and out of the clinic. All her patients were either black or Puerto Rican and all were young. At least their stated ages were all under thirty but many looked haggard and sad. They had various forms of vaginal or bladder infections. None with any potential surgical problems. One unsuspected pregnancy was diagnosed in a sixteen-year-old much to the patient's and her mother's disbelief. Undoubtedly the patients were being triaged, selected so the less promising patients, surgically speaking, were sent into Angie's cubicle. Angie didn't mind. Perhaps it was just as well since it would require the patients to be examined twice if surgery were indicated. Once by Angie and again by a surgical resident and then perhaps again by another surgeon.

It was four-thirty when Sandra Blaklee walked into Angie's cubicle and handed her a thin folder. It was Sandra's first visit to the clinic so her chart was one piece of paper with her name, age: twenty-six years old plus a few other statistics. What made her interesting was the chief complaint filled in by the nurse who wrote: "the patient states she is having a miscarriage."

It wasn't the only thing that made her interesting. It was her calm and efficient manner. She wasn't complaining at all. She had merely stated a fact to the nurse . . .

This twenty-six-year-old black woman was elegantly coiffed. Her straightened ebony hair was pulled back tightly around her scalp and tied in a bun in the back. She had sharp, delicate features, a sharp, almost pointy nose. Even the standard hospital gown did not diminish her poise and personality.

Angie had seen her earlier sitting on the bench waiting to be seen. Only then she didn't think she was a patient. She sat staring silently trying to ignore her surroundings like a black swan amid a cacophony of bandycoots. There was nothing to suggest she was a clinic patient waiting to be seen. She sat there with her coat folded on her lap, her back straight and her blouse collar turned up. The pattern was a pink-red floral against a white background but her black skin made it look like the flowers were painted in rich natural earth.

"When was your last regular menstrual period?" Angie asked trying to match Sandra Blaklee's poise.

"Three month's ago," she replied calmly.

"When did you realize you were pregnant?"

"As soon as I missed my period."

"Have you seen a doctor—when you thought you were pregnant?"

The question aroused the first hint of annoyance or discomfort in the patient. It quickly passed as she was determined to be cooperative.

"I haven't seen a doctor at all," she said.

"Then you may not be pregnant," Angie suggested. "Has there been any vaginal bleeding? Any pain?"

"It started about eleven this morning. It started with a cramp here," she held her hand over the lower abdomen indicating where the pain was," and then I could feel the blood oozing down the inside of my leg."

Angie looked at her legs but saw no blood. The patient seemed undisturbed as she related the events to Angie.

When the patient got on the table with her legs in the stirrups, Angie saw a small clot of blood at the vaginal opening. As she wiped it away, Sandra Blaklee flinched involuntarily. The muscles of her thighs contracted spasmodically from the pain caused by the adherent blood but she said nothing. Angie put a speculum into the vagina. As soon as she opened the blades of the speculum, a well-formed six-inch fetus was ejected through the orifice. The ejection force propelled the fetus into the basin suspended at the foot of the table just below the vagina.

The forceful ejection caught Angie by surprise and she stepped back instinctively to avoid the missle. It lay immobile in the stainless steel pan curled up and perfectly formed, distinctly human, attached to the umbilical cord hanging from the vagina. Angie pulled the cord gently. The attached placenta slippery with blood eased out of the vagina and plopped into the pan splattering blood up the curved walls of the basin.

Angie wiped the inside of the vagina with a sterile gauze sponge, removing the puddle of blood that had collected there. She examined the cervix of the uterus. It was still open with very little bleeding coming from there. With a gloved hand, she felt the uterus. It was contracted and there was no danger of any serious bleeding. The abortion was complete.

Angie stepped into the next cubicle and asked Dr. Gordon to check her patient. Gordon followed her back to the examining cubicle. He picked up the specimen of the fetus and its attached pancakelike placenta. The fetus didn't interest him as much as the placenta. He studied it carefully to be sure there were no missing or torn segments. A retained portion of a placenta could cause severe bleeding later on or worse it could degenerate to a hydatidform mole which can bore its way through the uterine wall as if it were a malignancy.

A strange creature with an appropriate name is a hydatidform mole. It is created in part from the mother and in part from the fetus. It is from the body and from another. It starts out as the placenta with an indispensable function for the fetus. The placenta bores its way into the wall of the uterus completely controlled knowing just how deeply to penetrate. Deep enough to cannibalize the uterine blood supply without injuring it. Left in place without a fetus, it may disappear but more often it bleeds the host.

The retained placenta doesn't penetrate any further but left without a fetus it sometimes changes character. Even a tiny remnant will start growing in an uncontrolled way. It becomes a hydatidform mole boring through and taking more and more blood slowly. It can invade a large blood vessel, rupture it and cause a sudden hemorrhage.

The mole can degenerate further. It can get into the blood stream and spread through the body like a cancer. It becomes a cancer called a choriocarcinoma. Once it was dreaded complication, causing death in young women by cancer disseminated through their bodies. It became the first cancer that was completely curable, even in the metastatic state, with chemotherapy. In some ways it was like other cancers but in a very important way it was different. It was not wholly of the body and the body could reject it with the help of chemicals.

After examining the placenta and the patient, Dr. Gordon was satisfied the abortion was complete. Angie agreed and the patient simply said thank you and left.

About an hour later, Angie met Martha in the hospital cafeteria for dinner. It was quieter, well below the lunchtime capacity.

"I never saw anything like that!" Angie said to Martha who was leaning back sipping coffee. "It was a perfectly formed fetus, a miniature wrapped up in itself." Angie held her hands close to her chest imitating the fetal position.

"Sounds cute," Martha quipped.

"It wasn't cute but it wasn't ugly either. I was just surprised by it being there more than anything. Also that woman, she was so—so cool! I can't explain it any better. She looked like she just stepped out of Harper's Bazaar or something. She just didn't seem to belong in the clinic."

"Maybe she spent all her money on clothes and couldn't afford a doctor," Martha said smiling but the look in Martha's eyes said more.

"Maybe, but don't be so inscrutable. Even your eyes become Oriental when you talk like that. What do you really think about her? How do you explain her almost bland attitude like she was having a hem repaired instead of a miscarriage?"

"If it were a few years ago," Martha said taking a deep breath, "I would say the abortion was induced. It used to be quite common you know. A girl would go to some midwife or some soothsayer to start the abortion. Then they'd come running into the hospital to have it finished. Many of them came in almost dead from bleeding or infection. Some knew what they were doing or were just lucky."

Angie was caught off guard. She never considered the possibility of a self-induced abortion.

"She wouldn't do that!" Angie insisted. "She's not the type."

"What type do you have to be?"

"I mean she seemed too smart considering the danger compared to the availability of a safe, legal abortion today."

"Maybe she was smarter than you think and she knew just how to do it. It's available but it could still cost her a hundred and fifty bucks. Maybe more."

"But—"

"But maybe it was spontaneous."

"No, that's not what I was thinking about. It was her attitude. The way she accepted it. No tears, no sorrow, not even worried about herself."

Martha waited silently watching the expression on Angie's face. Angie's eyes opened more widely, her jaw slackened and then she pursed her lips.

"You are right!" Angie said pointing a finger at Martha. "She did it herself. She had to! And I was so concerned about her, worried about how she was taking it all. But that was just the way she wanted it. I bet it wasn't the first time for her either."

"You sure run hot and cold," Martha said sneering at Angie's changing opinions. "Now you're ready to stick knives in her back. She's still the same person. You probably didn't like her from the beginning because she didn't react the way you expected her to. You do that a lot. Expect people to react like you."

"Martha!" Angie said feeling abused.

"You do!" Martha continued undeterred. "Either they have to feel the way you do or else they have to be dependent on you so that you can forgive them or somehow—I don't know what else but there has to be something for you to do."

"I don't think you're right but I don't want to argue about it," Angie said feeling hurt. It wasn't only their seemingly different attitudes about abortion that stung Angie. It was Martha's implication that she had to be selfishly dominant that stung more.

"I'm sure the world can go on without me," she said.

"It's not that bad, Angie. You really do make a difference in your own way but you can't have it your own way all the time. Let's forget it. How are you and Peter doing?"

"So far so good," she smiled and shrugged her shoulders. "I haven't seen him since yesterday. It's okay when we're alone but it's different in the hospital. I'm not sure I can handle it the way he wants to."

"Are you seeing him this week?"

"Er—Friday for a drink. He's got so many meetings this week. Tonight . . . , well, I'm working anyway but he's going to a party at Comerford's."

"I hope you have a quiet night. Don't stay up too late if you can help it. You're only required to help out in the Emergency Room until midnight so get some sleep. Tomorrow's a regular working day but I put you on some easy cases.

"Thanks, I'll see you tomorrow, and Martha—I will think about what you said."

Thirteen

The Comerford penthouse occupied the thirty-fifth floor of a white brick apartment building on Fifth Avenue across the street from Central Park. A small bronze plaque on the wall of the building near the entrance bore the simple inscription *Evergreen*. There was no clue as to why the building was so named, unless the builders or occupants lived there only in the summer and spring. It was possible that the very wealthy people who owned apartments there only returned in the spring from Palm Beach or Majorca or wherever wealthy people go to avoid the muddied, caked snows of New York in winter.

Whatever the origin of the name, *Evergreen* was synonymous with entrenched financial holdings that weathered the economic dips and folds of depressions, recessions, inflations, oil embargoes, assassinations and resignations. That may have been the cipher of *Evergreen*.

Almost all the guests arrived within minutes of each other for the evening of cocktails and talk about the new Institute Comerford was proposing. For the project to develop smoothly more than money was needed. Several state legislators and congressional representatives were there. The Governor had sent his regrets but said he would support the project. The Certificate of Need law required the approval of various state and federal agencies before changes and additions to the hospital could take place.

Arthur Comerford's brother Alex, who was five years younger, headed the delegation of bankers, financial moguls and other business people who would raise the bulk of the initial money for the Institute.

Alex Comerford could almost have passed as Arthur's twin. Arthur looked like a rumpled copy of his brother. They both had balding gray hair with strands going across the top trying to provide limited coverage to the scalp. Arthur's was usually out of place while Alex's was neatly plastered down and more effective. Alex's white moustache was carefully waxed and Arthur's was bushy and unruly. Alex was tanned a deep brown compared to Arthur's almost pale skin. Alex's eyes were sharper and more critical, devoid of compassion. Overall he gave an impression antithetical to the warm, congenial Dr. Arthur Comerford, although they shared a common ancestry.

Arthur Comerford as the oldest son had been expected to be the head of the Comerford family finances. Instead he rebelled so he could study medicine saying he wasn't interested in ledgers and balance sheets. It was only in a family like the Comerfords that such a choice would be construed as a rebellion. The family sceptre was passed on to Alex, who shouldered the responsibility happily. He still remained Arthur's kid brother and devoted follower.

Beatrice Comerford's beauty aged with her, taking on a patina which confirmed its depth. She had encouraged Arthur's rebellion and supported his battle with his father. Throughout their marriage she was there to share his triumphs and pitfalls. She was only an inch taller than he when they married. She remained slim and straight. He had become paunchy and walked with a slouch, so she seemed even taller now. Her gray hair was tinted blue and there was a small bit of loose skin under her chin. Her deep blue eyes remained clear and somehow she had avoided the eyebags and wrinkles of age.

The evening was meant to be a kind of pep rally for the Institute. No hard bargaining or selling was planned. The invited guests already had agreed to nominal support for the idea and the preliminary plans. Soon it would gather the necessary momentum but for the time being the concept had to first take root.

"Of course there would be a place for the study of sexual functions in The Institute for Gynecology," Eric Potter was saying to a group gathered around him. Elaine Potter, standing in another circle with two state senators and their wives, caught his authoritative tone. She excused herself to join him.

"Arthur gave us the impression that this Institute was for the treatment of women with cancer," a short chunky woman said. Her eyes squinted suspiciously. Potter wasn't sure who she was or whether she approved or disapproved of sex.

"That would certainly be a major focus at the Institute but there are many other problems which require intensive study," Potter said gaining silent approval from his wife. "Sexual function, reproductive biology and several other areas require attention."

"I'm certainly glad to hear that," the woman said, "I can't bear those hospitals for cancer where you know everyone has that damned thing. It's depressing."

A waiter interrupted Potter telling him he was wanted on the phone. He excused himself while Elaine took over the discussion. He took the phone in the entrance foyer.

"This is Dr. Reese at the hospital, sir," the voice at the other end said. Potter recognized one of the Chief Residents.

"Yes, what is it?" Potter asked harshly.

"Er—there's a twenty-nine-year-old Puerto Rican female admitted with a boardlike abdomen," Reese said reverting to a clinical cadence to force the message through without sounding nervous.

"So?" Potter said still annoyed by the interruption.

"I think she has a ruptured ectopic pregnancy, sir."

"Why are you calling me?"

"You're 'on call' tonight."

Potter had forgotten the schedule and it was too late to find a substitute. He had to find a way to stall. It was too early for him to leave the party. He wanted to make his pitch to establish himself in the minds of all these potential members of the Board of Trustees.

"What makes you think she has a ruptured ectopic?" he asked challengingly while trying to think of a way out.

"She was in the clinic this afternoon and it was suspected. We tapped her belly and got back free blood. Also—"

"Well then take her up to the O.R. and operate!"

"I can't do that without an Attending Surgeon. I don't have privileges for independent surgery until January."

Potter hesitated as he was torn between staying and leaving. No one saw the frustration and anger in his face as he sighed and bit his lips.

"You're not sure she has an ectopic." It was almost a command from Potter.

"I'm—er—"

"You can't be sure! And you'll be up the creek if it turns out to be another one of those aneurysms they presented last month at Grand Rounds. If I were you, I wouldn't make the same mistake Trenton made or you'll never get to operate on your own. You better get an arteriogram and call me back."

"But—"

"Just call me when you get the results." Potter hung up. He felt reprieved and ready to resume politics.

Dr. Reese stared into the speaker of the dead phone.

"Schmuck!" he said softly but audible so Angie and Dr. Gordon could hear him. They were in the surgeons' lounge of the O.R. expecting to operate.

"What did he say?" Gordon asked.

"Get an arteriogram," Reese ordered passing the buck to Gordon.

"Are you crazy?" Angie stood up angrily. "She has a ruptured ectopic and if you don't take her in right away she's going to die."

"You take her in, big mouth!" Reese matched her anger. "Why am I arguing with you," he said more softly, seemingly confused as he tried to straighten out his priorities. "Joe, ask them to do this as soon as possible. Just one injection to prove the aorta is intact."

Dr. Gordon nodded and left without commenting.

"Miss Palmeri, I appreciate your help but don't make diagnoses. There's more here than—he's got a good point and it's not your ass that'll be in a sling if—"

He stopped in midsentence as Angie stood there quietly listening to him trying to justify the delay. He just waved his hand at her and walked out. Angie sat down on the couch depressed and sulking.

Eric Potter returned to the guests shaking off his displeasure. Elaine tried to catch his glance for some hint about the phone call but he ignored her. He rejoined the circle of people, finding the discussion had not progressed very far.

"I wouldn't say gynecology has been neglected at University Medical Center," Elaine Potter answered Mrs. Carney's question. She was now able to put together the name and face of the wife of the Senate Majority leader in Albany. "An institute can physically focus on so many interrelated problems. Sex, reproductive biology, for instance, is a meshwork of disciplines, endocrinology, DNA research, metabolism and biochemistry and so on. The Institute can be very beneficial."

"For whom?" Mrs. Carney asked.

Elaine was caught off balance because she did not expect a challenge. She was already thinking of other selling points under the assumption that the benefits of the Institute were self-evident. Her pale white skin darkened with a bit of blush.

"For all of us, Mrs. Carney," Elaine recovered her poise.

"One can't be too specific. A successful program should discover relationships not previously considered. It's in the nature of good research to take things apart and put them together in new ways."

200

"But the Institute, as I understand it," Mrs. Carney said in a way to assure everyone she understood correctly, "is primarily a treatment facility. How can it be justified with the surplus of hospital beds already in the city? More importantly, I want to know who would have access to this facility? It seems to me that 'institutes' tend to be restrictive and it gives the staff considerable economic advantages."

"It would seem so," Eric took over from Elaine, "but on the other hand the real issue is to establish the best possible conditions for the best results. To accomplish the possible we—the Institute—should be selective. Yes, that's a much better way of looking at it," he smiled pleased with himself. "Of course, I mean selective in a scientific sense."

"I don't see the difference," Mrs. Carney objected. "The Institute would take a disproportionate amount of resources compared to the number of people who would use its services."

"But we are talking about quality services, not quantity," Eric said intently as he brushed aside a waiter with a tray of hors d'oeuvres. "It will certainly be an important resource for the general hospital to refer the more difficult problems, to properly test new ideas and to set standards of care."

"It sounds like a double standard to me," Mrs. Carney said with raised eyebrows. "Why can't everyone be treated with the same care and decency?"

"You said so yourself—there aren't enough resources," Eric said. "Why can't everyone drive a Mercedes or a Rolls Royce?"

"I'm sure we are all closer to agreeing on the priorities than we think," Elaine interjected. "It's difficult to see all these things at once."

There were other groups gathered throughout the living room and a few men gathered in the den. Most of the talk was general, light and seemingly irrelevant to the purpose of the evening. Eric was scheduled to present a more formal overview of what the Institute could accomplish. The conversation between the Potters and Mrs. Carney soon drifted away from the problems of the Institute. An hour after the first phone call, Dr. Reese called again.

"The patient died on the X-ray table," Dr. Reese said coldly without recriminations.

"What patient?" Potter asked. He wasn't being purposely obtuse. His mind was concentrating on opportunities elsewhere. The earlier phone call had been an intrusion which he had buried in the back of his mind. Now there was a patient to bury.

"The one I called you about earlier, the one with the ruptured ectopic," Reese said easily as if he was reminding a friend to pick up a sweater left behind. It wasn't necessary for Potter's memory was already jostled.

"What did the arteriogram show?" Potter asked hoping his diversion had turned into a lucky guess.

"It wasn't done," Reese told him. "She had a cardiac arrest before the procedure started and we couldn't resuscitate her." There was silence waiting on both ends of the line. Reese waiting for a reaction, a suggestion, advice, even a direct order while Potter let the facts sink in. The fact was he didn't go to the hospital when he should have. There was a painful stiffening in his neck which radiated to his shoulder as he regretted his earlier hastiness. Finally, Dr. Reese broke the silence on his end.

"I'll ask the M.E. if he'll do the post," he said.

"The Medical Examiner?" Potter said breaking out in a cold sweat but controlling his voice so his question made the prospect sound more dubious than frightening. "He won't be interested in this. You said the patient was in the clinic earlier so she was under a doctor's care."

"But she died as she was about to have a diagnostic procedure," Reese protested. Potter ignored it.

"Besides," he said, "there must be some family around. The M.E. won't do it if there's family and no consent."

"But we need a post," Reese insisted. "There'll be a lot of questions about this case."

"I know, I know," Potter said wiping the sweat from his lips. "That's why we need a good autopsy. Find the family and get them to consent to a hospital autopsy."

Dr. Reese slammed down the phone after he was sure Potter had disconnected. He was very thin and slouched with his forehead against the instrument on the wall. After a moment he wearily pushed himself away from the wall and straightened up. He tugged on the black belt going through the loops of his starched white cotton pants.

Dr. Joe Gordon sat in the armchair of the surgeons' lounge watching his Chief Resident contort his face as the options were considered. Gordon was worried, almost frightened and he was counting on his Chief to work out the problem.

"Call the Medical Examiner's office," Reese said thoughtfully squinting and biting the inside of his cheek. The squint made him look more alert than his tired eyes permitted a few minutes earlier.

"Is that what Potter said?" Gordon jumped up nervously.

"Call the Medical Examiner and tell him to forget about doing the autopsy," he said calming Gordon's agitation.

"What about Palmeri?"

"Where is she?"

"I saw her talking to the woman's sister explaining why we needed an autopsy."

"Oh, shit!" That's none of her fucking business!" Reese said as he pushed his hair back and held his head as it if were painful. It was a slow boil calculated to make sure he didn't lose his head.

"You get down there and find her family," he said. "I don't give a shit if you have to go up to 125th Street but get a consent for a hospital autopsy."

"What about the M.E.?" Gordon asked already jumping toward the door.

"I'll call. If you get the consent signed he won't give a shit who does the post."

"What if I can't find anyone to sign," Gordon asked anxiously hanging on to the open door halfway out.

"Then don't come back," Reese said in a soft, menacing monotone. "I'll spell it out for you. Your future is tied to Dr. Potter. I'm stuck in between ready to jump off depending on where the shit flies."

Eric Potter returned to the guests searching out his wife Elaine. She was leaning on the piano listening to Senator Carney singing in a pretty fair tenor accompanied by Beatrice Comerford on the piano. Potter tiptoed up behind her unnoticed by the other guests.

"Elaine," he whispered in her ear, "we've got to go."

She turned around mystified by his urgency but she could feel his subdued anxiety. His skin was blanched and the beads of perspiration were hanging on his upper lip. She wanted to ask why but it was not the place to do it. She followed him to the foyer where the butler was waiting with her coat.

"We can't just leave like this. Are you crazy?" she said ignoring the butler holding her coat open for her.

Eric was embarrassed but the butler pretended he heard nothing.

"It's an emergency at the hospital. I'll explain to the Comerfords. I'm sure they'll understand," he said agonizingly hoping she could read between his words.

"But I don't understand. We have discussed how important this evening could be for —" she stopped not wanting the butler to hear anymore despite his attitude of indifference. She let him help her with her coat as Eric was relieved to be on his way.

In the elevator, he explained the situation to

her. She stared stiffly in front of her listening but refusing to look at him.

"Why didn't you switch your call with someone," she asked bitterly. She was tense with hope when the evening began. There was the hope she was being accepted socially, that the Potters were attaining some stature. It was the first time she had been invited to *Evergreen*.

He started to explain but she cut him off. She pulled her coat tightly over her burgundy evening dress she had bought for the occasion. She even allowed herself a gold brooch that Eric had bought years ago but which she had refused to wear until now.

"Was Reese sure she had a ruptured ectopic pregnancy?" she asked as she looked up from staring at her sensible flat shoes.

"He was very definite," Eric said and was about to explain further when the elevator door opened to the lobby.

Further discussion of the problem was suspended as they entered the gold-carpeted lobby with the mirrored walls. The potted palms and the doorman to assist the departure of the nonresident aliens from the halls of *Evergreen* intimidated their speech. In a taxi on the way to the hospital, Elaine recovered first.

"Why am I going?" she demanded. "I could have stayed and presented your talk."

"Reese wanted the M.E. to do the post," Eric said secretively hiding the conversation from the driver. "An autopsy has to be done and we don't want the M.E. to do it."

"Eric, you make things very complicated," she said sadly as she put her head in her hands. She looked up again a few moments later.

"Is he getting the family to sign a consent for a hospital autopsy?" she asked.

"Yes."

"What am I supposed to do?" she asked sounding innocent and put upon. It was calculated to make him worry while she tried to sort things out in her own mind. Eric had made assumptions based on the past joint endeavors. He hadn't figured out the details but the general strategy was laid out. The details were up to Elaine.

"You're supposed to do the autopsy," he said squirming uncomfortably, annoyed by her coyness.

"I don't know if I should," she said. She waited for his reaction but he remained silent. He turned to look out the window as the taxi accelerated through an intersection.

"Even if I did," she resumed talking in a normal conversational tone when he refused to be baited, "I don't think it would help you, aside from it's educational value of course."

"What is that supposed to mean?" he asked sharply as he turned toward her.

"It's another example of your sloppiness. Last month it was McCrae. I warned you then!" she said with her voice rising in anger.

"This is different," he insisted.

"It was poor judgment," she taunted him. "All you had to do was to show up. Everything else was up to Reese."

"It wasn't even an hour between calls," he said

hoping for some sympathy. "She may have ruptured hours ago. It wasn't all my fault."

"You refuse to admit responsibility for
anything," she chastised him. "Dammit! That's the
problem. You think I can work miracles."

"I told Reese to get the arteriogram because it
might be another case like Trenton's, the dissecting
aneurysm?"

"So?"

"So cut the crap!" he said angrily. "You have the
specimen from that case. Do what you usually do."

"What if I don't?"

"I'll be on the carpet and the chances of being
Director of the Institute will be out the window,"
he said with resignation as the cab pulled up to the
Emergency Room entrance.

They hurried through the waiting room past the
patients and family or friends waiting to be seen.
At the nurses' station Eric asked the clerk at the
desk if she had seen Dr. Reese.

"He was here about an hour ago," she said.

Potter picked up the phone and asked the
operator to page Reese for the E.R. Angie came
out of a treatment cubicle. She stopped at the desk
to write some notes on a chart. Elaine didn't
recognize her or else merely turned away because
she preferred not to. Eric, because he saw her
almost everyday in the operating room, could not
afford that luxury.

"You're too late," Angie said flatly without looking up from her notes.

"I'm aware of that, Miss—" he hesitated,
withholding full recognition. Angie held up her

lapel with her ID card for him to see.

"Miss Palmeri, thank you. Did you see the patient?" he said condescendingly.

"I saw her this afternoon and this evening," Angie stopped writing to look at Potter. "She wasn't ruptured this afternoon. She should have been admitted then," she said confidently, matter of factly and without sounding accusatory. Still her tone caught Elaine's attention and made her turn around. She remembered Angie now.

The phone rang relieving Eric of the necessity of explaining the other possible diagnoses in a case like this. Not that he thought her opinion carried any weight but because he was already preparing the arguments in his favor. Eventually he might really believe them himself. It was Reese on the phone.

"I got the consent for the post from the family. The M.E. agreed but he wants a copy of the report," Reese said.

"Who notified him?" Potter said with only a hint of anger.

"Palmeri."

Potter looked at Angie without giving any hint of how disturbed he was. She finished writing and walked away feeling his conversation was inhibited by her presence. As far as she knew, the M.E.'s office had accepted the case.

"Where's the patient now?" Potter asked watching Angie walk behind the curtains of an examining cubicle.

"In the morgue," Reese answered. "The consent is on the chart. We didn't get any X-rays. She went into cardiac arrest as soon as they put her on the X-ray table."

He hung up the phone and took Elaine by the arm without saying a word. He guided her into the corridor leading to the main part of the hospital and her office. The nightime corridors were silent and empty.

"She was the one who notified the M.E.," he said in a stage whisper. Elaine turned around to look back through the deserted hallway.

"Who?" Elaine asked. "That girl? She looked familiar. She's the one who was looking at McCrae's specimen. I told you to be careful when she's around."

When they entered Elaine's office, Eric paced up and down, in and around the desk and lab table. Elaine sat at her desk without taking off her coat. She sat perfectly still while Eric was preoccupied with how to proceed. He stopped suddenly, staring at her inactivity.

"Are you just going to sit there?" he asked anxiously.

"I'm going to sit here until you calm down," she said. "Look at how you are sweating. Go wash your face or something. Take a Valium."

"I don't need a Valium, Elaine," he said harshly with the words sticking in his throat. "And I'll calm down when you have finished the autopsy."

"That may be awhile yet," she said calmly as she tossed her purse on the desk. "How does your upper lip sweat like that? I didn't think any human had so many sweat glands in that area. It's not hot in here. I feel rather cool myself," she said pulling her coat together.

"Okay, Elaine, what's the purpose of all this?" he said resolutely. He folded his arms and leaned against the waist-high laboratory table. "Why are you holding out? Have you had enough? Are you tired of this partnership and ready to sacrifice me? That's it! You have enough money to make it on your own now. God knows you must! You never spend it on anything. I'd rather quit right now than beg you, Elaine."

"Oh, shut up!" she said slamming her hand down on the desk. "Don't get hysterical! I want you to seem unconcerned like you were out there talking to Palmeri. Why do you always act this way when we're alone?"

"Let's say it's your charisma," he said sarcastically. "I don't really know but throughout all these years, not once, have you ever had a kind word for me. Never! I know what you have done for me but it was also for yourself. I've never held anything back from you. And you've been able to do it secretly while I'm out there in the open . . . waiting . . . just waiting for you to—I'm not sure what you're capable of."

"After ten years, you can really think that?" she asked hurt by his accusation. If she could really feel anything toward Eric, it was the feeling that they had a trusting partnership.

"I never knew you felt that way," she continued. "I never made any demands on you except for our original bargain. Otherwise you've been free to do as you please."

"But after living together for almost ten years,

you haven't changed one bit," he said more calmly as he wiped his face with a handkerchief, "Not even a pretense of warmth or concern."

"That was part of the bargain, Eric. Do you want to change it?" It was a cold challenge beset with practical pitfalls. He felt no love lost between them. At this point any renegotiations would come out in her favor. As always because she had the upper hand, it bothered him most. He declined to answer.

"Neither do I," she said. "I have greater ambitions for you and for myself. It has worked better than I expected. I was getting tired of just working. Comerford's Institute means a great deal more than money. He has spoken to me about the research program and the Pathology department. It's because of you that he even thought of me. I appreciate that, Eric. I knew you wouldn't let me down."

"You are a good pathologist—"

"Hold it! I know you wouldn't dream of having anyone else at your side when you become Director. Right?"

"Right," he said softly, "but you could have let me say it."

She was satisfied with the reaffirmation of their vows. In a way, a warmth of understanding of some sort had grown between them since their first heated meeting in Elaine's office ten years ago.

"Call Reese and tell him I'm going to start the autopsy in an hour."

"Why?" Eric stood up surprised and upset at the prospect of having Reese present.

"Because we need witnesses."

"That's crazy!" he said nervously as he began pacing again. "We don't want him to see this . . . , not when you open the belly."

"He'll see what he wants to see and I'll be there so he'll see what he expects to see. If I make it look like a ruptured aneurysm he'll be relieved."

"Why should he?"

"Why did he call the M.E. and get permission for me to do the autopsy? He doesn't want to challenge you. The patient was in his clinic. We all make little mistakes that come back to us. Whatever it is, he's hoping you were right."

The morgue attendants placed the body of Rita Algrin on the stainless steel table. Four other gleaming prosecting tables stood unused in a row. The concave surface of the tables were movable perforated sheets of stainless steel that rested in a canoelike basin running the length of the table. At one end a water faucet emerged about a foot above the table.

The room was well lighted with recessed fluorescent lighting. In addition, there were broad banks of spotlights suspended from the ceiling over each table just like those in the operating room.

Elaine Potter was dressed in a green O.R. dress but without the cap and mask. She stood ready before the table adjusting a microphone suspended from the ceiling. With her head and arms raised, she was preparing to dictate her findings as she went along. With her head raised and her arms above before the table holding Rita Algrin, it formed a silhouette of human sacrifice.

"Dr. Elaine Potter dictating," she announced into the microphone, "autopsy on Rita Algrin, U.M.C. case number 78973. Also present are Dr. Potter and Dr. Bedford Reese."

She stopped to look at the two doctors standing behind her at the cabinets. She took her foot off the pedal controlling the microphone. "Is Dr. Gordon coming?" she asked.

"He'll be here as soon as he can," Reese answered.

"And Dr. Joe Gordon," she said turning back to the microphone. "The patient is a twenty-nine-year-old female Caucasian. There are no external marks or injuries on the body," she went on as she scanned the naked body before her.

"The abdomen is severely distended." With the microphone off, she turned around again. "Something's ruptured in there," she said to both men, "or else she's about nine months pregnant with twins."

Both men pulled out stools from under the cabinet without comment. Elaine returned to her subject.

"The front teeth are absent and there is dried blood staining the lower teeth," she said with her gloved hand everting the lips. There was a scalpel blade concealed and taped to Elaine's right index finger which made her keep the finger straight out but neither Eric nor Reese noticed.

Elaine turned on the faucet at the head of the table letting the water run freely under the perforated surface of the table where it could wash away the blood expected from the open body. She picked up a very large scalpel sitting at the edge of the table.

The incision was started at the left shoulder and continued diagonally down along the rib cage to the beginning of the abdomen in the midline. The cut went deeply through all the muscle and fat down to the bones. A twin of this incision was made starting at the right shoulder and joined the first one just below the margin of the rib cage in the midline of the body.

There was no active bleeding from the dead body which had no pump to force the blood around. There was streaking of the yellow fat with dark blood that spilled without pressure from the blood vessels cut along the path of the incision. The incision was made longer down the middle of the belly. Elaine was careful not to penetrate the blood-filled abdominal cavity, which would spill its contents once the restraining muscles and connective tissue were divided.

The big Y incision traversed the entire trunk. Elaine undercut the skin at the apex of the Y raising a triangular flap which bulged on each side along the line of the breasts. The muscles of the chest wall were divided so the flap including the breasts was raised and folded over the face.

Focusing on the upper half of the body gender and identity were lost. The ribs with tattered pieces of muscle and fat were exposed. Elaine used an electrical saw with a semicircular blade to cut through the ribs along each side of the chest. She lifted the chest wall out as a unit, cutting the underlying connective tissue adhesions with the scalpel.

Dr. Joe Gordon came in in the midst of the harsh buzz saw sounds when the breastplate was being divided. He saw that Elaine had not reached the critical or diagnostic point in the autopsy. Through it all Potter and Reese had not exchanged more than a few worried words of reassurance to each other. Neither had anything sincere to say to each other anyway and Gordon had enough sense to remain silent.

Elaine worked competently giving a brief description of the normal findings in the chest cavity for the benefit of the microphone. She tied off the two carotid arteries, one on each side of the neck, along with the parallel jugular veins and then divided the vessels. She used thick postal twine. The same thing was done to the trachea and esophagus thereby freeing the major organs of the chest from their superior attachments. The heart, lungs and the esophagus along with the thymus gland and assorted lymph nodes were lifted up in a block. The lower attachments of each were cut through and the entire mass of organs removed from the chest cavity. They were placed on the table between the legs of the cadaver.

Blood dripped down from the mass of soggy flesh and stained the pale morbid skin of the cadaver's legs. The heart rested on top, darkened like aged beef, streaked with yellow fat obscuring the outline of the four chambers within. The great vessels, pulmonary artery and vein, aorta and vena cavae, divided and empty, stood out like stovepipes of disassembled plumbing.

With a large scissors, Elaine separated the heart from the lungs dropping each organ into a large formalin containing bucket. She stepped back to the almost empty chest cavity which still held the descending aorta.

"There's no aneurysm or evidence of dissecting aneurysm in the chest," she said to the three men behind her. She waited silently for their reaction, looking from one face to another.

"I never said she had an aneurysm," Dr. Reese was first to speak. He said it quietly without real assurance, without committing himself to anything that might be construed as sounding critical. He was maintaining his middle ground by disagreeing with Potter but doing what Potter told him to do.

Potter worried silently about Elaine because he didn't trust her. He began sweating again at the thought that she had set this all up to embarrass him or worse. She had always worked secretly in his behalf, for both of them actually, but she had a sadistic streak that liked to see him squirm. It seemed pointless to him that she began in the chest when the answer, one way or another, was in the belly. He wanted to leave, just to run away so as to cheat her of the pleasure she might find in his misery.

"All of you come over here," she ordered them and they slowly came around the table. As she cut through the restraining muscle and fascia, very dark burgundy fluid came rushing over the side walls of the abdomen as it collapsed. The thick fluid spilled over the table splattering the trousers

217

and shoes of the three men watching her.

The ectopic pregnancy within the confines of the fallopian tube had first cannibalized the blood supply. It was a normal process for the placenta to seek out and attach itself to the available blood supply to nourish the growing fetus. Then the fetus and the placenta grew and grew within the narrow confines of the tube distending it to its maximum.

And then catastrophe! The tube ruptured, tearing the placenta and allowing the life blood to spill unimpeded into the abdominal cavity. With the placenta still attached, the normal mechanisms for inhibiting the hemorrhage were abrogated. The placenta, unknowing, uncaring with its only function to maintain the flow of blood from the mother to the fetus kept the blood flowing freely into the abdominal cavity. It is a space within the body that is functionally outside of it. The blood could not find its way back to the heart, the lungs, the brain or anything else that needed to survive.

Elaine dipped her gloved hands into the cavity still overflowing with wasted blood. The fluid was deep so it reached above the rubbery protection to stain her forearms almost to the elbows. She manipulated the stomach and bowel and cut the attachments. The snakelike mass was lifted out of the pool like a watery boa constrictor coming up for air. Even in the short time since death, the fecal degeneration of the bowel wall exuded a fetid repulsive odor that made the three other doctors retreat further away from the table.

The coils of small and large bowel were put in a large stainless steel pail on the floor. The remaining contents of the abdominal cavity were drowned in the pool of blood contained by the walls of the abdomen. It was almost black in there if anyone cared to see but the three other witnesses kept their distance.

Elaine put her hands back into the pool of blood. She felt the outline of the aorta, identifying the bifurcation where it divides into two arteries, one going to each leg. As she moved her hand upward, she loosened the scalpel blade taped to her right index finger so she could control its cutting edge. A jagged cut was made through the thick fibrous rubbery wall of the aorta, simulating a ruptured aneurysm.

With the large scissors, Elaine cut the aorta and vena cava just below the diaphragm. She lifted the two vessels out of the pool carrying the attached kidneys on each side. The lower attachments were severed and the specimen was free.

She dropped the complex specimen dripping with blood once more across the legs of the cadaver. It was hard to identify details as the kidneys flopped over the vessels. No one but Elaine was watching too carefully anyway. She opened the tubular aorta which was lined with calcareous atherosclerosis. She cut the lining and insinuated the scissors between the lining and the muscular wall. She did it quickly. She might have been opening the wall as one normally did in an autopsy. She might have fooled someone who was actually watching but the fetid odor and the spillage of blood distracted the witnesses. The dissecting ruptured aneurysm was complete.

"Here it is," Elaine announced and the three surgeons immediately approached the table. "Torn over here," she pointed to one jagged hole in the lining, "worked down to here and then ruptured."

They didn't look too hard or too long but there was relief among all three, which they tried to hide.

"I think you did the right thing," Eric Potter said graciously to Reese. "Unfortunately, it didn't matter except if you had gone in without the arteriogram there'd be a big stink at Grand Rounds. I don't think they'd be as kind to you as they were to Trenton."

Reese and Gordon left Elaine and Eric alone at opposite sides of the table. Elaine reached into the bloody abdominal cavity and pulled out a macerated, exploded piece of flesh. She held it out in the palm of her hand toward Eric.

"What is that?" he asked.

"It's what's left of the ruptured ectopic," she said calmly. "In case you're wondering, I'll keep this for my private collection.

Fourteen

The T.G.I.F. crowd gathered round the bar at the Second Avenue Pub only a few blocks from the Medical Center. In the world of medicine, Fridays do not come with assured regularity. Someone has to work Saturdays and Sundays which makes scheduling an administrative art satisfactory to no one. The Medicine Ship morosely chugs through the weekend in low gear unable to stop completely or else it would lose all the mileage gained in the week passed. Because of this, participation in the celebration of T.G.I.F. might seem eratic by ordinary business standards but it is no less devoted when the end of the work week coincides with Friday.

Angie sat with Martha at a table against the wall. It was past six o'clock and the crowd was thinning out. Another idiosyncracy of medicine was to start the day at seven A.M. giving three shifts: 7 to 3; 3 to 11; 11 to 7. This gave another twist, putting it out of *sync* with the rest of the world. Six o'clock on T.G.I.F. was like eight o'clock for the rest of the world.

"I'll wait with you if you want me to," Martha said.

"No, you go ahead," Angie said unable to hide a touch of sadness in her voice. "I don't want you to be late. I'll stay a little while longer. If he doesn't come, I'll be home before you go out."

"It's only a little past six. He'll be here. Doctors are never on time," Martha assured her.

"Peter Trenton is," Angie said wistfully as she looked at her watch. "Sometimes he's awfully compulsive, especially about being on time."

"Did you see him this week?" Martha asked.

"When could I see him? Except in the hospital. I scrubbed with him once. He was a perfect gentleman. I wanted to pinch his ass," she said with her teeth clenched in mock anger.

"I don't blame you. He's got such beautiful buns!" Margha said with rising laughter. Her eyes wrinkled in astral radiations.

"He does not!" Angie stamped her fist on the table. "He's so thin back there. Every pair of pants he puts on looks baggy."

"I know. I just wanted to see if you really noticed."

"What if I did?" Angie blushed not sharing Martha's good humor.

"Don't take it so personally. I was only teasing you," Martha said. She stood up slowly and refrained from giving her too much advice. She didn't want Angie to fall too much in love with Trenton. "Anyway, don't wait too long for him. It's not good for his ego. He might explode."

"I won't have to," Angie replied with a warmer glow. "He just came in. Send him over this way on your way out."

Peter saw them and made his way through the maze of tables meeting Martha about halfway.

"Stay for another drink," he offered happily.

"Got to go!" Martha nodded and waved goodbye without stopping.

"Well, what time did you get here?" he asked sitting down. He unzipped the front of his jacket made of knitted wool with leather pockets and leather edges.

"Around five-thirty," she answered glumly. "I went to the Pathology conference this afternoon.

He turned around looking for the waiter and didn't seem to be paying much attention to her. The waiter came right to him.

"Two scotch sours," he ordered.

"How do you know what I want?" she said making sure he knew she was annoyed. It really didn't matter but she was annoyed at him for having other plans without her.

"When I came in you looked like you were glad to see me but as soon as I sat down it was like Dracula at the blood bank."

"What is that supposed to mean?" she said look-ing wide-eyed and demanding an explanation.

"I've been welcomed more cordially than that. I never saw such a rapid switch. The minute I sat down your eyes almost crossed."

"That's your own fault, Dr. Trenton," she said. "You weren't paying close enough attention."

"You don't have to call me Dr. Trenton," he said with a pleading, placating look.

"You told me to call you Dr. Trenton," she said arching her back and pursing her lips.

"That's not necessary. Dr. Pete will be sufficient," he said with exaggerated smugness try-ing to make a joke out of it, but it backfired.

"That's it! I'm leaving," Angie said quickly. She gathered up her purse and coat as she made a move to stand up. Peter reached across the table to grab her hand and easily unbalanced her back into the chair. He continued to lean forward gently holding her hand. He kept looking into her blue eyes which gradually softened. She leaned forward and they kissed across the table. It was a long soft kiss ignored by everyone around them.

"Ahem," the waiter in a white shirt and black vest intruded and waited for them to disengage. He placed the drinks neatly on square napkins and left without asking if there would be anything else. There were too many answers not on the menu.

Angie's eyes twinkled and she had difficulty focusing for a moment. She felt confused. A bit angry still and a bit of glowing warmth throughout her body.

"Angie, I was only trying to be funny," he began

apologetically, "to make it a joke at my expense. I know I can be very dense at times."

"Peter," she said staring at him and shaking her head slowly from side to side, "It's not funny! I tried to talk to you all week at the hospital but you were too busy."

"What did you want to talk about?" he asked.

"Never mind!" she said turning her head away.

"Oh, for godsakes, Angie," he raised his voice in frustration, "we only have a little time now. Say what you want to!"

"That's your problem, I've got all night," she said petulantly.

Peter give up the argument and sipped his drink instead. He wasn't getting anywhere with words but Angie wasn't getting ready to leave again. They studied each other with soft intensity. Peter wasn't ready to make the commitment he felt for Angie. Instead, he tried a more neutral area where he felt he had more control.

"Why did you go to the Path conference?" he asked.

"Don't you know?" she said with sad amazement. "Didn't you hear about Potter's case Tuesday night?"

"Of course I did," he said unconcerned but curious about Angie's reaction. "He left the party early to go to the hospital. He told everyone about it between apologies."

"Was he sorry that woman died?" Angic leaned forward aggressively narrowing her eyes.

"Of course he was sorry," he said with shocked anger because of her tone, "just like I was sorry when my patient died. But that doesn't change anything, does it? Now what are you pissed off about?"

"Did I say I was pissed?"

"No, but you sure look like you are!"

"He could have come right away and she would still be alive! Okay? That's what I'm pissed about," she said slumping back in her chair as the anger diffused.

"I don't think so . . . , well maybe if he was very lucky," he said conceding the possibility. "But it isn't likely with a dissecting aneurysm, if you remember anything from Grand Rounds a few weeks ago."

"She didn't have an aneurysm! She had a ruptured ectopic!" Angie said banging her fist on the table.

Peter looked stunned. For a moment Angie made it sound possible to him. Perhaps a sudden discovery at the autopsy revealed at the conference. Then he recalled Reese and Gordon confirming Potter's description of the autopsy findings.

"Are you crazy or are we not talking about the same case?"

"No, I'm not crazy and no, we are talking about the same case."

"And the case was presented as a ruptured ectopic and the cause of death was not a dissecting aneurysm?"

"No and yes."

"What does that mean?"

"If you can't follow the train of thought, don't ask compound questions!"

"Okay," he said unperturbed by her jibe, "we take it step by step. We're talking about Tuesday night, a twenty-nine-year-old Puerto Rican female—"

"Rita Algrin," she reminded him.

"I didn't get the name but there can't be more than one since last Tuesday. What was I going to ask you?" he said as he lost the thread of his thought.

"The case was presented at the Path conference as a ruptured dissecting aneurysm due to cystic medial necrosis but I saw her in the clinic and when she came in that night. She had an ectopic pregnancy and she ruptured!"

"That's your opinion. You were wrong. How can you dispute the autopsy findings?"

"It wasn't only my opinion. Gordon and Reese thought so too!"

"So that's three out of three wrong. At least they admitted they were wrong. How can you be so harebrained as to ignore what's right in front of your face?"

"That's it! If you're going to be insulting, I'm leaving. Don't worry about being embarrassed anymore. I won't speak to you at all," she said gathering her things again but this time with tears in her eyes.

Peter flushed deep red hating himself for getting carried away with his arguments.

"I'm sorry, I really am sorry I said that. A million times over I'm sorry!"

"No, you're not," she said wiping a tear away as she controlled herself once more. "That's just what you think of me. Some harebrained hick from the farm."

"It's not true! You were never on a farm," he said smiling.

"Don't try to joke your way out of this Peter Trenton," she said pointing a finger at him. "I don't care what you think of me anymore. I'm just trying to tell you there's something strange going on at that shrine you call a hospital. Forget it! Just go on to your card game and I hope you lose all your money."

She took a deep drink of her scotch sour and then stared at the table. He watched her thoughtfully as her facial muscles tightened around her jaw. He couldn't see all of her face. Only the gentle slope of her nose and her fine long lashes. He knew they would have to be more than just friends. He wanted to reach out and touch her again but dared not because she might run away for good.

"Angie," he said softly and then switched to his full voice, "Angie, we can have our own opinions about this thing and fight over it and still be in love."

"Who said anything about being in love?" she said as she turned toward him slowly.

"I did so let's not talk about the hospital anymore."

"But that's not fair," she said looking at him with pleading eyes. "You won't even listen to me without making some wisecracks."

"Okay, I'll listen and I'll be serious but I won't promise to agree with you."

"You won't agree with me," she agreed, "but why did you dismiss my diagnosis so flippantly?"

"It wasn't flippant. I know Reese and Gordon made the same diagnosis but you can't stick with it when the autopsy proves you're wrong."

"The autopsy was faked," she said quietly. Peter resisted the temptation to frown contemptuously.

"How can you fake an autopsy," he said instead. "Gordon and Reese were there. The specimen is still there for anyone to see."

"I don't know how she did it but that woman had an ectopic pregnancy that killed her and she could have been saved."

"It's Elaine that's bugging you and the story I told you about Eric. That's over with and even if it had the slightest bit of truth to it, it has nothing to do with this. If you had given me a chance, I would have told you the case has already been discussed privately. There is no question that this woman had anything but what the official autopsy revealed. It was almost exactly like my case. The autopsy specimens were reviewed and the findings were exactly the same.'

"That's it! She's using the same specimen. She's been doing it all along. I know it. I've seen the difference between what comes out of the patient and what's in the bucket a few days later."

"That's ridiculous! How could the same specimen be used twice?"

"What happens to the old specimens?"

Peter shrugged his shoulders in ignorance.

"It doesn't matter," he said, just forget about it and don't tell anyone else about it."

"I won't forget it. I'll prove it! No," she raised her hand to hold off his objections, "you said you would listen. Eric Potter whips out those uteri like crazy and nobody gives a damn as long as the results fit the pathological expectations."

"I see where you're going," he said with a painful expression, "but there are six or seven pathologists besides Elaine, which shoots your theory to hell."

"Not necessarily. I'm not saying how it's done just that the specimens are switched. Now listen! Don't interrupt. Some of his hysterectomies are legitimate. But some are very questionable. I mean nobody but him examines these patients. No one until I started. If I can mark a specimen beforehand, it would be possible to tell if it's been switched after it gets to the Path lab."

"That should be easy enough," he said none too enthusiastically. "All the specimens are labeled in the O.R."

"The buckets are labeled," Angie said. "I've got to label a specimen before it gets to the O.R. so Eric Potter doesn't know about it. What if I bury a metal clip or something right in the cervix when I examine one of his patients? The cervix isn't very sensitive."

"You can't do that," he said almost laughing. "Please forget the whole thing. Seriously! You'd be endangering the patient and if anything happened—she could bleed or get infected—you'd be responsible."

"I need a reliable witness. If you—"

"Forget it I said!" He stood up very quickly.

Angie pouted her lips childishly which cooled down Peter's indignation. He sat down.

"Promise me you'll forget about this," he asked very softly and pleadingly.

"I'll think about it," she said.

"Promise me so I won't have to worry about you tonight," he said leaning forward. As he did so their legs crossed under the table and she began caressing his thigh with her foot.

"Don't worry about me," she said softly and seductively. "I'll just go home and take off all my clothes. Maybe shower, wash my hair. Don't worry about me. Have a good time tonight."

"Okay, I won't worry about you."

"I'll just walk on home and probably get mugged and raped on the wonderful streets of New York."

"Forget it, they don't rape the willing," he said sarcastically.

She kicked him very hard in the shin she had just been caressing so lovingly.

"Ow!" he said stifling a stronger desire to scream. "Why did you do that?"

"Do what?"

"Kick me?"

She hit him again in the same spot only harder.

"If you insist," she said smiling.

"I was only joking," he said rubbing his eye as he absorbed the pain.

"So was I," she said as she caressed his arm. She gave him a sisterly kiss on the cheek and left.

Fifteen

Trenton's poker game lasted until two A.M. and he didn't get to bed until three. Saturday morning he stayed in bed long after the clock radio went off wondering why he had set it at all. It was the one Saturday morning in the month when he excused himself from attending Grand Rounds. It was his one full weekend off.

Angie's accusations about the Potters had been on his mind throughout the poker game. He won easily with extraordinary luck. He was dealt two straight flushes early in the game. Both were highly improbable, almost as rare as two cases of cystic medial necrosis in one month. The two straight flushes were worth more than the immediate pots. He found himself bluffing and winning with very little effort. The superstitions of the amateur players did it for him by assuming his luck was inviolable.

Angie's scheme wasn't very practical. It was even dangerous for the patients and if she discussed it with anyone else, it would be enough to get her fired for just suggesting it. On the other hand, surgery wasn't much different from poker when it came to pure chance. Two rarely occuring aneurysms could show up in a short span of time. There might not be another one for twenty years. But how could someone average like Potter get consistently superior results from surgery unless he was playing with a stacked deck?

Trenton's body ached as if someone had stuck a crowbar between his muscles and bones. He lay there listening to the music as he pondered on the peculiar hour of his awakening. 8:05 was too late to get up for surgery or to make rounds and too early for the lazy weekend he had planned. Coming home last night, he felt it was urgent to get in touch with Angie before she acted on her ideas. Now he couldn't remember why it was so urgent as he struggled to wake himself.

Turning over, he felt a painful tightening of a muscle on the left side of his chest. It inevitably happened after he periodically decided to do some calisthenics. He either had to do it regularly or forget the whole idea of physical fitness. Ten pushups too many. Maybe five.

He looked at the clock again: 8:37. Digital clocks were another modern marvel of precision he felt he could do without this morning. Eight more minutes to silence when the clock would turn off the radio. Once the music stopped he was afraid he'd fall asleep again and be late. Late for what? There wasn't anything Angie could do Saturday morning. There was no one else she would tell.

He sat up on the bed stretching his right arm over his head while feeling the other side of his chest. It began to feel better as he moved.

"Do it, do it, do it!" he silently encouraged his sluggish brain and body to get into the bathroom before the temptation of falling back to sleep overcame him. Suddenly the radio went dead cuttiong off a commercial for OTB in midsentence. "Get a horse . . .," then a mechanical clunk made the radio go dead. He couldn't believe he had been sitting there for eight minutes but there it was, precisely 8:45.

No room for interpretation. No big hand or little hand with which to estimate the time. Demanding and even intimidating him, the clock stared at him: 8:45. But still it didn't seem as urgent as it did last night. Maybe she had forgotten the whole thing by now. Maybe he had convinced her she couldn't be right.

He made it into the bathroom, bracing himself at the sink. There was a constricting scratching pressure in his chest which was painful when he took a deep breath. His tongue felt swollen. He coughed violently and cursed himself for smoking one cigar after another last night.

Once the spasm passed, he was able to begin his morning lavage by brushing his teeth. Quickly his body functioned more smoothly as he lathered his dark beard and scraped away the stubble. His mind was still foggy when he turned on the shower in the pink-tiled stall. The water was too icy, making his whole body shiver just from sticking his hand in to test it. He adjusted the knob and the shower stall filled with steam. The water was now too hot and he scalded his fingertips testing it. After playing with the hot and cold knobs unsatisfactorily, he just let the water run hoping some equilibrium between hot and cold would be established.

He went back into his bedroom standing naked before an empty dresser drawer wondering what had happened to all his underwear. A package of clean laundry from his valet service, neatly wrapped in brown paper, sat on the kitchen table. He carried the bundle into the bedroom and tossed it on the bed. He tore open the paper and the neatly stacked layers of jockey shorts and T-shirts crumbled into a pile.

The empty dresser drawer had produced a mild transient angst and a feeling of loneliness. He had become accustomed to a full drawer of clean white underwear first provided by his mother and later by his ex-wife. Perhaps it was fortunate he was divorced if the saddest feelings of separation were evoked by the empty drawer.

He selected his underwear from the pile provided by a surrogate laundry person and returned to the shower. Afterward, fully awake, he called Angie.

The phone rang and rang until a muffled voice answered.

"Angie? Angie's gone," Martha mumbled almost incoherently in a drowsy monotone.

"Gone! Gone where?" Peter shouted anxiously into the phone.

"Who is this?" Martha said waking up suddenly.

"It's Peter."

"Who?"

"Dr. Trenton."

"Oh, for godsakes, what are you shouting for?"

"I'm sorry, I didn't quite understand what you were saying. Where's Angie?"

"She left early this morning. What's the matter?"

"Where'd she go?"

"I don't know. Is something the matter?"

"No, er—, I just wanted to talk to her. If you—, never mind. I'm sorry if I woke you."

Martha didn't sound worried. It was perfectly natural for Angie to get out early if she wanted to. He slipped into a pair of jeans and then changed his mind. Maybe Angie went to Grand Rounds this morning. He thought she might talk to someone else, like Comerford for instance. He couldn't very well show up at the hospital in jeans so he picked out a pair of light gray slacks to go with a blue blazer.

He kicked off the jeans letting them lay crumpled on the floor as he pulled up the gray slacks. He found a shirt to go with it. As he was tying his tie, he stopped to reconsider why he was running off to the hospital. Once he went into Grand Rounds, he'd be there all morning. Angie might not even be there.

Off came the tie and the gray slacks. He had the jeans half way up when he fell back on the bed letting them dangle around his feet. He had no place to go since he planned to sleep late. He couldn't very well search for Angie in New York and expect to find her this morning. His plan to help her wasn't much better than her own. If they were found out and they were wrong, she'd be fired and his career would be down the drain. Even if she were right, it was no skin off his nose. His practice was booming and neither Elaine or Eric had ever tried to hurt him.

But Angie! Oh, Angie. He loved her and she could get hurt while meaning to do the right thing. She'd get chewed up even if she was right and much worse if she was wrong. They'd lock her up for abusing patients, for practicing without a license, for conspiracy. No, it's only a conspiracy if more than one person is involved. Maybe he shouldn't get involved. His personal feelings toward her were blunting his better judgment. Dammit, she could be right he thought as he kicked off his jeans and dressed properly for Grand Rounds. If he didn't meet her this morning, he might learn something useful there anyway.

Dr. Peter Trenton entered the darkened auditorium as slides were being projected on the large central screen. The x-ray picture showing reminded him that the main topic of the day was kidney transplants. Dr. Leslie Carelton, a Visiting Professor from the State University of New Jersey was the guest speaker. Trenton was not very interested in transplants and he had never heard of Carelton. It didn't matter as he had other things on his mind.

When the lights came back on, Peter carefully scanned the rows in front of him for Angie. He was sitting on the student side and far back so he wouldn't be noticed. Angie wasn't there.

He barely listened to the proceedings finding himself more fascinated by his candid staring at Elaine and Eric Potter sitting on the other side of the room. Eric was restless as Trenton would have been if he didn't have his present diversion. The subject was interesting but it suited neither of them.

Occasionally Eric whispered in Elaine's ear and laughed softly. More often than not she turned to rebuke him disdainfully. After awhile she merely ignored him. She listened to the speaker with interest and jotted down a few notes.

Trenton had known them both for over ten years but realized he only knew them at the Medical Center. Even here the relationship was limited to professional interchanges. They both seemed very rational. Angie's accusation seemed less tenable than ever now that he saw them sitting among all the other doctors.

Elaine hadn't changed much in the last ten years. If anything, she looked better. She didn't appear to have aged. Thin people seem to look younger anyway. She was a little more attentive to her personal appearance. She now combed her short hair more often. Maybe even had it styled regularly. If she tried harder, she could almost be attractive. Anyone could with the right style, clothes, makeup but Elaine never tried.

Eric had improved his appearance much more. He had lost a lot of weight, probably from sharing a table with Elaine. His thick curly hair was now more in vogue since men started having permanents for that Afro "natural" look. Maybe he was learning from Elaine about medicine legitimately. Trenton always thought she was smart and maybe she was passing it on to him. When they got together, Eric's practice really grew, Trenton recalled.

He dreaded to think of Comerford's reaction to Angie's cock-and-bull story. Not only Comerford but McDermott, Wright and all the rest of them sitting row behind row. He had a horrific image of Angie standing up in front of the auditorium shouting "J'accuse, J'accuse" while pointing at the Potters. Their baser instincts would have them hurling stones and rocks until she fell unconscious. Their civilized training would forbid it. Instead she'd be rushed by the crowd, pumped full of Thorazine and carried off in a straight jacket to the Psych ward.

When Grand Rounds were over, Eric Potter came up to Trenton in the hallway.

"Trenton, let's get together and write up our two cases," he said. "It's a rare enough occurrence and I think the two cases would be of some interest."

"Why?" Trenton asked, "we didn't do too well. They both died. Why bother to publicize it?"

"Nonsense, you see that all the time in case

reports. Besides, not too many read that sort of thing anyway. It'll look good in our bibliography."

"What could we say to make it interesting enough to be accepted in any journal?"

"We'll come up with something. I did make the diagnosis preoperatively. That should be of interest. How often is that done?"

"I don't know off hand. I'll have to check the literature."

"That's it. I'll do the same and we'll get together on it."

After Potter left, Trenton wondered how the diagnosis was made by Potter. It had to be a lucky guess. Trenton decided not to jump to conclusions. There was nothing illegal or unethical about lucky guesses. Everyone is entitled to make them. Even Angie.

It was twelve thirty when he called Angie again. This time she was home and she agreed to meet him right away at the coffee shop on First Avenue.

After the waitress finished pouring the coffee and left, Trenton told Angie he would help her. Angie jumped up across the table to kiss him. The table was snuggled in tightly between two upholstered benches of the booth. She violently jostled the table spilling the hot dark coffee on his lap. His light gray slacks were obscenely stained.

"Holy shit!" he said as he quickly wiped the hot liquid from his lap barely avoiding a scalding too. "I knew I should have worn my jeans."

"What? I'm sorry," Angie pleaded.

"It's okay, it's okay," he said. "Forget it."

The waitress came over to help clean up the mess and get them fresh coffee. After calm and order were restored, Angie sat back to listen to Peter while she tried to control her enthusiasm.

"What made you believe me?" she said smiling happily.

"I didn't say I believed you. As a matter of fact, I still think you're wrong both ways. The patient died of a ruptured aneurysm as proven by the autopsy and you have no business doing what you're doing."

"Don't start, Peter!" she said glaring at him. "Don't start telling me what to do for my own good. You'll drive me to do something desperate."

"I don't want to see you stoned by an angry mob."

"What?" she asked dumbfounded.

"What, what? Why are you always saying 'what?' "

"You're not making any sense, that's what!"

"Your way of marking the uterus is dangerous," he said taking a deep breath. "It can start bleeding, it can migrate up and get lost, it can cause infection. There are too many potential problems and too many risks for the patient. And it could even be missed in the Pathology lab because of its small size."

"Go on," she encouraged him, "I'm listening."

"All you have to do is to inject the uterine cervix with methylene blue," he said calmly holding up his hands in revelation. "It's a safe dye and won't cause any problems. You can inject it right into the cervix when you examine the patient through the vaginal speculum. She won't feel it because the cervix is not sensitive to sharp pain. With a very small needle the patient won't feel a thing. She won't even know what you are doing."

"Peter, I'm surprised at you for suggesting anything like that," Angie said disapprovingly.

"What the hell are you talking about?" he shot back at her. "This was all your idea in the first place. I'm just trying to stop you from committing mayhem."

"No, no," she said shaking her head, "you don't understand! I would never do anything like that without the patient's consent. We'll have to tell her just the way you explained it to me. We'll even have her sign a consent form."

"Okay," he threw up his hands in submission, "we'll also tell Potter. We might as well since his patient will tell him."

"Your idea is much better than mine but the patient can be informed without Potter finding out. We tell her this is a double-blind study. That Potter isn't supposed to know which patients are getting the dye. And you'll explain how safe it is."

"How did I get into seeing Potter's patients?" He looked worried about his own safety.

"I'll tell her you're a medical student. You can put on one of those short white coats and mess up your hair. When your cowlick stands up you look like a little kid anyway."

"I'm not getting personally involved in this," he said smoothing down the back of his hair. "I gave you this alternative so you wouldn't get arrested if something went wrong with your old plan. And it won't prove a thing anyway."

"You don't think it's possible?" she asked in a soft skeptical tone.

"Anything is possible," he said, "but—"

"I need someone there as a witness," Angie said. "When Elaine shows the specimen without the stain, I need someone to back me up or else it will be my word against hers. By the way, won't Eric see the stain when he removes the specimen?"

"No. It'll be blood-stained. He won't see the blue. The blood on the surface can be washed off, the blue will hold fast."

"Oh, Peter, you are so smart," she gushed happily.

"If I'm so smart, why am I still here with you?" he said glumly. "Who's the patient for this experiment?"

"I don't know yet. Not all of his cases are normal. He does take out some bad organs. There'll be one soon enough. I'll let you know as soon as I find one that's just right. I think we can only hope for one shot at this and it has to be perfect."

"Thank God for small favors. Maybe I'll get lucky and have smallpox when you call."

Sixteen

Two and a half weeks went by before Angie found a patient who was ideally suited for her test. There were one or two other candidates but Angie wanted to be absolutely sure Potter was depending on a switch.

"Peter," Angie said calling from a pay phone in the hospital lobby, "I found her!"

"Found who? What are you talking about?" Peter asked.

"The patient for the methylene blue test. Remember? Potter's patient? I found one he's trying to pawn off as cancer of the cervix."

There was dead silence on the phone. Peter Trenton couldn't speak because he felt a strangling kind of nausea in his throat. Angie waited silently for his response.

"I—, I can't make it. My office is full of patients. Are you sure?"

"Peter, I've already spoken to the patient about it," Angie said. She felt the evident resistance and the weakness of his excuses. Her tone of voice made it equally evident that she wouldn't accept any excuses and she would do it herself if she had to.

"But are you sure? How the hell can you be sure?" he said sounding very annoyed. "How did Potter make the diagnosis? Wasn't there a Pap smear?"

"Of course there's a Pap smear on record," she said. "I don't know how he does all this exactly but— are you or are you not going to be there when I inject methylene blue?" she asked leaving no doubt she would proceed on her own.

"I'll be there! But tell me first why you picked this patient?" he asked calmly trying to stall and hoping to find a reason not to do anything to this patient.

"She's only thirty years old and doesn't fit the pattern for having cancer of the cervix at such a young age," Angie explained patiently. "She was a virgin until she was twenty-two, when she got married. She has only one child and she uses a diaphragm. She's never had sex with anyone except her husband, who is circumcised. Did Potter's statistics include an analysis of the usual epidemiological variable like frequency and onset of sexual intercourse, partners—you know what I'm talking about."

"I don't know about Potter," Peter answered, "but it's an interesting point. What else?"

"The best part is this gal's got a Master's Degree in computer science and knows all about double-blind studies and statistics. She wanted to know why the study was being done but accepted that it was part of the protocol that neither the patient or her doctor know why. And she agreed not to tell Potter."

"What happened to all your honesty? You said you would never lie to a patient."

"I didn't lie!" she said indignantly. "I told her the scientific truth. The experiment would be useless if Potter knew the specimen was labeled."

"But what about the patient? Shouldn't you tell her why and what you think?"

"I can't do that! It would ruin everything. I can't tell her that her doctor is a phony, that she doesn't really need the operation. She'd be screaming her head off to see Potter in a second if I told her that."

"Angie, please understand me," he said slowly and forcefully. "If you're really sincere and I know you are, think about it without giving me ultimatums. If you think this patient shouldn't be operated on then tell her so and let the operation be postponed. There'll be a lot of flack but we'll get someone else to examine her and repeat the Pap smear."

"I thought about that but what would it accomplish? It would only prove that he made one mistake and he would go right on practicing. Even if he and Elaine stopped their little game, what about all those women he operated on in the last ten years?"

"Angie—" he hesitated unable to argue any further against her reasoned analysis. He felt a penetrating sense of guilt when she emphasized the ten years in which this may have been going on. It was staggering to him if it were possible. There were the earlier suspicions of Potter's sudden rise and success. Yet if they were caught tampering with Potter's patient. . . "Angie, what else have you figured on?" he asked in capitulation.

"Come up to the examining room on the seventh floor about nine-thirty. Make it nine-thirty sharp! All the visitors will be gone and the nurses will be taking a coffee break. I'll have the examining room all set up. I told the patient you would be there."

"You gave her my name?" he asked worriedly.

"I couldn't lie about that, Peter. She's a very smart girl and knows a lot about scientific studies. She wanted to know who the principal investigator on the project was. She would never accept a medical student so that disguise won't work. Don't worry! She won't say anything to ruin a double-blind study."

"Angie—" he stopped, not knowing how to protest.

"I'll see you at nine-thirty sharp," Angie said. Gotta go! Peter, I love you."

Peter Trenton accepted this assignment with complete calm but still he arrived at the hospital a little after nine. Angie said nine-thirty sharp and he didn't want to be early or late. He planned to make postoperative rounds to pass the time until nine-thirty. Unfortunately, he had done only one operation that day and had already seen the patient at five-thirty.

Visitors were just leaving the rooms and hall traffic was congested. He went to the surgeons' locker room to put on a long white coat he had hanging in his locker. He hoped Potter's patient would be less likely to remember him in the common white uniform. He took his I.D. card with his name and photo off the lapel and stuck it in the pocket.

He walked pass the nurses' station on the eighth floor on the way to see his patient. He thought he was unseen until his name was called behind him.

"Dr. Trenton," a remarkably overweight nurse with a rough, ruddy complexion called after him. She seemed to be bursting through her white uniform as she hurried after him. Her enormous arms swung widely from side to side as she barreled down the corridor to catch up with him. He stopped so she wouldn't think he was trying to escape her.

"Can I help you, Dr. Trenton?" she asked without seeming out of breath. Trenton could barely detect any breathing at all beneath her huge breasts.

"No, I was just checking on Mrs. Browder."

"She's doing fine. We just medicated her and she's asleep. Did you forget something? Weren't you here about six?'

Her question jostled his confidence. She would expose his clandestine rendezvous with Angie. Ridiculous! Keep cool he thought.

"Just thought I'd check again," he said smiling. "I was called in to see another patient," he added as he went into Mrs. Browder's room.

She followed after him. The patient was in a drugged sleep, very comfortable and relieved of all postoperative pain. The light above her bed did not disturb her nor did the television that was being watched by the patient in the bed next to her. The soft regular breathing and the remarkably good color in her cheeks made it evident she was doing well. There was nothing for him to do, nothing he wanted to do to disturb her rest or awaken her to pain. It was also evident that the "big white momma" who followed him into the room felt the same way as she hovered beside him.

"How are the vital signs?" he asked a sure fire pertinent question. He would be greatly surprised if they were anything but normal in this peacefully reposing healthy patient.

"They're fine. We just took them. B.P. 120 over 70, pulse 72, temperature 98.6, respirations 14."

"Thank you," he said and walked out of the room much to the nurse's relief. Assured of her charge's uncompromised composure, she left Trenton to himself. It was only 9:20.

The seventh floor examing room was right next to the stairwell, which is why he came to the eight floor. He planned to get there without passing the seventh floor nurses' station but it was still too early. Mr. Cohen was in the room next to Mrs.

Browder. He was a seventy-five year-old-retired furrier. Trenton had repaired his hernia the day before. He decided to pass the time with Mr. Cohen, if only to get out of "big white momma's" line of sight.

"Who's der?" Mr. Cohen asked suddenly recovering from dozing off in the dimly lighted room. He was a cherubic little man with sparse white hair at his temples giving the impression of a cue ball.

"It's Dr. Trenton," he assured the mildly startled little man.

"Oh, Dr. Trenton, come in, come in. What are you doing here so late? Always working. What a job!"

"How are you doing?" Trenton asked.

"Terrific! You did a wonderful job. But I didn't take any of that Demerol you ordered. Come here," he said in a secretive whisper, "I want to show you something."

Trenton approached the bed as Cohen reached into his pajama breast pocket. He pulled out a small bottle containing a brown-colored fluid. He held it partially hidden by his bathrobe.

"It's brandy," he whispered putting his finger over his lips enlisting Trenton in the conspiracy. "I didn't use much, maybe a half ounce every four or five hours. But I wouldn't mix it with the Demerol. Is it okay?"

"If that's all you need, sure it is. I'll order some for you and cancel the Demerol."

"Really? You mean it." Terrific! The last time when you fixed the other side, the Demerol made my head swim and without it, it burns in the cut.

That's terrific."

It was 9:29 and Trenton was ready to move downstairs to see his last patient waiting for him with Angie.

"One more thing, Doctor," Mr. Cohen held him at bay with urgency in his eyes. "I haven't had a bowel movement since I came to the hospital."

"You only came here two days ago. You had an enema and then nothing to eat yesterday. Give it some time."

"If I don't have a bowel movement every day I worry. I feel terrible."

"Don't worry. I'll give you something for it tomorrow."

As he hurried out of the room he could here Mr. Cohen say "terrific!"

Trenton arrived at the seventh floor examining room at 9:31. Angie and Potter's patient were talking quietly when he walked in. The room was brightly lighted by overhead recessed fluorescent lighting filling most of the ceiling space. The white walls and white furniture gave a sensation akin to snowblindness after he descended through the dimly lighted stairwell.

"Margaret Kelly, this is Dr. Peter Trenton," Angie said making formal introductions.

Peter blushed feeling his ears burning intensely. He stood there with his hands in his coat pocket squeezing his plastic I.D. card. Angie told him on the phone she had used his name but he still hid his picture and name in his pocket. The only thing worse he could imagine was for Potter to stumble in and catch him red-handed.

251

"Er, did Miss Palmeri explain the procedure to you?" Peter asked regaining his composure and his clinical confidence.

Margaret Kelly was a pleasant-looking woman, smiling expectantly from the moment Peter walked in. She wore a long robe over her nightgown. Her face tended to be somewhat round with little angulation except for a cleft chin. She wore no makeup and in the bright white light she appeared slightly pale.

"Yes, I understand what you're going to do. She even injected some of the dye into the back of her hand to show how safe it was. But she didn't say why."

"Why? Er—" he cleared his throat nervously, "why are we doing this?"

"I understand perfectly why you can't tell me," Margaret said smiling and relieving Peter. "If it ever gets published, please let me know. Should I get up on the table?"

"Put on one of these hospital johnnies," Angie said offering her a short cotton gown that tied in the back. "It would be a shame to stain this beautiful pink nightgown you're wearing."

Margaret took the johnnie and changed behind a screen in the room. It was one of the anachronisms of civilized behavior for the patient to undress behind a screen away from the eyes of the physician who was about to probe her clinically. It was as much a benefit for Trenton as it was for the patient. With his back turned to the screen, he busied himself with the instruments Angie had prepared. There wasn't much: a speculum, gloves, lubricating jelly, a syringe filled with blue dye and a long fine needle. When he turned around, the patient was lying on the table, her feet in the stirrups and her body covered with a sheet.

Trenton placed the speculum in the vagina and gently opened the speculum blades to expose the cervix. Angie's description was accurate. There were no erosions and the opening to the uterus was consistant with only one pregnancy. It was a dark pink, very healthy-looking cervix tinged with blue from blood in the veins. It certainly wasn't suspicious for a malignancy judging from the physical appearance, but it didn't matter if the Pap smear were accurate.

He picked up the blue-filled syringe and needle. Through the opening maintained by the speculum, he passed the needle through the cervix. It painlessly penetrated the lining. He injected the blue dye slowly watching it spread through the cellular interstices. He moved the needle to distribute the dye more evenly. The cervix and part of the vaginal vault was a deep blue-violet hue when he was done.

"How do you feel?" he asked to reassure the patient as well as himself.

"Fine, I hardly felt it," Margaret smiled.

With nothing else said, not even a word to Angie, he walked out of the room and down the stairs to the lobby and then up the elevator. By this circuitous route he made his way back to the surgeons' locker room to change his coat. Somehow, despite the gloves, one finger was stained with blue dye. He stared at it thinking of

Lady Macbeth and wondered if he had committed a sin.

The act itself was harmless. If it turned out that Angie was completely wrong, it might be construed as a practical joke done in very poor taste. If she were right, his dilemma was worse. If she were right, then he was allowing Margaret Kelly to be subjected to unnecessary surgery but for a greater good from which she could not benefit directly. He had to console himslf with the belief that she was the type of person who would have agreed to do so if she knew. But she never volunteered for the duty.

The next morning, Trenton carefully avoided Potter. They were both in the surgeons' locker room. When Trenton heard him talking in an adjacent row, he stuck his head in his own locker pretending to search for some missing item. He waited until Potter had gone into the surgical suite before he finished dressing. It made him late for the start of his own case but he couldn't risk speaking to Potter. He pictured their encounter with a mixture of guilt and hate. He wanted to confess his machinations while throttling Potter by the throat for this arrogant misuse of the skill he had acquired.

Angie scrubbed with Potter. She watched Potter remove the stained uterus without a hint that she had any special interest in this case. Potter handed off the specimen when he finished removing it from its attachments in the pelvis without examining the specimen. It wasn't as blood-stained as

Trenton had suggested. The cervix was a blue proboscis extending from the body of the uterus.

Angie watched as Potter, with Gordon assisting, wiped and suctioned away a small amount of blood from the area of the vaginal cuff. This was the vagina from the inside with a hole in its wall where the cervix normally passed through. The edge of the vaginal cuff was clearly stained blue but neither surgeon mentioned it as Potter sewed the defect with a running stitch.

Leaving Angie and Gordon to close the wound, Potter stepped out of the operating room just as Trenton was leaving his. Trenton made a quick retreat back into his room to avoid Potter. About fifteen minutes later, he stepped out again face to face with Angie this time.

"You were wonderful last night," she said whispering and snuggling as she took his arm in hers. One of the porters who cleaned the rooms was standing nearby and heard it all. He smiled broadly imagining an evening of sensual delight.

Trenton unhooked his arm from her as they walked slowly down the central corridor of the O.R. suite.

"Don't even talk about it," he warned severely. "Don't say a word! Even if it turns out you're right, don't say anything. Let me handle it. And if you're wrong—" he hesitated with a sour expression causing him to squint painfully," just don't say anything to anybody."

Angie didn't argue and didn't pursue him down the hallway since it was obvious that he wanted to get away from her.

Martha came up behind her. She had witnessed Trenton's departure as Angie held back in the hallway letting him go.

"You and Peter at it again?" she said wondering if they had another public exhibition.

"No, nothing serious," Angie said glumly. She wanted very much to confide in Martha but she hadn't been able to reveal her suspicions. She wasn't sure how Martha would react and wasn't sure she could trust her. Martha was her friend but also her direct supervisor, who couldn't very well approve of her special activity.

"We'll talk about it tonight if you like," Martha said then left Angie standing alone.

For the first time Angie felt guilty. She consoled herself as she saw Margaret Kelly being wheeled into the recovery room. She would be fine but there was nothing Angie could do for her. It seemed like the right thing to do last night but Angie wouldn't know until tomorrow afternoon when the specimen was presented at the Pathology conference.

Later that afternoon, Angie went to see her. Margaret was awake with some pain but was glad to see Angie.

"How did it go?" she asked in a hoarse voice irritated by the anesthesia. She tried to turn over on her side but was restrained by a tight muscle spasm around the wound which made her grimace.

"Excellent," Angie assured her. "Everything went just fine. No problems at all."

"How about the experiment? Don't forget you promised me a reprint of the paper."

"I won't," Angie sighed.

"You look awfully tired," Margaret said sleepy herself. "Did you have a rough day?"

Angie straightened her shoulders trying to perk herself up. It was an ordinary day, perhaps slower than usual but she felt she had carried more than ordinary weight today.

"Just the usual. Get some sleep youself. I'll see you tomorrow."

Martha was preparing dinner for them both when Angie got home. She offered to help but Martha had everything almost ready, so Angie slipped into the shower and avoided Martha until she was called to eat.

Angie came to the table wearing a white terry-cloth robe and a blue towel covering her dripping hair. A large plate of spaghetti covered with red sauce steamed in the middle of the neatly set kitchen table.

"I'll just get the garlic bread out of the oven," Martha said. "Go on and start."

Angie absentmindedly shoved her plate under the serving plate. She took a heaping portion of spaghetti leaving about a fourth of it for Martha. She played with the food spiraling the strands on her fork and then letting them slide back into the plate.

Martha thumped the plate of garlic bread on the table and quickly pulled Angie's plate away from her. She placed it beside the serving plate. The suddeness of her action startled Angie who stared at the two portions.

"What am I doing?" she said surprised at the inequity. "I didn't mean to make a pig of myself."

"You can have all the spaghetti you want," Martha said waving a serving spoon at her, "but first tell me why Peter Trenton did a frontal lobotomy on you."

"Sit down and take some spaghetti off my plate," Angie said forcing a smile. She reached for the plate but Martha pulled it away.

"Come on, Martha! There's nothing to talk about. Everything's just fine."

"It's not fine or you wouldn't let me cook the Ragu sauce without sticking your fingers into it. Now you come on and tell me what's making you walk around like a zombie. No man's worth all the grief that's showing on your face."

"It's nothing like that, Martha," Angie said trying to sound lighthearted about it but only making it more obvious. "Honest," her voice cracked, "Peter and I didn't have an argument today."

"What about yesterday? How come you went out in your white coat last night? You weren't on call."

"I haven't had a chance to have all my clothes sent down here. The white coat is handy. Why the third degree?"

"It's up to you," Martha said sitting down and letting go of the spaghetti plate. "I thought it would help if you talked about it. Just tell me one thing. Did you see Peter last night?"

"It has nothing to do with Peter. Really! Not the way you think it does."

Martha scooped her share of the food onto her plate. They both sat silently playing with the spaghetti more than eating it. It rolled around the fork and slipped back. Neither had the necessary gusto needed to attack the spaghetti properly.

"Martha, if you weren't a supervisor I'd tell you," Angie said as she dropped her fork and folded her arms across her chest.

"What! What the hell are you talking about? I'm the supervisor of nothing!" Martha said pleading for Angie's confidence. "That's just a title. They got supervisors for everything or else they think it can't work. I only work there like you do. If you're in some kind of trouble let me help."

"I'm so glad you said that, Martha," Angie said with great relief. "I was just dying to tell you. You've scrubbed with Eric Potter a lot in the past six or seven years."

"Sure I have. He's so damned busy all the time. So what?"

"Have you ever looked carefully at his specimens? Or compared them with your physical findings?"

"I never examined his patients. He didn't want them to be examined by the staff and I don't go where I'm not wanted."

"Did you ever see him examine a specimen in the O.R. before he sent it down?"

"How should I know something like that? Never even thought about it except Dr. Johnstone once asked me—" Martha started to laugh as she recalled the incident. "He really got me on this. I had just started working and he asked me if I knew why it was so important to open the uterus before it was sent to the lab. I didn't know. He said there might be a mouse inside. I just nodded like a dummy thinking he was serious but I didn't know what he what talking about. Do you know what it means if they find a mouse inside the uterus?"

"A mouse? You mean one of those tiny little furry things with a long tail?" Angie asked unbelievingly. "I haven't the faintest idea."

"It means," Martha said starting to laugh again, "it means the pussy's asleep."

Angie's mood was far too serious and troubled to even concede an understanding smile. Martha stopped laughing seeing that Angie didn't appreciate the story.

"It was funny at the time," Martha said.

"It's funny but this is serious," Angie said. "Were you here when Potter was investigated for too much surgery."

"He was?" Martha's eyes shot up in great surprise. "When did they do that?"

"You never heard about it?" Angie matched her surprise.

"No way," Martha waved her hand. "That kind of thing wouldn't be announced. Even if something were wrong you wouldn't hear about it. If it were really bad, Potter would just fade away from the Medical Center without a fuss. They'd just let him resign and no one would know why."

"They didn't find anything wrong with his work. All the hysterectomies were justified by the pathology at least."

"What is bugging you about Potter?" Martha asked, looking at Angie with a sideways glance.

"The first day I worked here, remember we talked about it. There was something peculiar about Elaine Potter, the way she reacted when I was looking at Helen McCrae's specimen. After that I noticed a lot of discrepancies in Potter's cases. Everybody said I didn't know what I was talking about."

"Who's everybody besides me?"

"Peter mostly, well, Peter only," she conceded. "It wasn't until a couple of weeks ago when that woman came in with the ruptured ectopic pregnancy and died—"

"When did that happen? I didn't hear about it?"

"When I was on call a few weeks ago. They called it a dissecting aneurysm."

"Hold on a minute!" You're not talking about Potter's case?" Martha asked doubting Angie's accuracy.

"That's the one. I didn't tell you about it because Peter gave me such a hard time," she said sounding distressed while trying to apologize to Martha.

"Angie, don't mix your love life with your work. What I mean is—" Martha hesitated to catch Angie's full attention, "don't try to outsmart the man you love because if you win, you lose."

"If you were in my shoes, you would have done the same thing!" Angie said angrily. "You wouldn't stand by and let some—whatever, you wouldn't turn your back on negligence."

"So you think Potter was negligent for not coming in that night," Martha said indignantly. "Well, if he was, no one else thought so. Don't get worked up about things you can't change."

"It's more than that! I saw that woman in the

clinic the same afternoon and made a diagnosis of an ectopic pregnancy, unruptured. Gordon missed it and wouldn't admit her. She came back the same night in shock. Reese saw her and made the correct diagnosis. Potter wouldn't come in and she died. Suddenly I'm wrong and the woman has a virtually untreatable disease."

Martha let her carry on her angry diatribe while she waited for a good place to interrupt her. Angie sounded so angry that it seemed unreasonable to Martha. It sounded like nothing more than a difference of opinion in which the more experienced Potter turned out to be right. Martha needed something more objective to be convinced Angie was right.

"Don't look so dumbfounded," Angie said more calmly. "That's not the whole story. This woman turns out to have the exact same disease and the identical specimen as Peter Trenton's patient had a month ago."

"A coincidence! Just a coincidence."

"Maybe but Peter wasn't as sure as you are."

This bit of information changed Martha's expression dramatically. She had been sitting back almost mockingly and daring Angie to prove herself. She was almost ready to insist that Angie drop the whole subject, but now was more interested. Angie continued.

"Remember, put this case in perspective. You said you weren't aware of anything strange about the way Potter operated. But if he's so successful—if he had some help all these years from Elaine—" Angie drew in a deep breath and exhaled slowly. "I think Elaine has been substituting specimens for Eric Potter all along and tomorrow I'll prove it. Last night—Martha, swear you won't say a word."

"I swear," Martha said excitedly. "I told you I just work here and unless you killed someone—go on," she was fascinated by Angie's tale.

"This patient Potter operated on today just doesn't figure to have cancer. I know anything is possible but not in this case. Last night Peter injected methylene blue into the cervix. Tomorrow afternoon the specimen will be presented at the daily Path conference. If it's not blue then it proves my case."

Ho-ly shit!" Martha said slowly, looking stunned from the enormity of Angie's enterprise. "You—I wouldn't want to be in your shoes for anything!" She shook her head from side to side as she thought about the possibilities. "No, no, no! Don't tell me any more."

"Martha," Angie pleaded.

"Don't 'Martha' me! I can't help you."

"I don't need any help. It's all done."

"That's just the start. If you're right, you'll be up to your ass in litigation. You and Peter! Poor Peter. How could you do this to him? And if you're wrong, he's never going to forgive you."

"Why?" Angie pleaded. "Never mind why. You're right about Peter. I know from the way he looked at me today. It's all over if I'm wrong. But I had to do it. Somebody had to stop him. And Elaine! I don't want to lose Peter."

"You're crazy," Martha said consoling Angie,

"and maybe there's something that protects crazy people. If he cares about you he'll get over being mad at you so long as nobody gets hurt."

"I could be right you know."

"I certainly hope not," Martha said with her hands clasped in prayer.

The daily Pathology conference was primarily attended by members of the Pathology department and second year medical students who were taking the required course. It was commonly referred to as the daily "organ recital" because the bulk of the conference was devoted to describing the organs removed the day before.

Everyone was welcome but only those who were required to came. The conference room in the Pathology department was a smaller replica of the great hall used for Grand Rounds. There were about forty seats arranged in tiers, a semicircular pattern of seats fanning out from a shallow well where the specimens were arranged on a high table. The only entrance was past this stage. When Dr. Peter Trenton walked in, Elaine Potter stopped her presentation to give him a special welcome.

"What have we here? A new student in Pathology?" she said watching him walk up the aisle to an empty seat in the third row. Peter spied Angie on the other side of the room but did not look long in her direction.

"We're all students," Peter said gracefully as he took his seat.

"True, very true, Dr. Trenton," Elaine said, "but we don't often have the privilege of educating a surgeon of your experience. Is there something special you came to see?"

"There is but don't interrupt your agenda. I came to hear about the colon I removed yesterday. Dr. Ito couldn't tell if the lymph nodes were involved. I wanted to take a look at it myself."

"Very commendable," she said, "But you're just a bit too late. Dr. Ito just finished his presentation. There were no positive nodes and the cancer did not invade the deep muscle of the colon."

Peter made no comment and Elaine continued where she had stopped when he walked in.

"This is a very interesting specimen taken from a thirty-year-old woman. A routine Pap smear showed class five cells. That is usually quite definitely cancer but a few cells cannot tell how deep and extensive a tumor is. It may also be quite superficial and the Pap smear could still be class five.

"The next step is a cone biopsy of the cervix and a D and C. This gives a better idea of the extent of the tumor. A cone biopsy is a wedge of tissue from the cervix. This was done about a month ago and it was positive for cancer. The unusual thing about this case is the final specimen."

Elaine reached into the bucket and pulled out a uterus dripping with formaldehyde. She washed off the excess fluid in the sink and then passed it around on a wooden board for the students to examine it closely. It was sliced through and through several times like a melon. The fringes that were left of the cervix were definitely blue.

"As it turned out," Elaine continued, "we were not able to find any evidence of malignancy in that specimen grossly. We may find some cancer microscopically," Elaine stopped talking while the specimen was being passed around, "but suppose we don't?" she continued. "Would anyone care to comment?"

None of the medical students volunteered, afraid of some trap laid by the instructor. Angie's heart pounded with excitement. She bit her lip to restrain her impulse to get up and tell what she thought of it. She looked to Peter who was listening to Elaine without any visible reaction.

"Could she have been cured by the cone biopsy without any further surgery?" a young man in the front row asked.

"What do you think, Dr. Trenton?" Elaine called on him.

"It's certainly possible," Trenton answered without hesitation, "but it would require at least one or two more cone biopsies to be sure. Even that wouldn't make it absolutely safe. What did the margins of the biopsy show? Was the tumor cut across in the biopsy?"

For the first time, Elaine lost her poise. She looked startled by the question and was unable to answer right away. With her head bent, she nervously pushed her hair back along the side of her head. Dr. Ito, a short man with closely cropped salt-and-pepper hair stood up with the patient's record in his hands.

"It was not a free margin," he said reading from the chart. "The tumor was cut across very extensively on the original slides. It is very strange," he said smiling at the unexplainable inconsistency, "that it has been so difficult to find the remaining tumor."

Angie was very alert to the discussion. For once, someone else, someone she had no contact with was questioning as she had. It was an avenue she never would have thought possible. If only Peter would follow through.

"Not so strange, Dr. Ito," Peter said from his seat. All the students turned toward him as he explained, "It was cut right on the margin of the tumor which means the remaining border was either sutured or cauterized. Either way the effect would be to destroy the cancer."

Angie couldn't believe her ears. It was Dr. Peter Trenton explaining away Potter's discrepancy. He completely ignored the side of the room where Angie was sitting. To the rest of the audience, his tightly clenched jaw and knitted brows were signs of thoughtful pondering. To Angie he was cold, distant and full of anger. She wanted to run out but it would require her to pass before the whole group.

"What about the blueness of the cervix?" another student asked as the specimen was passed to him.

Angie felt a quivering in her stomach. This was it, she thought. Trenton would get up and confess the whole thing while denouncing her for her meddling interference. He had already gone over to the Potter's side with his explanation of Ito's objections. Ironically it seemed, Elaine had a ready explanation also.

"That is a vital dye," she said. "There are several

types and some are used in douches. We'd have to check back with the patient to find out which one she used. Actually, it is little more than a curiosity."

The conference continued but mercifully for Angie, it ended fifteen minutes earlier than usual. Peter was the first one out the door giving Angie no chance to catch up with him. It was over between them.

Unhappy, alone in the corridor rapidly deserted by the medical students, she kicked the base of the walls with the sole of her shoe. Slowly, with no desire to be any place, she walked toward the main corridors of the hospital. The traffic around her picked up. White coats flashed by her, visitors coming and going, no one having the slightest interest in her.

She looked up at the two-story ceiling near the main entrance. It was more enormous and distant than it ever seemed before. There was no one to talk to. In the short time she had been there only two people had come to mean anything to her and she didn't feel like talking to either Peter or Martha. They had forewarned her.

It was because no one seemed to give a damn that she felt so empty. Peter had tried for awhile but skipped out at the first chance to redeem his faith in his colleague. Martha never wanted to get involved in the first place. Angie could go back to her by merely suffering a few "I told you so's."

Peter was lost to her. It just didn't seem fair to her when she still believed so strongly she was right.

Seventeen

Angie's desperate calmness was matched by an equal but opposite rage by Elaine toward Eric Potter. It had more time to simmer and was finally put under pressure by the application of blue dye so it was ready to explode. While Angie felt constrained by rejection and self-doubt, Elaine was sure someone was on to her.

"I know it has to be that blue-eyed bitch," Elaine gritted her teeth so her pale skin turned red while leaving a white halo around her lips.

Eric sat motionless in a chair beside her desk. His shoulders were tightly rounded as he listened to

Elaine's angry analysis.

"I saw her jump when I took that specimen out," Elaine went on in better control of her anger. She spoke almost softly and then swallowed hard with a sucking sound because there was too much spit in her mouth. "It was more like a twitch or a shudder. I saw it out of the corner of my eye."

"Then Trenton must know," Eric said worriedly. "He has to. She probably told him."

"She told him! That's why he was there," Elaine said with a thin smile. "I was going to bluff him. He's not that smart but it wasn't necessary. As a matter of fact, he defended you vigorously."

"Trenton?" Eric looked quite surprised. "He was very cold toward me all week. Not that we're so close but he seemed to be avoiding me."

Eric relaxed a bit. He unfolded his hands and let his shoulders sag. Elaine was letting her angry intensity diffuse after it had boiled so vehemently. Less than a half hour earlier, she had been tensely wound up with anxiety as she presented the case of the blue-stained cervix. She was so well prepared, so ready to blunt any challenges that she didn't realize how close she came to exploding until now.

She had the scene well rehearsed in her mind if it came to the point where Trenton actually accused her. She was ready to shred the heavens with indignation if necessary. But Peter made it so easy for her that when she returned to her office she let it all out in front of Eric.

It wasn't what she had in mind for Eric but the unexpected good fortune by which Trenton explained the whole case for her left her a trifle confused. She felt elated and yet the anger lingered. She had planned to rage against Eric but Trenton blunted that too because Eric's mistake was minimized. That left only Angie to diffuse her pent-up passion.

There was no point in continuing her denunciation of Angie to Eric who looked more frightened than bored with her anger this time. Her diatribes in the past had usually driven him into a shell. He was more receptive to a conversational tone.

"How's your operating schedule?" she asked walking around the desk and then over to the sink where she leaned backward.

"It's full for the next two weeks and then it slows up as usual before Thanksgiving. If you think I should, there are some I could cancel. Maybe I should? Let's wait and see how this blows over. We can take it easy for six months until the whole thing is forgotten."

"That would be bad, very bad," Elaine frowned thoughtfully. "We've got to keep up the volume. The demand for surgery has to keep pace or else the urgency of the Institute will fade. The next twelve months could be critical when the Certificate of Need is evaluated. If the trend is downhill, the state agency will wait and see if it continues. They won't approve anything if it looks like a down trend."

"I understand that," Eric said, "but I don't think Palmeri is giving up so easily. That's quite a stunt she pulled. I think she'll try something again."

"So do I. That's why we have to get rid of her!" Elaine said, letting a little venom seep through.

"Comerford will never fire her," Eric said as he rotated his chair to follow Elaine who walked to the other side of the laboratory office. "If I make up a complaint about her, he'll investigate it. I can't put enough pressure on her to make her quit."

"There is another way," Elaine said looking straight at Eric. "Just sit there a minute. I'll be right back."

Elaine left the room almost at a gallop. Five minutes later she walked back in slowly carrying two glass slides. She held them up to the light in front of Eric.

"This is a Pap smear taken from Miss Angelica Palmeri," Elaine said with a victorious smile as she handed them to Eric.

Eric's eyes widened in dismay and he squirmed in his chair.

"They haven't been read yet," Elaine said taking out an uncompleted lab slip that went with the specimen.

"How did you know about this?" Eric asked. He held up the transparent glass rectangles streaked with dry mucus.

"There's a whole stack of employee Pap smears waiting to be read. They're backed up in the cytology lab. I got a complaint from the Employee Health Clinic last week."

"What's the point?" Eric said disturbed by the idea percolating between them. "She won't fall for this. She won't buy it and even if she did, so what? She certainly won't come to me."

Elaine's head snapped back and then she leaned forward toward him.

"Forget it, Elaine!" Eric said angrily. "I could never do anything like that. Never! If I ever had to do a hysterectomy on that girl, I'd be sure it was the best I could do. I would never deliberately hurt her. Your idea stinks! I know you could keep substituting her biopsies until someone else has to operate but a young healthy girl like that would be back to work in six weeks. Nothing would be accomplished."

"She wouldn't be back so soon if she had a melanoma of the uterus," Elaine said casually as she walked over to a stool. She sat down and waited for Eric's reaction.

"A melanoma? Of the uterus?" Eric's voice was deep but full of disbelief. "Where'd you get that from?"

"It's in the Pathological Museum."

"A primary melanoma of the uterus?" Eric said doubtfully.

"A very rare specimen I grant you," Elaine said getting up to pace the floor, "but no one will miss it. It's been there forever gathering dust on the back shelves. It wasn't even catologued until last year when I cleaned up the shelves."

"Very interesting. What happened to the patient?"

"I don't know. The specimen wasn't even labeled. I took it out of the jar and recut it because it looked so peculiar. But that's what it is. I could scrape it to get cells for a Pap smear," Elaine said expectantly.

Eric thought about it. He rested his elbows on the desk and then turned to Elaine.

"It would certainly put a lot of pressure on her to have the surgery," he said thoughtfully, "but how much longer would it keep her out of our hair?"

"At least two years!" Elaine said enthusiastically. "By then we'll be the Directors of the Institute."

"Two years?"

"The specimen has positive lymph nodes," Elaine said quickening with excitement. "She'll have to have a radical operation. With the positive nodes, they'll give her chemotherapy. She won't be able to work and she'll probably go back home to—wherever she came from."

"What if she dies from the chemotherapy? It's too risky. I don't want to be responsible for that," he said shaking his head.

"It's not your responsibility. Anyway, she won't die. They'll monitor her carefully. She'll be sick but she won't die!"

It didn't take Eric long to make up his mind. He played with his eyebrows a bit and pulled his lip but finally said:

"Okay. What do you want me to do?"

"Pick up your schedule for November and December. There has to be a pressing need for the Institute and Comerford has to recognize your contributions to that need."

Eighteen

Martha could tell the Pathology conference was a disappointment by the way Angie slouched through the door. Angie shuffled through to the living room where she threw herself down on the couch with her head on the armrest and her legs hanging off to the side. It was almost comical the way she let her handbag drag along the floor and Martha had a tough time not to laugh.

But Angie's immobile figure with her forearm slumped over her eyes touched a sympathetic nerve in Martha who resolved not to be sarcastic. Anyway she tried. She sat down in the armchair placing her just to the side and behind Angie. After a few minutes of silence, Martha could no longer control herself.

"I told you so!" Martha said slapping her thigh through the white linen pants that were part of her uniform. "I didn't want to say it but I told you it wouldn't work."

Martha was happy and energetic without sounding spiteful. It had a ring of friendship so clearly modifying the words that Angie had to move her arm from her eyes to check Martha's expression. It wasn't angry, sour or grinning with spite. It was wide-eyed, knowing and sympathetic. It made Angie more comfortable with her failure by offering acceptance.

"You're such a smart-ass," Angie said sitting up prepared to accept Martha's friendly criticism. "You were hedging before it all came out so you told me nothing."

"I told you it would work out badly for you. I didn't hedge on that," Martha said with a soft touch of sorrow.

"Well, nobody got hurt," Angie said weakly as she puffed up one of the throw pillows.

"Nobody but you! You look like you hemorrhaged," Martha said.

"It's nothing a tourniquet around the neck won't cure. I'm just kidding," Angie added quickly seeing Martha's horrified expression.

"That wasn't funny! No man is worth doing that for so don't even joke about it."

"What has that got to do with anything?" Angie asked defensively as she threw down the pillow.

"You weren't even there so you don't know what happened."

"I didn't have to be there. I told you before he wouldn't stick by you when it came to a showdown. Whatever happened, Dr. Peter Trenton will blame you for getting him involved."

Martha's aggressiveness stimulated Angie. She liked her honesty and down-to-earth analysis which separated her own feeling about Peter from her feelings about the defeat by Elaine Potter. Despite Martha's own views, she said nothing to condemn Angie.

"That's his problem, not mine," Angie said confidently. "I don't understand why he acted the way he did. Even Dr. Ito, who didn't have the slightest suspicion, thought there was something weird about the specimen."

"A blue-stained cervix is unusual but I wouldn't say it was weird," Martha interrupted. "You have to be more precise or else it's just a waste of time. It has to be scientific criticism."

"Elaine explained the blue cervix," Angie said thoughtfully. "Why would she do that? You know what our problem is?"

"Hold on!" Martha said holding up her hand. "I don't have a problem and neither do you unless you want to make one for yourself. Really, Angie, you saw how it works. There's always an explanation for everything. It can get very complicated. They're always arguing about something but somehow they are all right even when they totally disagree with each other."

"Who are you talking about?" Angie asked

breaking out of her own train of thought.

"All the doctors at the Medical Center. It sounds like a debating society sometimes but in the end everyone comes up smelling like a rose. You've heard it all at Grand Rounds. Peter's not going to jump all over Potter unless he kills or maims someone with his surgery. And then only if it's repeated blatantly and Peter can get the mob to join him."

"They have the same problem we do," Angie said tossing her head back. "They go on the basis that everyone is trying to do good."

"Do good?" Martha's voice squeaked with incredulity.

"They start with the premise that each and every doctor is purely motivated to do what he thinks is best for his patient," Angie explained. "The arguments are only what is comparatively better. They can't imagine someone fouling up the system on purpose. Especially someone who is just like they are!"

"Just like innocent lambs, huh?"

"Worse that that! Innocent shepherds who can't tell a wolf from a sheepdog. Elaine is so smart! She didn't make an issue of the blue cervix because it would draw attention. It's now been quietly filed away, explained and no one will ever hear about it again."

"Hallelu-yah!" Martha clapped her hands over her head.

"What's the use!" Angie said throwing up her hands. Her spirits were much better than before she walked in. Martha remained firm in her own opinion. Without converting Angie, she managed to cheer her up.

"Let's go out to eat tonight," Angie said. "My treat."

"How come?"

"A good loser always picks up the tab."

"You're not a loser," Martha sighed. "You just got in over your head in something you don't know enough about."

"Stop!" Angie pleaded. "You were doing good until you started to tell me what's good for me."

"What about Peter?"

"He'll do whatever pleases him," Angie said quickly and then stared at her outstretched finger-nails. A moment later she looked back at Martha. "It never would have amounted to anything anyway. He's married to his practice and surgery. He probably feels he was irrationally seduced into committing a traitorous act."

"Did you seduce him?"

"Only in bed and he was more than willing."

The contagion of Martha's spirit had only a temporary effect on Angie. The next morning she saw Trenton come out of the surgeons' locker room wearing the baggy green pants and shirt. With the first eye contact, she was betrayed by hope which was completely shattered as he walked by with only a cold, polite "Good Morning."

His meaning was clear: keep away! It wasn't done with the shy coyness of the first morning after which Angie had publicly penetrated. This hurt much deeper but was not fatal. Severe injuries usually leave the victim surprisingly calm. Like a mouse in the mouth of a cat, she didn't resist. She simply shrugged her shoulders and walked down the central corridor of the O.R. suite behind him.

He stopped next to an alcove containing scrub sinks to adjust his mask. Angie was headed for the next alcove thirty feet further down the hall. As she passed him, she pinched his behind.

"Nice buns!" she said loud enough and kept walking.

His back arched upward as he was startled by the contact. His ears blushed red over the green surgical mask.

It took about a week for their unavoidable meetings in the hospital to normalize. The sudden stops and breath holding when they first spotted each other gradually became a slowed pace and a prominent nod so there could be no question of rudeness. It progressed satisfactorily to the point where they could ignore each other without taking offense.

Angie gained some personal understanding from the short-lived love affair and its uncomplicated aftermath. She had no thought of leaving or going back home. In two months she had become acclimated to the faster pace of New York. By just coming to work and doing her job, she was integrated into the gridiron of passing activities.

It was a week before she realized she had not considered going home as an alternative. When she did think about it she was pleased with herself. Her work was satisfying after all. She was more involved with patients at the clinic. They asked for her and she was building a small following already.

Except for Potter, she admired all the surgeons

for their skill and competence. She even thought Potter was good but not as good as his statistics.

In a week it all seemed to blow over without recriminations. No one talked about Rita Algrin, her death or her autopsy. No one mentioned the blue-stained cervix.

By the end of the week, Angie received a note from the Employee Health Clinic saying she had an appointment with Dr. Gillis.

Nineteen

Angie knew Dr. Nancy Gillis but had not seen her too often in the operating room. She was a young Instructor at the Medical School who had finished her residency about two years ago.

Dr. Gillis was thirty-two years old. She had dark straight hair pulled back in a bun. Angie had once seen her with her hair down and it reached almost to her buttocks. She was short and only a little plump but gave the impression of being heavier because of her round face.

Envy prevented Angie from liking her better. She was the physician and surgeon Angie wanted to be years ago. It wasn't bitter envy. It was more like a feeling of regret.

"Have a seat, Angie," Dr. Gillis greeted her warmly as she indicated the chair in front of her desk.

The office was tiny with just enough room for the furniture and a pathway around it. The diplomas on the wall confirmed Angie's rationalizations that perhaps Nancy Gillis had more opportunity than she did. There hung a B.A. from Bryn Mawr and her M.D. from Columbia College of Physicians and Surgeons. There were others but Angie was right. Nancy Gillis's father was a prominent physician in New Jersey and had supported her all through her training from college to the present.

"I haven't seen you much in the last two weeks," Angie said as she sat down.

"It's been slow and I expect it will be for a while," Nancy said. "You'd be surprised how many women don't want another woman to operate on them. But it'll change. How do you feel about it?"

Dr. Gillis wanted to be in private practice. She had taken postresidency fellowships in GYN cancer surgery. Her appointment as an Instructor was a parttime one which enabled her to have a small but steady income. Usually the post was abandoned after a year by most new surgeons.

"Why not," Angie said, "if I needed surgery I'd let you. What am I doing here?"

"Don't look so concerned," Nancy said. "I'm sure there's been a mistake or else it's nothing anyway. Your Pap smear was reported back abnormal. It was sent to me for follow-up."

"I know it was a mistake," Angie said gruffly. She felt her stomach flutter but was surprised she wasn't more agitated by the news. She controlled herself very well.

"Pardon me?" Nancy asked, not understanding Angie's sudden hostility.

"It's all a mistake," Angie said. "Just forget the whole thing."

"Perhaps I said the wrong thing. You had a definitely abnormal Pap smear. You need a second examination," Nancy said firmly.

"It's not necessary," Angie said just as determined. "I can't explain it all to you," Angie said, standing up to leave.

"Wait a minute, Angie, please," Nancy said quite worried. "Please sit down." Angie complied. "If you'd rather have another doctor, say so. I'll call Dr. Potter right now if you like. Or whoever you want but don't be so flippant about this."

"It's not you. I'd be pleased to have you operate if it were necessary," Angie said politely.

"You're not taking this in the right way," Nancy said, suspecting Angie's politeness was a ruse to leave. "Who are you going to see to have this checked out? You can't just forget about it," she said pursuing the need.

"I won't. I have to think about it for a while," Angie said looking straight at Nancy. She was trying to evaluate Nancy's part in this. "Why don't we just do another Pap smear and see what it shows."

"I think a D and C with a cone biopsy is indicated," Nancy said definitely after a slight hesitation.

"No, I'll go for another Pap but no surgery," Angie said shaking her head. Her attitude was bewildering and upsetting to the doctor who had no idea why she was so resistant.

"You're making a big mistake," Nancy said taking off her round spectacles. "I — the report showed there were melanotic cells in the smear. Do you know what that means?"

"It means there are black colored cells," Angie said shrugging to indicate the obvious but then added, "What does it mean?"

"You may have a malignant melanoma. I didn't want to discuss it or even mention it because it seems so unlikely . . . ,"

"There's no such thing," Angie interrupted but for the first time she recognized her anxiety. Nancy looked very disturbed by the revelation as well.

If the Potters were trying to get back at her, it would be ironic if the Pap smear were genuine and she refused treatment.

"There is such a thing as a melanoma of the uterus," Nancy pleaded. "More often that not it is a metastatic lesion from a primary melanoma somewhere else. On very rare occasions, a primary one of the uterus has been reported."

"Has there ever been one here at University Medical Center?" Angie asked as her eyebrows raised up suspiciously.

"No, there hasn't," Nancy said. "I checked. I looked at the smear myself and tried to find another example of this lesion in the files."

This bit of information was disconcerting to Angie. At first Angie felt relieved because it meant

Elaine wasn't trying to get back at her. On the other hand, she quickly turned apprehensive at the prospect of real disease.

"Couldn't it be another patient, someone here now?" Angie asked.

"No, there wasn't any mix-up in the slides," Nancy was positive. "You were the only one in the clinic to have a Pap smear that day. The slides were labeled and dated in the clinic so they can't be mixed up."

"What do you want to do?" Angie said with resignation.

"The first thing is a complete physical with special attention to the skin. I'm going to go over you with a magnifying glass and anything that seems suspicious comes out and goes to the lab."

"Except for a few freckles, I don't think there's a mark on my body."

"We'll see," Dr. Gillis said. "Go into the examining room next door and take off your clothes. All of them, including your stockings."

"There are no moles on my body," Angie resisted.

"Don't be too sure! One of the favorite questions they like to ask students in physical diagnosis is, "What disease can be found between the toes that would save someone's life if treated early enough?""

Angie thought about it then got up and went into the examining room. While she was waiting for Dr. Gillis, she spread her toes but saw only a little cracking due to athlete's foot.

Dr. Gillis throughly examined every crack and crevice of her skin with the magnifying glass as promised. There were no black moles hiding anywhere. She did a pelvic examination and took another specimen for a repeat Pap smear.

Back in her tiny office, Dr. Gillis put down the details of her examination. Her head rested sadly in the palm of her left hand as she concentrated. Angie came in and sat down.

"I found nothing on your skin," Dr. Gillis said. "You must have the D and C and the biopsy."

"I don't have to have anything," Angie said testily. "It's my body and I want to think about it."

"I'm sorry," Nancy said sincerely. "I'm sorry if somehow I antagonized you. I don't know what I did but whatever it is, don't let it affect your judgment. Go to someone else. Get someone else to do the biopsy. Angie, this is a very deadly disease. It spreads quickly and you can't put off making a decision."

"It's not you, Nancy," Angie said apologetically. "It's too hard to explain just now. I need more time."

Angie needed the time to learn more about melanomas. She suspected Elaine's hand in this but wasn't sure. If it hadn't been for her suspicions, she would have been more upset and afraid of the disease. She had a general idea that melanomas were treacherous tumors that usually began in the skin. Sometimes they occurred in the eye but rarely elsewhere. But rarely elsewhere wasn't reassuring if you were the one with the unlikely cancer.

She considered leaving now. Perhaps going to Boston for the biopsy but decided against it. If she had a melanoma, she was in the best place to get treated for it. If it was the Potters' vengeance then they were really sick and had to be stopped. There had to be a way to prove it one way or the other.

Angie had no intention of keeping this all to herself. For one thing, she was not entirely sure what was going on. It would have made no sense to Dr. Gillis if Angie had told her about the blue cervix and the Potters. She wasn't even that sure any more now that she had a personal stake in it. Her mood vacillated from unrestricted anger when she thought the Potters were behind it all to fear of a hopeless disease that could end her life. The worst feeling was that of helplessness and the possibility that she had brought this down upon herself.

By the time she got home, she was exhausted by the crosscurrents of anger, fear and helplessness swirling within her. She dragged herself to the couch past Martha who followed right after her into the living room.

Dr. Gillis had called Martha because Angie had acted so strangly. Martha defended her without answering any questions directly. When Dr. Gillis told her the diagnosis, she took it much harder than Angie because she believed it. This made it worse. There was no way for her to know how hard Angie would resist going for treatment. She decided to approach Angie as if she were dealing with a mad woman perched on a high ledge ready to jump.

Angie's agony was already apparent. She lay on the couch with one hand pressed feverishly on her head while the other hung flaccidly toward the floor. Her eyes were painfully closed tightly and her lips twisted and contorted her face.

Martha moved cautiously. She chewed on her lip as she walked on tiptoes toward the couch. Angie opened her eyes and Martha stopped in midstep as if the gaze were a light shining on a midnight burglar.

"Are you alright?" Martha asked.

"I'm fine," Angie said without moving. "You don't look so good from here." There was an unsteadiness in Martha's stance that Angie had never seen.

"Sit up and I'll improve," Martha said. She sat down while Angie sat up.

"You know I went to see Dr. Gillis this afternoon," she said lamely.

"What'd she say?"

"Nothing much. It was all straightened out," Angie said.

"Bullshit! She just called me and told me all about it," Martha blurted out, no longer able to restrain herself.

"Holy shit! Isn't anything sacred around here?" Angie shouted back at Martha. "I knew it! The way you were pussyfooting around here like it was a wake," Angie slapped her hands down hard on the sofa pillows.

"Angie, I'd be scared to death if it was me," Martha said in a firm soft voice, "and I hate to think what's going on in your head."

"I'm scared, Martha, I'm really scared!" Angie said as she put her hands over her face. Martha thought she was crying and moved to her side. As soon as she put her arm around Angie's shoulder,

Angie looked up gratefully. She wasn't crying but was obviously perplexed.

"Can we talk about it?" Martha asked.

"Of course we can," Angie said smiling and sat back against the arm of the sofa. "I was going to tell you but I had the feeling you found out, that Dr. Gillis called you and it really burned me."

"Don't blame her for that. She did the right thing. Who else should she call when she thinks you won't go for the biopsy?"

"Did you tell her why?"

"No," Martha said hesitating, "I know what you've been through and you know how I feel about it."

"No, I don't. I only know you don't want to be involved in anything affecting you directly. But it's changed now. It's possible — I'm only asking you to say it's possible . . . ."

"Anything's possible," Martha conceded with embarrassment.

"Don't be condescending!" Angie said pointing a warning finger at her. There was a mean intensity in her face to back it up. "I need your help but you have to believe I'm not a fruitcake."

"I wouldn't go that far. I told you you were crazy to get mixed up in this to begin with. It had nothing to do with you. It wasn't your fight." Martha stopped as they looked at each other in revelation. "I guess it is now," Martha said.

"It really is," Angie said softly.

"But you could be wrong. I don't want you to be wrong this time," Martha said, very upset and on the verge of tears. "Oh shit, Angie, you've done it again! I don't know what to say. You can't let this slide because you think the Potters are behind it."

"I'm not going to," Angie said. "I'll go in for the biopsy but you have to help me. More than ever I have to be right about the Potters. I don't want to die with a malignant melanoma."

"Oh, God, I hope you're right," Martha said squeezing her hands together. "You won't die, stop talking like that. It can be removed, eradicated, treated. I'll call Nancy Gillis right now."

"No, not now!" Angie said holding on to Martha who started to get up. "If I'm right . . . , I have to be right. My life depends on it! I don't think anyone has ever survived a melanoma of an internal organ. I'm right about them, Martha! What'll happen to me if the biopsy is positive?" Angie said rapidly and anxiously.

Martha sucked in a deep breath awed with fear as if Angie's words were indeed true. She couldn't answer but Angie was prepared to go on.

"I'll have a hysterectomy followed by chemotherapy. Remember that woman with the melanoma of the vulva and vagina. Two years of chemotherapy and she was sick all the time."

"But she's alive," Martha said widening her eyes hopefully.

"That's beside the point," Angie said. "If they wanted to get me out of the way without making a fuss, this would be perfect. Two years of therapy would get me out of the way permanently.

"You have to keep an eye on the specimen. It's got to be labeled the way I did it before. We've got to get Gillis to stain the cervix before she does the biopsy."

"Did you tell her about the other case" Martha asked. "She'll go along, I think."

"No, she won't," Angie said disappointingly. "Not if I have to tell her the whole story myself. She needs to hear it from someone she respects professionally. Someone who can change her mind. That leaves no one but Peter Trenton. What do you think?"

"You should know more about it than I do," Martha said with gloom spreading from her voice to her face. "If he feels he made a fool of himself once, he won't do it again."

"It wasn't that bad," Angie said dismissing Martha's sympathy for Trenton. "He was afraid to take the risk, just like you said. This time you can get him to do it for me if you tell him I won't go for the biopsy unless my specimen is stained before it goes to the lab."

"Do you mean that?" Martha asked worriedly. "Would you risk your life if he won't do it?"

Angie thought about it a while wondering if it would make any difference in the way Martha approached Trenton.

"You've got to make him believe I won't," she said out of sympathy for Martha's concern.

Martha was greatly relieved.

"Why do you have to make things so complicated?" Martha asked. "I'll do it your way but maybe you should have it done at another hospital. Make it clean and simple so you know if you're sick or not. All this scares me."

"It scares me too," Angie said.

"Then have it done someplace else!" Martha

pleaded. "This will probably be another standoff like the last time."

"Standoff?" Angie said surprised at Martha. "Do you really believe the Potters pulled a fast one on Margaret Kelly? It wasn't a standoff. They won."

"Oh, Jesus! You're driving me crazy!" Martha said with anguish. She stood up holding her head as if she were in pain. "The only thing I want is for you to be well. The hell with the Potters. It doesn't matter."

"It does to me," Angie said calmly. "Look, if the biopsy is positive, I'll go to another hospital, another state even and get another biopsy. But if the Potters are involved, this could slow them down a lot. So long as you're there to keep an eye on the specimen I'll feel better. And I want to have it done under spinal anesthesia so I can see what's going on, too."

Twenty

Martha called Dr. Trenton at his office. She said it was urgent but could wait until he finished seeing his scheduled patients.

She arrived at his office just as his last patient was leaving. The receptionist, a fiftyish-year-old woman who spoke with a distinctly British accent despite having lived in New York for the last thirty years, was surprised to see another patient walk in. She did not know Martha and was annoyed at her for being there without an appointment.

"Don't you remember? I just called a couple of hours ago," Martha said trying to establish her legitimacy for being there.

"You called," the receptionist said in clipped tones, "but you didn't request an appointment. The doctor said nothing to me."

"Just tell him I'm here," Martha assured her.

Trenton came out to usher her into his consultation room as soon as he heard the name.

"She's really touchy, isn't she?" Martha said waving a thumb toward the door as she sat down in a leather upholstered armchair. Trenton settled in behind a six-foot walnut desk. There were a few charts stacked in front of him and a stack of journals off toward the edge of the desk. The walls were lined with diplomas.

"I forgot to tell her you were coming and she gets flustered when I don't confide in her," Peter smiled.

"I came to talk about Angie," Martha said bluntly. Peter frowned uncomfortably so Martha could not miss it. She expected such a first reaction as she figured he would think she was intervening in their personal affair.

"Her Pap smear came back positive," Martha said before he could raise any objections to her presence. His face went blank with disbelief. He was totally unprepared for this kind of news. It was much worse because in his own conceit he was thinking of reasons why he should reject Martha's pleas for a reconciliation.

"Did you see the report?" he asked studying his fingernails as he nervously scraped one against the other. He looked up suddenly. "Was it class four or five?"

"Dr. Gillis phoned me. She said there were melanoma cells in the smear."

Trenton rubbed his eyebrow with his left hand. He looked very angry to Martha, who couldn't interpret his reaction. He didn't say anything but stared at her with his head tilted to one side. She shifted uncomfortably in the chair.

"A melanoma? From where?" he asked doubtfully.

Martha shrugged her shoulders and said, "She said it was in the smear and could be from the cervix or the endometrium. And she also said she went over every part of her skin. She thinks it's a primary."

"It doesn't necessarily mean she has a malignant melanoma. Don't be so upset by it until they get a biopsy. Did Gillis see any lesion on the surface of the cervix?" Peter said calmly and reassuringly.

Martha took a deep breath and closed her eyes momentarily.

"Angie won't go for the biopsy unless you stain her cervix like you did on that other patient," Martha said then opened her eyes. Trenton was sitting there with a fierce scowl on his face. His lips were pouting and his eyes focusing hard on Martha.

"Who else did she tell about that?" he said bitingly.

"No one! I twisted it out of her," Martha said apologetically. "That's why Gillis called me. She couldn't understand why Angie refused to go for the biopsy. I couldn't either until she told me about the Potters."

"And what did you think of that?"

Martha felt moist and physically uncomfortable. Her breathing was difficult. She made a conscious effort to breathe more deeply and slowly.

"It doesn't matter what I think or what you think! The point is she thinks the Potters are behind this and won't go for the biopsy anywhere. She thinks it's unnecessary unless she can prove a point."

"I think she's crazy! And before you jump all over me," he said holding up a hand, "I also love her. But this is carrying it too far. I can't do it!"

"Why not?" Martha said rising out of her seat. "She's scared to death and needs us badly."

"I can't do it because the stain will screw up the specimen," he said sounding badly troubled and scared himself. "It's a strange lesion. It's in the wrong place. They have to do special stains on the biopsy specimen to be sure if it's malignant, to be sure it's melanin. In the other case the diagnosis was established. You don't really think the Potters would plant something like that. My God—tell her it can't be done. I'll tell her myself."

Trenton's troubled face transferred the anxiety to Martha. She was more worried than ever that Angie might have lied to her. Perhaps she wouldn't have the biopsy except on her own terms.

"Wait!" Martha held up her hand as Trenton was reaching for the phone. "Can't we fake it? Can't we just go through the motions without injecting the dye? She won't be able to tell."

"Jesus!" Peter said flopping back in his chair. "I have never lied or cheated and in the past month she's had me do both."

"Oh, come off it, there have been times when you didn't tell the patient everything," Martha said. "Do it for her sake!"

"What happens when she wakes up and wants to see the specimen?"

"It's going to be normal. Oh, God, it has to be normal. You just said so. The smear doesn't mean a thing. If it's normal, then she's wrong about the Potters, isn't she? You said she was wrong," Martha's tone wavered at the end seeking assurance from Trenton.

"Tell her I'll do it but you better be there to back me up. I'll come up to the treatment room and fake it without talking to her so you have to be there. Just tell her I think she's wrong but I'm doing it because of her stubbornness. Just as you planned!"

Martha was pleased, almost happy with the outcome until she remembered one other detail.

"She insists on spinal anesthesia so she'll be awake. What happens if she wants to see the specimen when it's out?"

"It'll be over by then," Peter said. "If she makes a fuss she gets zonked."

As a patient, Angie entered the hospital with apparent placid calmness. Mechanically, she went through the preliminary testing procedures.

The prospect of exposing the Potters provided an aura of hope antagonized by a crawling gritty fear harbored within her womb. It played see-saw with her confidence. Before this, she never understood why women accepted Eric Potter's diagnosis and recommendations for surgery so readily and often without question. From moment to moment, more than once, she found herself wishing the uterus gone if only to be free of doubt.

The same feeling assured her that her suspicions were correct. He offered salvation from a dreaded disease and who could resist even if the disease were only a possibility and the cure a sure thing? The ignorant and the cynical were not affected. They shared a common faith. The ignorant by revelation found with their heads tucked firmly in the ground; the cynical by selective reasoning. In the end, they shared a common fate which Angie had seen too often when the diagnosis was correct. The ignorant died bewildered and forlorn; the cynical to prove a point.

Being neither ignorant nor cynical, Angie had no faith to sustain her. She was depending on Martha Daniels and Dr. Peter Trenton but the biopsy was only a baptism. If it were positive, she had already decided to seek salvation anywhere but University Medical Center.

Angie wasn't surprised or angry because Peter didn't believe her story about the Potters. He agreed to help if that's what it took to get her into the hospital. It meant to her that he still had some feelings and concern for her.

His belief was made clear by the conditions he insisted on. He would not talk to her or even see her. Martha prepared Angie in the examining room. He waited outside while the sheets and drapes were put over her legs in the stirrups. The linen barrier separated them and hid his feelings.

He was nervous, not shaky, but his face displayed the duplicity he was planning. Angie might have guessed if she could see him.

He said nothing to either Martha or Angie as he sat down on a stool. Professionally, he placed the speculum in the vagina and held out his gloved hand for Martha to place in it the syringe filled with blue dye. His hand extended to the side beyond the sheets so Angie could see the transfer. He squirted the dye into a test tube which he placed in his pocket. The action was covered by the sheets raised up by Angie's legs. From another pocket, he took out a syringe filled with saline. He carefully injected the colorless fluid into the cervix so there would be a faint sensation of stretching the cervical muscle fibers. He handed Martha the empty blue-stained syringe and left.

"Who was that masked man, Tonto?" Angie asked to break the tension for Martha. She was a little depressed herself.

"It sure wasn't the Lone Ranger," Martha answered also trying to lighten the mood.

Angie made no move to get off the table. She sat up resting on her elbows while Martha was putting things away and cleaning up.

"Would Erica Jong have called this a *zipless fuck*?" Angie remarked. It caught Martha off balance. She stared open-mouthed at Angie. It touched a thought she was trying to resist during the whole procedure.

"Don't look at me that way," Angie shrugged innocently. "I read it in a book."

* * *

With the help of two hundred milligrams of Nembutal, Angie finally found deep sleep about midnight. At five-thirty in the morning she was aroused from this drugged sleep to prepare for the operation scheduled for eight.

This strange inimical behavior of the nurses is part of the prescribed protocol before surgery. It seems absurd to awaken a patient so she can get injections of Nembutal or Demerol to put her back to sleep. It would be foolhardy not to distinguish sleep from coma whether drug-induced or pathological consummations. The nurse's responsibility is to document the patient's condition upon delivery to the operating room.

The patient comes to the operating room in the most natural state, bereft of hair pieces, prostheses for teeth, breasts, extremities. Colorful or opaque appliques of the skin and nails are removed. In surgery nothing must hide physiological deficiencies. Silicon implantations, skin stretched surgically smooth and even robust muscle tone count for little. It is the unseen visceral body, the vast pool of proteins that reconstruct the body after surgery that counts.

Angie had nothing to remove: no wig, no teeth, no makeup, no nail polish and no jewelry. She refused the preoperative medication in order to be alert under spinal anesthesia. The nurses coaxed her as if they were pushers and she a reluctant junkie. "It'll make you feel better so you won't remember a thing," they promised.

It was just what Angie wanted to avoid. There was no more prodding on the medication after the anesthesiologist said it was okay. He had been warned by Trenton that Angie had some idiosyncracy about surgery but would be a very good and cooperative patient.

Awake with a slightly fuzzy barbiturate hangover from the Nembutal taken the night before, Angie was wheeled through the halls of the hospital. She saw the hospital from an unaccustomed perspective. Flat on her back, it was the first time she had studied the ceiling. Lights flickered by as the stretcher rolled at an even pace. There were cracks and peeling paint no one would notice for awhile yet.

Almost all the O.R. staff stopped at the side of her stretcher when she was wheeled into the O.R. suite. Mrs. Beeson shooed them all away saying something about giving the girl a little privacy. In the operating room, she was able to crawl over from the stretcher to the table. The only problem was keeping herself covered with sheets and not exposing the lower half of her body. The top was covered by a short hospital gown. The nurses kept the stretcher from slipping away and the sheet from falling off.

Dr. Joe Flexner was the anesthesiologist she requested because he worked competently without a lot of fuss. He did things in a quiet systematic fashion which Angie found reassuring when she watched other patients undergoing anesthesia. He was about fifty years old, thin and short with a black moustache peppered with white hair.

"So you want to come in here cold turkey?" Dr. Flexner smiled at her as he took her arm and placed it on the armboard.

"I don't want to miss a thing," Angie smiled back at him.

302

He was studying her forearm at different angles of light by twisting it gently from side to side so he could follow the outline of her vein that curved gently from the thumb up over the forearm.

Angie's torso contracted but she managed to keep her arm perfectly still as the needle penetrated the skin and went into the vein. Flexner attached the hub of the needle to the intravenous tubing.

With the intravenous securely taped in place, Angie was asked to turn on her side. She did so awkwardly with the help from the nurses standing around the table so she couldn't slip off the narrow table. Her back was exposed from the shoulders to well below her hips. Knowing what to expect, she pulled her knees up toward her chest and bent her neck forward.

This curled-up position made her spinal vertebrae stand out in a straight line of repetitive peaks and valleys. The valleys were vertebral interspaces enlarged by the position she held. It separated the bony portions so the six-inch spinal needle could pass through the valley to the spinal canal.

After painting the lower back with antiseptic solution which felt icy cold to Angie, Flexner placed his thumb in the fourth lumbar interspace corresponding to a level equal to the top of her hip bone. The soft fleshy spinal cord densely packed with axons, neurons and ganglia encased in the protective bony armor of the spine did not descend down to this level. The needle entered the canal containing the watery fluid which bathed the long nerve fibers emerging symetrically like a horse's tail from the cord six or seven inches away.

First the skin was made numb by injecting lido-caine through a tiny thin needle that was little more than a mosquito bite. She didn't feel the larger spinal needle pass easily into the watery canal. Flexner injected the prepared anesthetic. Angie was able to turn on her back once more.

Within a minute she felt a warm flush pass through her legs and then gradually nothing. She didn't have any legs, or so it seemed, unless she looked at them. At first they were extremely heavy, needing extraordinary power to move them. And then they were gone. Not even a sense that she was trying to move them although she willed it.

Dr. Gillis came in with her hands and forearms dripping. Angie recognized her immediately behind the mask. Her round dark eyes were bright and serious as she said "Good morning" to Angie. As she finished drying her hands, Martha walked in and went over to Angie. She stood beside Dr. Flexner at the head of the table. Angie, lying flat on her back, looked upward and backward at her.

"Where have you been?" she asked Martha soft-ly. Dr. Gillis with the help of the scrub nurse put on her gown and gloves.

"I've been looking for you," Martha whispered as she bent over closer to Angie.

"What?" Angie asked not understanding why Martha was looking for her when she had been the center of attention for so many people. She was unaware of her legs hanging up in the stirrups. She was totally devoid of any perceptions from the waist down and could not feel the doctor washing her skin and vagina with antiseptic.

"You were scheduled for nine-thirty," Martha whispered. "You weren't in your room. The eight o'clock case was cancelled."

"I know that!" Angie answered. "Where else could I go? What took you so long to get here?"

"The schedule wasn't changed until this morning. How was I supposed to know?" Martha pleaded.

"Never mind. Get up there and see what's happening," Angie whispered.

Dr. Gillis finished dilating the small opening of the cervix with smooth steel rods of graduated sizes. She inserted a metal loop with fine sharp teeth at its end through the dilated cervical opening. Her wrists moved the scraper back and forth and rotated like an epeeist. The lining of the uterus mixed with blood slid through the cervical opening like loose tapioca pudding. The specimen was carefully collected in a small plastic jar.

The room was quiet except for the beeping of the ECG monitor attached to Angie. She was straining to see what was going on over the sheets covering her elevated thighs. As she sat up, there was interference with the oscilloscope because of the movement. Dr. Flexner assured her everything was fine. He pressed her shoulder forcing her back down on the table as he asked her to keep her head down.

A few minutes later she heard Dr. Gillis say the second specimen should be sent down separately. Angie knew this was the cervical biopsy. She tried to sit up again and was about to ask if she could see the specimen.

"Joe, keep her still please," Dr. Gillis said as she was bothered by the activity of Angie's upper torso. "There's a small bleeder down here I can't see when she sits up."

With only the slightest movement that Angie didn't see at all, Dr. Flexner twisted a valve on the I.V. tubing and injected pentathol into Angie's veins. Within a few seconds, she began to lose consciousness which was the only inkling she had before she blacked out. She was just able to turn her head toward Flexner and say "No" before the lights went out.

A half hour later, she opened her eyes in the recovery room. She recognized the tall thin nurse with the large hooked nose standing over her listening to her blood pressure.

"Where's Martha?" Angie barely whispered through a mouth that felt like sandpaper. There was no feeling in her legs and there wouldn't be any for a few hours. It would be another twelve hours before she was permitted to stand.

"What?" the nurse said taking the stethoscope out of her ears.

"Where's Martha?" Angie said more loudly after making a great effort to take in a deep breath.

"She told me to tell you she went down to Pathology with the specimen. How do you feel? Are you having any pain?"

"I don't feel a thing," Angie said then closed her eyes in sleep once more.

Twenty-one

By the time Martha came by to see her at four o'clock all the anesthetic effects had worn off. Angie was feeling fine but she still wasn't allowed to get out of bed. She was alone in the two-bedded room. Her roommate was discharged a few hours earlier, leaving Angie to ruminate most of the afternoon.

Now that it was over, she felt a little apathetic. Perhaps it was the effects of the pentothal or the isolation and the surgery. She felt indifferent toward the Potters as battle fatigue blunted her desire for victory. She was wounded.

Martha was a casualty, too, although her wound was undefined. Her mother died of cancer untreated and undiagnosed until she went to the hospital to die. She couldn't remember her mother being sick until that day she came home from school when she was twelve years old. The ambulance was there to take her mother away. Her aunt and her father later said she had been sick for over a year.

Martha could see Angie was recovered from the anesthesia but she asked anyway.

"How do you feel?" she asked.

"Tired and bored! I wish I could get out of here," Angie said as she rested her head propped up on her elbow. "Gillis and Flexner were just here. I told Flexner I'd get even with him. Some day I'll slip him a mickey and see how he likes it. What happened?"

"You were trying to sit up and Gillis was trying to clamp a bleeder," Martha explained patiently.

"Gillis said there was no problem. Flexner just shrugged his shoulders so I tore up his anesthesia bill and handed it to him."

"You got a bill already?" Martha said with amazement.

"It was on the nighttable when I opened my eyes. He claimed it was a mistake. I don't care as long as he took it with him."

"It was," Martha said. "The Employee Health Clinic is supposed to take care of it. What did Gillis say?"

"She'll let me know tomorrow," Angie said calmly but her eyes narrowed with concern. "Did anybody say anything about the specimen when you brought it down?"

"No," Martha said casually, "I gave it to Dr. Castle. He looked at it and cut it right away. It went right into the processor."

"Was it blue enough for him to see? Did he say anything?" Angie asked furtively.

"Er—no, it didn't look that blue," Martha stammered.

Angie immediately flopped down in the bed and stared at the ceiling.

"It's labeled with your number and it's in the processor," Martha pleaded. "No one's going to touch it until tomorrow morning."

"Peter didn't inject the dye last night, did he?" Angie asked as she turned over to look at Martha squarely.

"He said—"

"Never mind what he said. I figured it out for myself," Angie said distressed by the confirmation. "He really thinks I have a melanoma." Her eyes began to tear betraying her false indignation.

"It doesn't matter what we think or what Peter Trenton thinks," Martha said. "It's what Dr. Castle thinks when he looks at those slides."

"What if they're not my slides?" Angie said reaching for a tissue to blow her nose. "I know nobody believes me. Don't look so worried, Martha. You're witnessing a miracle. If those slides are positive, I'm going to Boston for another biopsy and everyone will say I was cured by the D and C."

"Angie, I—" Martha started to say something that was meant to be comforting but she stopped.

"It wouldn't have worked anyway," Angie said reaching out her hand to Martha. "No one wants to hear bad news, especially when they let something be put over on them. Trenton and Wright and Comerford and all the rest of them suspected Potter at one time but they couldn't prove it. Now even if they could, they would rather be silent about it."

The next morning no one entered Angie's room except the nurses and the nurses' aides. Dr. Gordon poked his head into the room to ask how she felt. Obviously she was okay sitting up finishing her breakfast.

She knew the task of reporting the results was left up to Dr. Gillis. As the morning passed on, it became more likely that the news would be bad. The good news would have been on everyone's lips.

Dr. Gillis came in a little after ten o'clock wearing a long white clinical coat. She entered with a smile but Angie could see a faint tremor at the corner of her lips. The tightness of the muscles around her eyes made them look puffy. After finding out that Angie had a comfortable night and no ill effects from the biopsy Dr. Gillis pulled over a chair and sat down beside the bed.

"The biopsies confirmed the Pap smear," she said keeping eye contact with Angie. She said it without hesitating and waited for Angie to react.

All morning Angie had been expecting this news. She practiced several variations of quick rebuffs designed to startle or enrage Dr. Gillis. When she actually heard it, she couldn't think of one. Her eyelids drooped heavily and her jaw felt like it was heavily weighted. The feeling lasted for about twenty seconds until Dr. Gillis took her hand sympathetically. Angie pulled her hand away abruptly.

"What does that mean?" Angie asked regaining her composure.

"There is a melanoma in the cervical biopsy as well as in the D and C. It means you need to have a hysterectomy," Dr. Gillis said trying to sound compassionate without pity. It had to sound like a suggestion with the impact of necessity.

"Do you really believe I have a melanoma?" Angie asked angrily.

The emotional response came spontaneuosly. It surprised Gillis, who had heard patients ask "Are you sure?" or something like that but never a question of belief. She didn't know how to answer.

"Is there anything you found in your own examination to give the slighest suspicion that I have this thing," Angie expanded.

"No, but it's there," Dr. Gillis answered quickly. "I saw it on the slides. Dr. Castle saw it."

"But is it my slides you saw? Does it look like anything that could have come out of me?" Angie asked insistently.

Dr. Gillis was first puzzled then worried by Angie's questions. She didn't understand what Angie was talking about so she labeled it irrational

"Angie, I'm sorry. The slides are a fact. It shows a melanoma and it is malignant. It's hard to face it but there is no other way. If we could be sure all the time by just examining there would be no need for biopsies."

That was it. Angie saw no further point in discussing or arguing about it. Dr. Gillis was practicing as she was trained. The answer was in the laboratory and the patient had to be made to fit the report.

"I understand your doubts and maybe it would be better if I called in a consultant for a second opinion. Perhaps Dr. Potter—"

"No," Angie calmly interrupted. "It's not because I—it's—let me think about it," Angie said.

There was no reason why Gillis should believe her any more than Trenton or Martha. If anything, she seemed less likely to do anything about it.

Martha was waiting outside the room until Dr. Gillis broke the news to Angie. She felt guilty without feeling she had done anything wrong. When she came into the room, Angie's expression did nothing to alleviate that feeling.

"I'm sorry, Angie," Martha said with great sadness.

"What are you sorry for?" Angie asked unrelentingly. "You think I might die from the tumor or are you sorry because you doublecrossed me?"

"I—I don't know," she mumbled. "You make it so hard. I just don't know."

"That's an excuse. You don't want to know," Angie said bitingly just as Peter Trenton came in. Martha was on the verge of tears. She ran past Peter without a word.

"You'd better go comfort your coconspirator or are you still bound by a vow of silence?" Angie said and then turned away from him.

"Don't blame Martha. She did what I told her to do," Trenton said, leaving no doubt he thought he was right. Angie turned to glare at him.

"Why didn't you say something the other night," she asked angrily. "I didn't need you to fuck things up. I would have gone somewhere else for the biopsy."

"I wasn't sure you would," he said softly looking away from her.

"She doesn't know," Angie's voice rose as she raised her hand toward the door, "and you're never sure! That's what my life depended on. That's what I trusted!"

"You don't trust anybody," he said disappointingly.

"Should I?" she said with feigned surprise.

"You have to!" he said angrily and then controlled it. "You have to," he said pleadingly. "Why must it always be your way?"

"Look who's talking! You're the one who expects everything to be done his way or it's not done!"

"This is not helping you," he said sadly. "I know I did the right thing. The proof is down in the laboratory and I'm sure Eric Potter had nothing to do with it. I'm sure of it. There's no place they could get a specimen like that."

After he left, Angie felt queasy. She had a cramping pain starting deep inside her which spread upward over her abdomen. She was going to ring for the nurse when it subsided.

"I'll sue the bastards, I'll sue them all," she thought. But it wouldn't work even if a biopsy somewhere else was negative. She knew they had the slides in the lab to prove they were right.

Relieved of the transient pain, she felt grateful things went as well as they did. She didn't suffer much discomfort so she couldn't complain. Some people were grateful for merely not getting worse. Some got worse but never complained.

Deep in thought and conscience, she didn't hear Dr. Comerford come into the room. He had a naturally soft step, perhaps cultivated and assured by rubber heels. The clickety-clack of footsteps in a hospital corridor was for him an unnecessary disturbance. He stepped to the foot of the bed where Angie became aware of his presence. She opened her eyes to his benevolent visage staring at her. His eyes were warmly comforted by his thick white eyebrows that curled around each side. They inspired Angie with their confidence and sense of knowing.

"Good morning, Miss Palmeri," he said.

"Dr. Comerford, I'm so glad you're here," she said sitting up on the side of the bed. "You know, don't you, the results of the biopsy."

"Yes, I do."

"They're wrong! Pull over a chair and sit down," Angie said as she got out of bed to move the straight-back chair closer. Comerford frowned but was always willing to listen when a patient talked.

Angie sat at the edge of the bed just a few feet from him. She started by telling him about Helen McCrae. He listened benignly not sensing any revelations or complaints. Angie was speaking calmly, mildly animated as she recounted her experiences, which Comerford expected to be good.

He expected her to say how glad she was to be here at University Medical Center. He thought her own words would give her confidence and courage.

He didn't catch the significance of her criticism of Elaine Potter. It was a doubt that could be usefully aired and he would reassure her afterward.

His attitude changed dramatically when she told him how she and Trenton managed to stain the patient's cervix blue. His ears pulled back on his head with a jerk. The deep creases on either side of his nose slackened as he sucked on his tongue. The redness of his skin gave a pink tinge to the roots of his white hair. He let her go on to the results presented at the Pathology conference but he couldn't contain himself any longer.

"This is despicable!" He said as he stiffened in the chair. His hands were rigidly pressed against his thighs and he pushed himself up. "Are you deliberately trying to ruin the reputation of the hospital and the medical school?"

"I'm trying to tell you something," Angie shouted but was visibly frightened because of Comerford's response.

"I've heard enough! And if it's true both you and Trenton will be gone from here. Is this melanoma something you conjured up?"

Angie fell back on the bed despondently. Comerford was shaking from a mixture of anger toward Angie and despair at himself for displaying his anger so openly. He apologized but his opinion was the same. He had nothing more to say to her and she had given up any hope of convincing anybody of anything.

He went straight to his office believing Angie had concocted the whole thing for her personal gain. Perhaps she was planning to sue the hospital for misdiagnosing. Perhaps the specimen wasn't genuine. As he thought about it on his way, he wondered if he had over-reacted. Perhaps she was unstable or worried about the consequences of the diagnosis and this was a psychotic denial.

Dr. Potter's results were going to be published. The journal's editor was a personal friend who had called Comerford to congratulate him on the great work that was being done at University Medical Center.

He considered calling in Potter and Trenton together but it wouldn't work. He would have to be objective to start and it would sound like he was accusing Potter. It could leave bitter feelings no matter how well he apologized afterward. It wasn't worth it. The girl might just be psychotic, which saddened him further.

It wasn't all her fault if the diagnosis was correct. She was trying to deny it all, he thought. But Dr. Castle couldn't be fooled, could he? It was a rare diagnosis. Even Dr. Castle hadn't seen a primary melanoma of the uterus before this. Castle's conclusion had to be based on comparison with other types of melanoma but not with one in the uterus.

Comerford charged into his office so he immediately had the attention of his two secretaries.

"Go down to the Path lab and get me the slides of Angie Palmeri," he said to the younger one with long blonde hair. The older woman, Madeline

Dempsey, had never seen his eyes burn so intensely in the twenty-five years she had worked for him.

"Pull Janice Pearson's folder and bring it inside," he said and stalked into his private office.

A minute later, Madeline came in carrying a brown aged folder in two hands balancing the contents of the thick file.

"Anything else?" she asked and waited trying to get a hint of what was agitating him.

"Bring in the other slides as soon as Karen gets back," he said while already reading the contents of the folder.

Thirty years earlier, Arthur Comerford had operated on Janice Pearson. She died three months after surgery. The autopsy showed she had extensive spread of malignant melanoma to the liver, bowels, lungs and brain.

The patient had three D and C's within a year for excessive uterine bleeding. In each instance, the melanoma cells were overlooked. The diagnosis was unsuspected and little attention was paid to the peculiar cells in the mass of uterine tissue removed by the curette. Afterward, after the uterus was removed and the diagnosis was obvious, the previous specimens were reviewed. It was all there.

At first, it didn't seem to have made much difference. The hysterectomy was uncomplicated and the melanoma seemed to be confined to the uterus. But no lymph nodes were taken and there was no way to know that the barn door had been closed after the horses were gone.

He planned to write a case report for a journal. He had all the materials together in the chart. He started the paper but then abandoned the project. There were too many errors in the management of this case. At least, in retrospect it was all wrong. Before she died he thought he had done some good. Afterward, he knew he had not altered the course of the disease.

Comerford's microscope from his medical school days sat in a glass bell jar on the table behind his desk. It was a beautifully polished brass microscope with a single eyepiece. It had an antique quality to its appearance but the optics were excellent.

He set up the microscope on his desk with a special light in front of it which was reflected by a mirror under the stage of the scope. He wiped the lenses with a tissue. The dust was nonexistent.

There were three glass slides taped to the inside of the folder and a small paraffin block containing the specimen from which the thin sections on the slides were cut. These had gathered dust since they were not protected by the glass bell jar. He wiped them vigorously without disturbing the glass cover slip protecting the specimen on the slide.

As he rotated the fine focus wheel on the side of the shining brass body of the scope, the blurred colors sharpened and became brighter. The individual cells lined up like brick masonry set by a master builder.

He moved the slide a millimeter or two on the stage to view another field of cells. It was out of focus. When he adjusted the fine focus something was wrong. The cells were heaped together going in random directions, no longer lined up straight to form an orderly layer. Was it vandals that destroyed the wall or did the mason have too much to drink? The cells were swollen, the nuclei were black and very large. They were strewn like rubble into the muscle fibers. There were four or five times the number of cells in this cancerous section compared to the normal line. The pressure of cellular growth distorted their shape and the line bulged deeply into the muscle layer.

The cancer spilled randomly through the field of normal tissue without design and without purpose. In one section, it erupted like a lava flow into the open space of a small gland.

Karen brought in Angie's slides while Comerford was still staring through the microscope.

"Just put them down," he said absorbed in his study.

He removed the old slide from the stage and replaced it with one of Angie's. Once the specimen was in focus, it took him all of ten seconds to confirm the diagnosis of malignant melanoma. He continued to scan different fields. It looked just like the pattern of melanoma in his old patient. As he continued to look through the scope, the pattern became more familiar. There was the lava flow erupting into the gland. He pulled the slide from the stage and looked at it with his bare eyes. He searched for his glasses and found them on the top of his head.

With the glasses he could see the label was correct. This was Angie's slide. He replaced it on the microscope stage. It was identical to the old slides. He checked the old slide again to be sure.

He held the two slides up, side by side, facing

the window to get the daylight to illuminate the thin sections. They were both cut from the same log. He superimposed one on the other. The thin sections melded into one.

He felt a sorrowful lump in his throat. It had to be a coincidence. He was looking for similarities between the two cases but he found identity. He wasn't ready to admit it. He tried to think of other cancers he had compared. There were always similarities. That was the value of comparisons when one case was doubtful.

Angie didn't have a chance to tell him the whole story. He didn't want to hear her preposterous accusation that someone was deliberately falsifying laboratory reports. It was worse than that, he recalled. Elaine Potter was systematically substituting abnormal specimens. He didn't want to hear it and yet he was now thinking it himself. It could be the power of suggestion. He had to be sure.

He picked up the phone and buzzed his secretary.

"Madeline," he said wearily, "have Karen go down to Pathology and get the paraffin block."

"What was that?" Madeline asked.

"The paraffin block on Angie Palmeri. Just ask the Chief Technician in the histology lab. Get it right away and if there's a problem have her call me. And get Alex Borden over here right away. Tell him it's urgent that I see him now."

Twenty minutes later, Dr. Alex Borden slumped his hulking body in the chair in front of Comerford. He had huge proportions, starting with a six feet four frame liberally larded with two hundred ninety pounds of flesh and fat. He had thick black hair and would have been handsome if his too solid flesh would melt a little, especially around his second chin.

"Well, Arthur, what's going on? Madeline sounded desperate," he said as he folded his hands over his ample belly.

"Did she?" Comerford said casually. "I'll have to speak to her. She's been edgy the last few weeks. Maybe she should retire. How's your research coming in the tissue typing lab?"

"You didn't get me here in the middle of the morning to discuss research," the laboratory director of the transplantation service said.

"I did," Comerford demanded. "Tell me about superfecundation."

The large man in the white coat straightened himself in the chair. He thought it strange that Comerford should ask the question that way. It sounded like an oral examination and he reacted accordingly. It was sort of a reflex brought on by a sense of deja vu from all the examinations he had had in the past. But he wasn't sure where to begin.

"Superfecundation refers to multiple conceptions and births from one mother but from different fathers. It can be the same father but fertilization can occur at different times. It—"

"Forget about all that," Comerford waved his hand, "tell me about your last paper."

"That arose from a contested paternity suit. The defense alleged that the woman had been having an affair with two men and that she had sex with

321

each of them within a two to four hour period. She gave birth to twins. I was called in to determine which one was the father. It turned out they both were.

"We compared blood group antigens and HLA tissue antigens of the two children with the alleged fathers. Of course half the genes and the antigens came from the mother but taking that into account, the frequency of antigens definitely proved there were two fathers and the two men involved matched separately with each twin."

"Could you do this with formaldehyde-fixed tissue?" Comerford asked

"To a certain extent," Borden answered thoughtfully. "To about ninety-nine percent probability we could establish identity. Of course if they were different, that is negative or non-identical tissue could be proven with a hundred percent reliability."

"I have two sets of slides and two paraffin blocks of tissue here." Comerford said patting his desk. "How soon can you run these tests?"

"I can start this afternoon. What's the problem?"

"Let's leave that out and do it as a double-blind study. It has to be objective and I don't want you to check . . . , you won't be able to anyway," he said as he stripped off the labels on the specimens. He applied new coded labels and handed them to Borden. "When can I expect to hear from you?"

"I don't know what you're looking for. If they're different, I should be able to tell right away, certainly by late this afternoon. Once they come up with an antigen that's not the same, the tissue can't be from the same person. But there are many common antigens in the human race. I assume these are both human. As we get to the less common ones, the chances of them occurring in the tissues of two different people become less likely unless they're identical twins."

"Let me know as soon as you find a difference," Comerford said with subdued hopefulness.

Twenty-two

Elaine and Eric Potter had just finished eating lunch in the hospital staff cafeteria. They were about to get up from the table just as Dr. Trenton walked in. He was frowning and preoccupied as he scanned the room searching for someone. It wasn't the Potters or else he just looked through them as if they were invisible.

"Looking for a place to sit," Eric called out to him. He was about ten feet away. The staff room was almost full and there were no empty tables. Trenton went over to the Potters.

"No thanks," Trenton said. "I was looking for

Dr. Comerford. Has he been in here?"

"Not since we've been here," Eric said.

"Well, thanks anyway," he said and started to leave but stopped to speak with Elaine.

"Did you see Angie Palmeri's slides?" he asked.

Elaine sat up stiffly as if she was startled by the name. Eric also tensed but only his legs beneath the table tightened together. Peter couldn't have noticed anyway since he was looking at Elaine. She pushed back her unkempt short hair on the side of her face.

"Palmeri?" she asked, "when was it done?"

"Eric, you know Angie Palmeri," he appealed to Eric Potter.

"Sure but I didn't know she was on the schedule," Eric said trying to sound surprised and sympathetic. "What does she have?"

"She had a D and C and a biopsy," he said as he pulled over a chair to sit down. He was talking directly to Eric and seemed to exclude Elaine. "I wish she had gone to you. Gillis is okay but Angie has some peculiar ideas about surgery. You could have convinced her. Maybe Gillis wasn't strong enough or she doesn't have that ability you have with some women."

"Gillis is pretty good," Eric said modestly, "but she needs more experience in talking to patients. I guess the biopsy was positive."

"It's bad!" Trenton said shaking his head and then turned to Elaine.

"Haven't you heard? Dr. Castle read the slides this morning. It was a primary melanoma of the uterus. I thought it would be all over the hospital

325

by now. Elaine, did you see the slides?'

"No, I got in late this morning. A primary melanoma? Are you sure? Eric, have you ever come across that? It should be worth writing up even as a single case report."

"Not off hand but it sounds awful," Eric said. "Is she balking on the surgery with Gillis?"

"She signed herself out," Trenton said as if Angie had burned down the hospital. "Before I go after her and try to talk some sense into her I wanted to look at the slides so I'd have some first-hand information."

"Why won't she have the surgery?" Elaine asked.

"It's quite irrational. I'd rather not go into it," Trenton said looking out over the room to avoid looking at the Potters. "Elaine, do me a favor, please. If Comerford returns those slides give me a call at the office. I'd like to look at them and go over them with you if you have the time.

As Trenton got up, Elaine and Eric stared at each other in a very startled, nervous way.

"Comerford took the slides?" Elaine said.

That's what the girl in the lab said. And the parafin block too. That's why I'm looking for him."

Trenton left the Potters staring worriedly at each other.

"It doesn't mean a thing," Eric said. "I'm sure Comerford's interest is no more than Trenton's.

"You're a fool!" Elaine said. "If it was so casual he would have just stopped by the lab and looked at them there. And where is Arthur Comerford now?"

Eric just shrugged his shoulders while Elaine got up and left. He followed after but by the time he caught up with her in her office she was already on the phone.

"Karen, this is Dr. Potter," Elaine said sweetly to Comerford's secretary. "I need the slides on Angelica Palmeri for a conference this afternoon. Would you ask Dr. Comerford if he's through with them?"

"He's gone for the day. I don't know when he'll be back," Karen said apologetically.

"In that case, could I have the slides back for this afternoon. I'll return them as soon as the conference is over," Elaine said biting her lip and nervously smoothing back her hair.

"I think Dr. Borden took both sets of slides with him."

"Both sets," Elaine said surprised.

"The other was an old case of his, over thirty years old. He never throws anything away," Karen giggled a little. "Interesting, the two have the same diagnosis."

"Yes—yes it is," Elaine looked very disturbed as she put down the receiver without saying goodbye.

Elaine slumped down in her chair with her eyes closed. Her usually pale skin was white as a sheet. Eric thought she had fainted and ran over to her. He straddled her legs and felt her moist sweaty hands. He gently slapped her cheeks between the palms of his hands. Her foot came up into his crotch. He doubled up and fell backward holding his lower abdomen and gasping with pain.

"You son of a bitch! I told you never to touch

me!" Elaine said glowering at the agonized Eric.

"But—I thought you fainted," Eric gasped. He staggered over to another chair in pain. He sat down with his head between his legs.

"I never fainted in my life, you schmuck!" The violence had moderated Elaine's anger but she still showed no concern for Eric. "We have a problem. Can you hear me?" she said to the bent over Eric.

"I hear you," Eric said softly as he lifted his head and sat back in the chair. Her blow had missed the mark causing little damage and much less pain than his reaction implied. But the natural defense of a man against female violence is to feign injury.

"The melanoma I found in the museum came from one of Comerford's patients," Elaine said anxiously.

"What are you talking about?" Eric asked.

"His secretary just told me he took Palmeri's specimen to compare it with an old case of his," she explained patiently.

"That doesn't prove it's the same case," Eric said trying to dismiss her concern.

"Will you shut up!" Elaine slammed her fist on the arm of the chair. "Of course it is! How many fucking melanomas of the uterus do you think there are?" Elaine turned beet-red with anger at his stupidity.

"It doesn't prove a thing," Eric repeated himself but this time he was trying to comfort himself but could not hide his worry. The sweat had already formed on his upper lip. He wanted a way out and was ready to believe in anything. "You said all along that all cancers look alike," he said appealing to Elaine.

"Maybe they don't, Eric, maybe they don't," she said reflecting on the possibilities. "How many cancers have you looked at through the microscope? All of Jackson Pollock's paintings look alike to me but if you study them they're obviously different. When you drop a pebble into a pond, are the ripples always the same?"

"You're reading too much into this," Eric assured her. "Comerford has more than a clinical interest in this girl. He hired her and he's always said he looked after her."

"You're right as far as you go," she said calmly, "but it's possible Palmeri told him about her — her suspicions."

"He wouldn't believe it," Eric jumped in quickly. "She certainly told Trenton and he hasn't done anything about it."

"I think he tried but was too afraid or too dumb to do anything. He's prettier than you but not much smarter," Elaine said through a thin smile.

Eric grew red at the jibe but didn't argue either point.

"Comerford would do anything to defend the reputation of University Medical Center except lie," Elaine said thoughtfully. "He might close his eyes if it were a minor fault and get rid of the risk quietly. On the other hand, if he were sure, why would he give two sets of slides to Dr. Borden?"

"For tumor specific antigen studies," Eric brightened up. "He's been working on that for years. He has anti-sera to tumors from different organs which can identify the organ or the tumor immunologically. He's looking for another primary site of the melanoma."

Elaine saw a ray of hope but was not quite as enthusiastic as Eric.

"What else has Borden been up to?" she asked.

"What do you mean?" Eric asked.

"You're going to the library and read everything Borden has published in the last few years. Just go through the abstracts until you find something. Do you understand?"

"Yes, I do, Elaine," he said sarcastically, "anything to do with tissue typing of individual people. What will you be doing?"

"I'm going to drop into his lab and ask him if I can have those slides for my conference," she said as she stood up to leave.

Martha ran back to the apartment as soon as she learned Angie had signed herself out of the hospital. She was still breathing heavily when she put her key in the lock.

There were Angie's bags sitting in the foyer while Angie sat silently in the living room doing nothing. Martha walked into the living room slowly as she controlled her breathing.

For awhile they merely looked at each other. Angie on the couch and Martha sitting on the armchair next to it. Twice they both started talking at the same time unable to hear what the other was saying.

"Go ahead," Martha," Angie said.

"Where are you going?" Martha asked softly.

"Nowhere."

"What are those bags for?" Martha asked surprised.

"I was going home," Angie said, "but then I got this call from Dr. Comerford just a few minutes ago. I told him everything in the hospital and he just blew up. It was awful."

"Everything?" Martha said with obvious concern.

"Everything!"

"Holy shit!" Martha said, looking up at the ceiling.

"It was worse than you can imagine but he sounded very different when he called. He didn't apologize but he was very polite. He didn't want me to leave today. He didn't say why but he wanted me to stay at least until tomorrow."

"What are you going to do?" Martha asked. She unbuttoned her white clinical coat with her I.D. hanging from the lapel. She was still in her green O.R. dress and white shoes.

"I don't know," Angie shrugged. "I told him I'd think about it. So I'm thinking about it. Would he play dirty pool?"

"What do you mean?"

"He changed his attitude so much like he would do anything to keep me here one more day. In the hospital, he practically fired me. He could keep me here in New York just so he could prosecute me."

Martha was shocked. Her eyebrows shot up and her mouth opened wide.

"Prosecute you?" she said, "for what? Nobody was hurt. Kelly consented. You had Trenton there. What makes you say a thing like that?"

"Anything is possible right now. He sounded so

damned mysterious in a way," Angie frowned. "Maybe I'm getting paranoid. No, forget that! I didn't say it."

"Nobody thinks you're paranoid," Martha said sympathetically.

"I am getting paranoid," Angie insisted. "I keep thinking up all kinds of terrible reasons why he would want to keep me here. Maybe he's out getting a court order to force me to have that operation. He could say I was paranoid."

"I won't let them. I'll swear you're as sane as anybody," Martha facetiously reassured her. "They'll have to take me first."

"Oh, Martha, can they really do that, get a warrant?" Angie said, a little frightened.

"No, I was only joking," Martha reached out to hold her hand.

"It's been done before," Angie said still worried.

"Not to someone like you," Martha said soothingly. "Those are cases involving children or patients in institutions. Come on, think of some good reasons Comerford wants you to stay."

"If it was something good you'd think Peter would be here to tell me," she said sulking.

"Why should Peter know what Comerford has on his mind?"

"They all stick together like rats on a ship," Angie said.

"Rats don't stick together when there's trouble," Martha corrected her.

"Whatever! I've got to find out what's going on. The Potters have been noticeably absent from my case. I bet they know what's going on. I'd like to have a few words with Elaine."

"Maybe you should if it'll make you feel better," Martha said. "You've got nothing to lose if Comerford already knows."

"You still don't believe me," Angie said without rancor.

"It doesn't matter what I think. I'm not your doctor," Martha said. "Whatever you do, I'm still your friend."

By two o'clock that afternoon, Dr. Alex Borden had determined that the specimens on the two sets of slides had come from patients with the same blood type. It didn't prove they were one and the same patient but it didn't prove they were different as Comerford had hoped. It might take a week to complete the survey for all the rare antigens needed to establish positive identity without doubt.

At three o'clock, Comerford was in the office of E. Norwood Dracut, attorney for the hospital, for the Comerford family and for most of the corporations in the Comerford portfolio at one time or another.

When they were at college together, Comerford and Dracut were quite different in appearance. Dracut was at least three inches taller and had blond hair compared to Comerford's deep black. But the years had brought with them a remarkable resemblance between them as if some makeup men had conspired to create twins. With crescents of white hair ringing their scalps and white thick moustaches over their lips, Dracut listened while Comerford told him the whole story about the Potters and what Borden was trying to prove in his laboratory.

"I understand what you are saying about Borden's work in a general way," Dracut said, "but if you are correct, how reliable are these tests?"

"If all the HLA antigens are identical then the probability for this to happen by chance is less than one in a hundred fifty thousand," Comerford said proudly.

"Very well," Dracut cleared his throat, "let's say you can be absolutely certain then. What can you prove about the Potters? Opportunity? She certainly had the opportunity but so did anyone in the laboratory or even the hospital for that matter. Motive? What's their motive in this case? You said they weren't involved."

"That's what makes this so horribly despicable!" Comerford said angrily. "Their only motive now is to harm this girl, to get her out of the way."

"But so far, no harm has come to this girl Palmeri."

"Enough I'd say. Can you imagine being told you have a hopeless case of cancer."

"But she doesn't believe it."

"Only through an agonizing process I would think," Comerford said feeling frustrated by the lawyer's cynicism. "What can you be thinking of?"

"I need an injured party," he explained coolly. "Forgive me if I sound unsympathetic toward this girl."

"Everyone who has ever been in contact with the Potters is injured. We've been taken in by allowing them to—" Comerford's head sagged into his hands distressed by the possibilities of the past ten years.

"I know how you feel, Arthur, but the Medical Center is an innocent victim too. I am just trying to establish a case for Palmeri without exposing the Medical Center to ridicule or worse."

"I appreciate that," Comerford said looking up more composed. "That is why I came to you first but I have no intention of letting them get away."

"How long would it take Borden to run tests on all the slide specimens Eric Potter was responsible for in the last ten years?"

"He couldn't" Comerford said dejectedly, "not without recalling all the patients. Not without a sample of tissue except in some cases I think a blood sample would be sufficient."

"But not all the specimens were fraudulent," Dracut said, raising a finger emphatically. "I also have to think like a defense attorney for the Potters at this point. The hard evidence is very complicated and a good defense attorney could easily make a jury disregard it by making them misunderstand. It would take patience and lots of time to overcome it. The trial would drag on sensationally. At this point we haven't even identified the injured parties."

Comerford banged his fist against the arm of the chair in angry frustration. Every passing moment made it more likely that Angie would be proved right. He told Borden where to reach him as soon as there was any evidence that the specimens came from two people. It was a false hope from the moment he compared the two slides.

"What can we do?" Comerford asked tasting the

frustration.

"You've got to get rid of them. Get them to resign from University Medical Center immediately," Dracut said.

"That's not enough!" Comerford insisted angrily.

"It's not," Dracut said sadly, "but it's all we can do without causing more damage to the Medical Center. Consider it. It's only two rotten apples. Why sacrifice the tree?"

Comerford sat silently, obviously reluctant to accept the advice of counsel.

"Arthur, look at me," Dracut said ominously. "You're got to do it right away before they have time to think about it. I'll come with you to back you up if they make a fuss or deny it."

"No, I have to do this myself," Comerford said with sad resolution.

Elaine Potter stormed back into her laboratory slamming the door behind her. She paced up and down rubbing her hands anxiously together. She didn't notice Eric sitting at the corner of the lab when she came in. When she did, she stopped pacing suddenly.

"I'm glad you're here," she said quickly. "Borden wouldn't tell me anything. He lied about the slides but he can't lie very well. He admitted Comerford gave him something but he doesn't know what it is. That could be true. Are you listening to me?" she said to Eric who was looking off distantly. Elaine was almost manic in her speech as she tried to tell him everything at once.

"I'm sure you're right, darling," he said looking

around the lab but avoiding Elaine.

"You weren't listening to me," Elaine insisted angrily but Eric still paid no attention to her. "Eric, we are in serious trouble. Can you understand that!"

Eric ignored her as she paced around the lab. She gradually calmed down and spoke more slowly.

"What did you find in the library?" she asked.

"Nothing. I quit looking two hours ago," he said with an air of released anxiety. "Comerford had me paged in the library while I was getting Borden's bibliography. He wants to see us in his office at seven tonight."

Elaine's shoulders tensed as she rigidly placed both hands in her lab coat pocket.

"Did he say why?" she asked as calmly as she could.

"That should be obvious," he said getting up and walking toward her. "Our little partnership is dissolved." He walked past her to the chair beside her desk.

"And what do you have planned for the rest of your life," she said shuddering. "Do you think you'll be happy selling life insurance?"

"I'm afraid we both may be making license plates for the state," he said.

"I'm not ready for that," she hissed. "I won't accept it."

"What can you do about it? Comerford has the evidence," Eric said, resigned to the outcome.

"Not yet! Borden's still working on it and he doesn't know what he's working on. He has two unknowns as far as he's concerned."

"Don't be too sure!"

"Of course he doesn't know," Elaine insisted angrily. "That's how Comerford would do it to get an unbiased opinion. And Comerford hasn't gotten his answer yet."

"So what? He will have it by seven o'clock tonight.'

"It means he probably hasn't told anyone about it," she said just as the phone rang.

"This is she," Elaine answered after Angie asked for her on the other end.

"I want to talk to you. Could I come over now," Angie asked urgently.

Elaine hesitated. She looked at Eric who anxiously wondered who she was talking to.

"Not right now," Elaine said. "If it's important, say about six-thirty. I'll be here catching up on some work."

"That'll be fine," Angie said.

"I'll be expecting you," Elaine said and hung up. She looked at Eric. "That was Miss Palmeri," Elaine hissed as she sucked in air through her teeth.

Elaine walked slowly around the lab carefully lifting her toe and heel with each step. She seemed preoccupied as she picked up different instruments and papers and laid them down carefully in the same spot. Finally she leaned against the sink with her arms folded across her chest.

"We don't have to surrender, Eric," she said calmly. "There's a way out of this and we can still keep what we have."

"I'm listening," he said.

"Comerford and Palmeri are the only ones with balls enough to expose us. If we could get rid of them—"

"You're crazy," Eric said disgustedly. "Enough is enough! We won't go to jail. Comerford will ask us to resign. He may even hound us so it'll be impossible to practice somewhere else. I don't need to work anyway and I'm sure you have more than enough money stuffed away somewhere."

"I don't think he'll be satisfied with only your resignation," Elaine said goading him. "His honor has been trampled and if he wants to drop it to protect the Medical Center, Palmeri will always be there pushing hard."

"I didn't think you were serious," Eric gasped. "We can't get away with double murder."

"We can do anything if we do it right," she said with her eyes opened wide and her pupils constricted.

"We won't get away with it and it's not necessary!" Eric argued, then wiped the sweat off his lip. As he loosened his tie and collar, his hand trembled.

"Do you know what will happen?" Elaine said and stalked across the room until she was directly over him as he sat in the chair more frightened than he had ever been.

"Comerford will have Borden review every case you've ever done," she stared at him. "He'll pay for it himself. He'll bring every patient back and have them tested against every slide with their name on it. And then you'll get sued and sued till there's nothing left. You won't be able to practice in Afghanistan!"

339

She walked away from him while he sat slumped in the chair with his hand covering his eyes. He seemed hopelessly resigned to an infamous end to his career.

"We can't get away with it," he mumbled. "There's still Trenton and Borden."

"Borden doesn't know anything about us and Trenton can't believe it," she said. "Palmeri will disappear and be forgotten. Leave it to me but you must take care of Comerford."

"How?" he asked weakly.

"You've got to make it look like a robbery, a mugging," she said slowly. "Hit him in the head with something heavy and ransack the office and his clothes. He's an old man and should die easily."

"What about Palmeri?" he said growing distinctly short of breath. "When they find her body the two deaths will certainly be linked together."

"No one will ever find her body," Elaine said with assurance and a thin smile. "It'll be right next door in those three big boxes in the Pathological Museum. The identifiable parts will be incinerated with the entrails along with the unused parts from some other autopsy."

"Stop it!" Eric shouted. "I don't want to hear about it."

"Forget it then," Elaine turned away from him. "I can't do it myself. I expect you back here to help me when you've finished with Comerford."

There was an awful silence between them after Elaine offered her ultimatum. Eric didn't move for several minutes. Then he sat up taking a deep breath while straightening his tie.

"Will she be dead?" he asked.

"Some chloral hydrate in her tea and pentothal in her veins will keep her near death until you get here," Elaine said grimly. "Think of it as just another autopsy. Go home and change your shirt. This one's a mess."

"What are you going to do?" Eric asked as he stood up.

"I'm going into the Pathological Museum to make room for Angelica. Then I'm going to make her some tea."

Angie knocked on the door. When no one answered she walked in and found the hissing sound was coming from a tea kettle set over a Bunsen burner. The water started to boil and the hissing became a shrill whistle. Angie lowered the flame and the sharp whistle groveled to a soft hiss again.

She felt Elaine's absence was a temporary respite. Once more she changed her plan from a frontal assault in which she saw herself flatly accusing Elaine to a quieter plea for advice. In this way, she hoped to trap Elaine into admitting how she was doing it.

Elaine came bustling through the door. Her long white coat trailed behind in the flurry of her breeze exposing a green cotton O.R. dress. She looked surprised to see Angie in her office.

"I'm sorry," Elaine apologized, "but I'm still tied up with my work. I just came up here to get a cup of tea."

"This won't take too long," Angie said.

"Yes, you said you had something to talk about," Elaine said casually as she poured herself a cup of hot water and added some tea from a tin can. "I'm awfully sorry but I thought I'd be finished by now. It's just some collating to do and the only place with clean tables was the prosecting room so I have to get those papers put together before I leave tonight. Let me fix you a cup of tea."

"Is that where you do the autopsies?" Angie asked.

"Yes," Elaine said. She reached for a cup on a shelf and quickly poured the hot water over a clear liquid sitting in the cup from the shelf. Then she added tea to the chloral hydrate solution in the cup.

"Bring this with you," Elaine said handing the spiked tea to Angie, "and we can talk as I finish up."

Angie agreed. She followed Elaine out the door carrying the steaming cup of tea with her. They took the elevator down to the first level basement which was deserted. Elaine's soft rubber soles made no sound against the concrete floor. Angie's wooden heels made a distinct click-click as they walked into the prosecting room.

There were no windows in this rectangular room lined mostly with stainless steel cabinets, some with glass doors and some with airtight insulated doors.

Five narrow stainless steel tables stood in a straight row. Each was a little over six feet long. There was a bank of spotlights over each table. Only the first two were turned on giving the only illumination in the room. One table was covered with stacks of papers Elaine said she was working on. The other table reflected the spotlight brilliantly off its perforated gleaming surface. The reflections produced strange shadows in the quiet room.

Elaine bent over one of the tables as she shifted the piles of paper around. Under the spotlight her skin seemed drained of blood. Her lips were tense and thin as she worked and ignored Angie completely.

Angie walked to the side of the table opposite Elaine. Elaine retreated into the shadows as she stood outside the spotlight. Angie couldn't see her face. Only her body and her hands caught some of the light.

"I heard you had some bad news today," Elaine said sounding sympathetic. To Angie it was a disembodied deep voice from the shadows.

"It's hard to keep a secret around here," Angie said then took a sip of tea. "This is an unusual tea, sweet without sugar added."

"Yes, it's a special blend I have made for me," Elaine said. "Would you like to take some with you?"

"Did they show you the slides?" Angie asked ignoring the offer but tasted the tea again. She thought it very pleasant.

"No, I haven't. I'm anxious to, please forgive me for sounding so clinical. I've never seen anything like it," Elaine's voice faded toward the end.

"Has anybody seen—a melanoma of the uterus," Angie said with a tremor creeping into her voice. She took a large sip of the hot tea to ease her dry throat.

Elaine resumed shuffling the papers. Her head in the light showed a barely visible clear streak of perspiration against her pale skin trickling down the side of her face. She stopped working, leaving her hands spread across the table as she leaned.

"I'm trying to think if it's ever been reported," she said with her head turned to one side. "If there was one found here at the Medical Center, the file should be available somewhere."

"Where would you look to find such an old case?" Angie asked. The tea was cooling as she took a large swallow.

"Medical Records should be able to trace it if there ever was such a case. Of course, it would have to have been diagnosed correctly," Elaine added quickly.

Angie felt tired and found herself leaning back against the other table. She finished the tea hoping it would stimulate her.

"There was more I wanted to ask you," Angie said weakly, "but I'm not feeling well. Excuse me."

Elaine came over to her. As Angie put her full weight on the floor, her knees buckled and Elaine caught her. She stood her up and pushed her onto the table. Angie was unconscious.

The flame from the match danced erratically each time Dr. Comerford sucked on the curved stem of his pipe. He blew the smoke in the direction of Dr. Eric Potter who was sitting in front of his desk. On the desk lay a worn brown manila folder.

"I was a great disappointment to my father,"

Comerford sighed. "He wanted me to join his business. When I asked him what he did in the business, he said he made money. I told him we had enough. 'There's never enough until you have it all,' he said. 'What happens then,' I asked him. He said, 'Then the game is over!' "

"Sounds like an interesting man," Eric smiled nervously.

"He was an awful bore even to his rich friends," Comerford said. "How much money did you make last year, Eric?"

"I don't know offhand," Eric said. He felt hot and was perspiring.

"Offhand, it was about four hundred thousand dollars," Comerford said calmly. "I checked your operative records. Anyone can add and multiply. My father would have been impressed. He liked people who made a lot of money. He never cared how they made it."

"I don't understand, sir," Eric said. He reached for the handkerchief in his breast pocket to wipe his lips. His effort was restricted by the sock weighted with heavy steel balls in his side pocket.

"He was a financier. Never knew anything about a business except the money part. He didn't care so long as the collateral was sound and the return more than he could get at a bank. He believed he never knowingly did any harm to another human being. That was true because he never knew what had to be done to repay his financing."

"Some people are like that," Eric said shifting his weight uncomfortably. The steel balls clicked in his pocket.

"Too many, perhaps," Comerford said. He put his pipe down in the ashtray and leaned forward on the desk. "Unfortunately, doctors can't have the luxury of such ignorance. There is nothing between us and our patients. No board of directors, no executive committees, no corporate reports! They always tell us face to face."

"Yes, very true, very true," Erick was quick to agree.

"Then in God's name how can you face a patient!" Comerford said angrily through gritted teeth. "How can you face yourself in the morning!"

Potter blanched, swallowed hard and gripped the arm of his chair until his knuckles turned white.

"You have perverted everything you touched, everything I believed in. Palmeri never had a melanoma and God knows how many others never needed you! But I swear I'll find every one and bury you!" Comerford said in a rage, fire spreading throughout his skin and being. He turned away from Eric in fulminating disgust.

Eric got up quickly. He pulled the rolled up heavy sock containing the steel balls from his pocket. He swung the deadly instrument in a wide arc over the desk directed to the side of Comerford's head.

"Potter!" Trenton shouted from the open doorway. He was soon on him with his arm wrapped tightly around his neck. His shout made Comerford look up and move so the blow was a glancing one from Potter. It knocked his glasses off and hit the bridge of his nose. Blood flowed profusely from

346

both nostrils. The nose was broken but Comerford was on his feet. As Trenton held on to Potter, Comerford hit him squarely in the face with a roundhouse blow. Potter sagged and Trenton let him fall to the floor.

"What the hell is going on here?" Trenton said flabbergasted by the melee. Blood was staining Comerford's white shirt and Potter was slumped on the floor.

"You should have believed Angie Palmeri," Comerford said as he sniffed back the blood from his nose without good effect. "She was absolutely right about the Potters."

"That's great! She doesn't have a melanoma," Trenton said joyfully.

"Maybe for her," Comerford said sadly, "But she was the only one who knew that besides the Potters. It's not great for everyone. It took us too long to find them out."

Potter raised himself slowly, climbing up on the arm of the chair. He fell back into the chair with blood running from his lip and his nose.

"Stop Elaine," he whimpered, "in the prosecting room. She's going to kill Palmeri."

Trenton was frozen by his words. He looked to Comerford who was also stunned.

"Get going, you damned fool! I'll take care of him," Comerford ordered.

Trenton raced down the four flights of stairs to the first level basement and through the catacombs of connecting corridors to reach the prosecting room. The door was locked. He felt desperate as he pushed hard against it. Footsteps came clattering toward him from around the corner. Two security guards appeared as directed by Comerford's phone call. One of them opened the door with a key.

Inside they found Angie lying on the prosecting table completely naked. Her head was propped up on a wooden block. She lay there motionless under the harsh spotlight. Slowly, they walked toward the table in the darkness.

"Eric blew it!" Elaine said as she stepped out of the shadows. All three men were startled by her sudden appearance. "Don't look so damned worried. She'll wake up in about twelve hours."

Angie woke up the next afternoon in the intensive care unit. She had an intravenous line going into her left forearm and electrodes of the cardiac monitor strapped to her chest. Comerford insisted on this precaution until she was revived. The danger to her diminished rapidly with each passing hour as her body metabolized and excreted the pentathal and the chloral hydrate Elaine had given her. Peter Trenton came in shortly after she woke up.

"You're okay," he said to her smiling. "You don't have a melanoma."

"I know that," she said, "but what happened?"

"You never had a melanoma," he said once more.

"I know that too," she said getting annoyed with him. "What happened yesterday? The last thing I remember was having tea with Elaine. She put chloral hydrate in the tea."

"How did you know that?" Peter said impressed

with her deduction.

"What else would you use? It had a sweet aromatic flavor. A very unusual tea. I didn't actually know it at the time," Angie admitted. "It was the after effects."

"After you passed out, Elaine pumped you full of pentathal. It was almost enough to kill you," Peter shuddered. "There was enough in the syringe to do the job."

"Poor training, Peter," Angie said holding up her right arm which was discolored by a large blue-black hematoma between her forearm and the arm. "She ruptured the vein and injected subcutaneously. It doesn't work fast enough that way. Don't hold it against her. She hasn't worked with live patients since she was an intern."

"Angie!" Peter's voice rose critically. "She tried to kill you and Eric to kill Comerford. Don't apologize for her. It's over now. You slept through the worst of it.'

"Did I?" Angie said looking hurt with a small tear beginning to form. "What were you and Comerford and all the rest of you doing for the past ten years. That was the worst of it! All those women who went to Eric Potter."

She turned away from him and let the tear fall on her pillow.

"You're right, Angie," Peter said softly. "You were right about everything but there's nothing we can do for them now. We can try to do better in the future."

Angie kept her eyes closed and her head turned away from him. He sat down on the bed beside her.

"Angie, when I saw you lying there in the morgue, I nearly died myself. I've seen a lot but nothing so terrible as that. Few people get a second chance. I thought I lost you forever. I never want to lose you again. I want to marry you. What do you say?"

Angie looked at him as she wiped her eyes.

"I don't know what to say, Peter," she said hesitantly. "I love you but you should have known that before you thought I was dead. I can't think about that right now," she said wiping another tear from her cheek. "You should have known about the Potters. You should have known better!"

Neither of them knew how long Dr. Comerford had been standing at the foot of the bed when he suddenly interrupted.

"Do you think you could have done better if you were in our shoes?" he said gravely. His face looked battered. His nose was swollen. The black and blue hematoma had spread under both eyes. One side of his face was twisted where his lip had been cut.

Angie gasped at the sight. She felt terribly sorry for him and for the pain she assumed he had.

"Oh, Dr. Comerford, I'm so sorry for you. You look awful," she said most sympathetically.

"Never mind that," he said. "It looks much worse than it feels. Answer my question. If you were a physician and surgeon, would you have acted any differently that we did?"

Angie pulled herself up and took a deep breath.

"I am the way I am," she said, "and no amount of hardship, training, learning in school or out will ever stop me from seeing the truth or speaking it.

You can't justify what happened at this hospital by hiding behind professional ethics!"

"You're fired," Dr. Comerford said softly.

"Wait a minute!" Peter jumped up from the bed. "You can't do that!"

"Cool it before you say something you'll be sorry for," Comerford smiled jovially but quickly changed to a grimace of pain from his battered face. "Cool it, I learned that from an intern. I can do anything I want. The Comerford Foundation has eighteen million dollars to spend at this institution and I'm the cashier. I had a long talk with Martha Daniels about you," he said to Angie. "She said you wanted to go to medical school so you're fired as a surgical assistant. You start school next week. You already know more anatomy, pharmacology and pathology than any first year student. So you can join the second year class with advanced standing."

"I don't think. . . ," Angie started to say quite bewildered.

"And you are the first recipient of the Comerford Foundation Scholarship for Women. The stipend is more generous than necessary but that's the way Beatrice wanted it."

"I don't know what to say," Angie said sinking down into her pillow overwhelmed by the offer.

"Of course, you could marry him instead," Comerford said deprecating Trenton with his tone but added, "or even both, I suppose. Come on Trenton, let's go. Let her sleep on it."

Angie closed her eyes but couldn't sleep. Two things kept spinning through her mind: Mrs. Angelica Trenton and Dr. Angelica Palmeri.

DISASTER NOVELS